The Summer of Perfect Mistakes

Also by Cynthia St. Aubin

Blue Blood Meets Blue Collar
Trapped with Temptation
Keeping a Little Secret

Visit the Author Profile page at Harlequin.com for more titles.

The Summer of Perfect Mistakes

CYNTHIA ST. AUBIN

HARLEQUIN

afterglow BOOKS

Recycling programs
for this product may
not exist in your area.

ISBN-13: 978-1-335-04165-4

The Summer of Perfect Mistakes

Copyright © 2024 by Cynthia St. Aubin

For questions and comments about the quality of this book, please contact us at CustomerService@Harlequin.com.

TM and ® are trademarks of Harlequin Enterprises ULC.

Harlequin Enterprises ULC
22 Adelaide St. West, 41st Floor
Toronto, Ontario M5H 4E3, Canada
www.Harlequin.com

Printed in U.S.A.

To those who live, or have lived, in the gray.
Your every breath is bravery.

AUTHOR'S NOTE

This novel contains descriptions of mental illness,
including depression, anxiety and panic attacks,
that might prove upsetting to readers
sensitive to those subjects.

One

Just unbuckle your seat belt.

Do it now.

Lark Hockney sat frozen to the passenger seat of her mother's pristine Land Rover, her stomach a cold ball and her limbs heavy as cement.

She never should have agreed to this.

She didn't know why she'd thought this would be any different.

Why she'd figured the basic act of leaving her parents' house would magically remove the barriers that had prevented her from completing even the simplest of tasks over the last several months.

"I can come in with you." Diana Hockney, painfully chic in the tailored cream-colored suit she wore on days when she met with patients, turned down the soothing music.

Lark knew her mother had chosen the music the way she'd been choosing everything lately: out of excessive caution for her daughter's fragile mental state.

"You don't need to do that," Lark said, drawing a line in the condensation on her window. They'd been idling at the curb long enough for it to fog.

"I know I don't *need* to. I want to." Lark's mother reached across the armrest to squeeze her clammy hand. "I know this must be intimidating."

Looking at the squat, uninspiring buildings of Spring Valley Community College through a windshield bejeweled by spring rain, Lark bit back a bitter laugh.

Her first days at *Dartmouth*—her father's alma mater—had been intimidating. And yet she had marched into the venerated Georgian edifice with a confidence bordering on hubris.

She was Dr. Anderson Hockney's daughter.

Excellence was in her blood.

Or so she'd thought.

"It's an art class, not an MCATs prep course." She'd meant the comment to lighten the mood, but seeing her mother's blue eyes darken, Lark felt a pang of guilt. Her extended hiatus after a single semester of medical school had been a source of angst for both her parents—husband-wife ob-gyns whose health clinic was a cornerstone of their tightly knit community.

A community that had fully expected Lark to follow in her parents' gilded footsteps.

Instead, she'd fallen flat on her face.

Spectacularly, and in public.

"Sweetie, if you don't feel ready—"

"I'm going." Lark scooted forward and clicked the seat belt open, wanting to avoid the last half of what had become a painfully familiar sentence.

We can give it more time.

It only reminded Lark of just how little she really had.

Twenty-seven days.

The countdown hanging above her head like the blade of an academic guillotine.

Twenty-seven days to decide whether she'd go back to the med school program that fall. Or surrender her coveted spot as one of the ninety-two students selected out of approximately seven thousand applicants each year.

"You have your phone?" her mother asked.

Reaching into the kangaroo pouch of her oversized hoodie, Lark held up the device up for her mother to see.

"You'll text me when class is almost over?"

Lark resisted the urge to sigh and roll her eyes. "Yes, Mom."

They'd reviewed the plan at least ten times since Lark had agreed to cooperate with her mother's latest scheme to coax her out of the basement.

She pushed the door open on a gust of air heavy with rain. "Lark?"

Fine mist cooled her cheeks as she slung her painfully new portfolio over one shoulder. "Yeah?"

The hope in her mother's eyes was a knife to the gut. "You can do this."

Lark's jaw tightened as she nodded.

Neither of them had any reason to believe it.

As witnessed by the fact that her mother remained at the curb until Lark pushed through the entrance to the humanities building.

The wet soles of Lark's sneakers squeaked on the linoleum as she stopped short, nearly capsized by a wave of nostalgia. The unguent mellow of linseed oil. The earthy pong of clay. Sensory memories associated with a version of herself she no longer resembled. The Lark who could effortlessly churn out sketches and paintings her teachers gushed over. Never imagining that one day, the prospect of even setting foot in an art classroom would represent a panic attack–worthy event.

Dragging in a deep breath, she walked toward the end of the corridor.

"…and I told him, if I wanted someone to criticize my wardrobe I'd still be married to Phil," said a lilting voice as sweet and smooth as sun tea.

"You did not," answered a husky feminine voice.

"Did so," the first speaker said. "So it's back to the app, I guess."

"Or you could just take our instructor home," the second suggested.

"Please," the first scoffed. "I'd sooner adopt a goat than a man in his twenties. Less house training required."

"I still say we should have just married each other."

The whoosh of the building's door behind her announced the arrival of either another student or the instructor in question. It was the jolt Lark needed to force her feet to move. Sucking in a breath, she held it all the way to an unoccupied table at the back of the classroom where she pulled out a chair and quickly sat down.

Both women, older than she was by at least a decade, turned to look at her with expressions of surprise and curiosity.

Even before they introduced themselves, Lark had pegged the lithe, tanned former-beauty-queen blonde in the vintage sundress as speaker number one—Tammy, as it turned out— and her blazer-and-boots-wearing friend with russet skin and a wild halo of sculptural curls as speaker number two—Linda.

"Lark Hockney," she mumbled, forcing a smile before hunkering down in the oversized hoodie that had become her emotional support talisman.

"Good evening, ladies." The instructor's deep, resonant voice preceded him into the room, his back turned to them as he set a messenger bag and a cardboard file box on the table at the front. Without turning, he began to unpack the contents. Rusty teapot. Several red and green apples. Some kind of seed pod. A black cloth.

Still-life components.

Even in her bleak fog, Lark noticed their instructor was

tall, broad shouldered with a mop of dark, disheveled curls that brushed the collar of his light blue dress shirt. Faded jeans hugged his lean hips enough to reveal a small but well-rounded backside. Taking a step back from the table where he had arranged the components, he dug a cell phone from his pocket and pulled up a picture of what she assumed was last week's arrangement.

"What do you think, ladies?" he asked. "Close enough?"

Lark's heart leapt when he spun around to face them, dizzying recognition flooding her.

She knew him.

Knew who he was anyway.

Nick Hoffman.

A name she hadn't thought of in years but that brought up a rich list of associations. Enthusiastic underachievement. Unsolicited philosophical debates with teachers. A permanent residency in detention. A computer virus that had taken down Spring Valley High's Blackboard app for an entire week. Hand-drawn graphic novel illustrations submitted in place of assignments he'd considered arbitrary.

Which had been most of them.

His aquiline nose was longer, broader and matched by angular cheekbones and a sculpted jaw. His large gray eyes were soulful pools behind stylish wire-framed glasses he hadn't worn in high school. But his scar was the giveaway. A pale, dime-sized patch just below his right eye. Lark remembered when it had been fresh and accompanied by a nasty scrape on his cheekbone and jaw. A result of the car accident that had taken his father the same year they'd had their one and only class together.

The whole school had watched Nick with an ugly brand of pity she only recognized now that she'd felt it too. Following "the incident," those same eyes were on her wherever she went, which was why she'd gone to as few places as possible.

A sleepy tourist trap nestled among the rolling green hills of Virginia, Spring Valley demanded its permanent residents be cast in roles as identifiable as its landmarks.

Lark had once been its darling.

Prom queen. Valedictorian. Waving from the flower-bedecked parade floats lumbering down Main Street. Fresh as the bouquet of pink peonies in her arms and bright as the tiara perched atop her naive head.

Lark knew Nick recognized her when he cleared his throat and rearranged his features into an expression of mild politeness. Would he ask her to stand up and introduce herself?

Nick only ducked his head and gave her a conspiratorial smile. "Welcome," he said. Then, "Who can name the four basic principles of design?"

The bangles on Tammy's wrist jangled as her arm shot up.

"Go ahead, Tammy."

The pecan-pie sweetness of her answer drifted away as Lark sank into a profound sense of relief to have escaped introductions.

"And what principle is it that makes a red apple look redder when it's placed next to a green apple?" Nick continued, gesturing to the still-life arrangement.

"Simultaneous contrast." The sound of Lark's voice startled her. Quiet, and raspy from disuse.

"That's right," Nick said, his grin revealing a flash of straight white teeth.

Had she ever seen him smile in high school?

The memories of the boy whose eye she'd occasionally caught in art class featured a sardonic smirk at best.

"Show-off," Tammy scolded with a smile meant to reveal it as a compliment.

"Take it easy, Tammy," Nick said, walking toward the back of the classroom to hit the light. "We don't want Lark thinking we routinely haze newcomers."

Plunged into darkness interrupted only by the lamp shining on the still-life objects, Lark immediately felt more comfortable.

"This week I'd like you to focus your attention on the role value plays in representing different colors of fruit in a gray-scale medium like pencil," Nick said as he returned to the front and set out a Bluetooth speaker. Elvis's smoky croon flooded the classroom.

"He could sing the panties off a preacher," Tammy sighed.

"I bet that would have improved Sunday sermon attendance," Linda said as both women rifled through their bags.

Grateful to have a task, Lark followed suit, pulling out a sketchpad of thick, creamy paper and a metal case of drawing pencils.

Like her brand-new portfolio, they'd been acquired by Lark's mother.

A clever gift to make her attendance in this class cooperative rather than compulsory.

Why her mother had chosen this particular tactic was as obvious as it was ironic: Lark had loved art once upon a time. Had lived for it, actually. In a senior year crammed with Advanced Placement classes meant to accelerate her college track, art had been the one nonnegotiable in the schedule she'd crafted with her father's help. The one place where she could create for the pure pleasure of it.

A motive that had seemed downright frivolous when she'd reviewed Dartmouth's premed program requirements.

We know how much you love oil painting, honey, but is adding electives really worth an extra semester?

And of course, with the father she idolized doing the asking, the answer had been no.

But now Lark sensed her former love being dangled like a carrot to lure her back to a more functional version of herself. She highly doubted sketching Granny Smith apples would restore her from gifted-kid burnout to overachiever in the allotted twenty-seven days.

And yet here she was.

"Don't forget your light source," Nick called, settling into a chair at the next table over and cracking open a laptop.

Resigned, Lark selected a pencil from the neat row and rolled it between her fingers. It had been so long since she'd held one it felt awkward in her hand.

Paralyzed, she stared at the still-life composition until it was embossed in glowing white on the backs of her eyelids when she blinked.

She had no idea how to do this.

Where or how to start.

Beads of sweat trickled down her ribs from her armpits as she forced the pencil down to the page.

Just make one mark. Anywhere.

The graphite tip made contact with the paper, and Lark tried to conjure the rounded outline of the red apple next to its bright green neighbor. But the second she glanced up to make a visual comparison, her efforts looked flat and childish.

What she hadn't found in the kit of expensive materials her mother had picked out was an eraser.

Lark tore the sheet off and started again.

The longer she stared at the composition, the more it bothered her. The airless closeness of the apple to the teapot. The discomforting proximity of the alien-looking seed pod to the teacup. When in real life would anyone stop in the middle of having tea to stack apples next to a kettle?

It didn't even make sense.

A hot gust of anger surged through her.

What was she trying to prove here anyway?

"Mr. Hoffman?" Tammy's slim arm lifted. "Could you come look at this a minute?"

"It's Nick," he said, pushing back from the table. "And you don't have to raise your hand."

"My nana would somersault in her grave if she knew I'd called a college professor by his first name."

"Nana can rest easy," Nick said. "I'm not a professor. I'm not even a college graduate. I dropped out of NYU my third year. Had to get a special dispensation from the humanities department chair to teach this class."

"Well, she must think pretty highly of you." Tammy leaned a hand beneath her chin, batting long lashes at him.

"I hope so," Nick said, "seeing as she's my mother." He leaned in closer, glancing between the arrangement of objects and Tammy's artwork. "Okay, see how in your drawing you have the shadow from the red apple extending parallel with the green one?"

"Uh-huh," Tammy said, looking not at her drawing but at Nick's smoothly muscled forearm. Following her gaze, Lark, too, couldn't help but notice the graceful, sloping lines from the crook of his elbow, swelling into the biceps rounded against the fabric of his shirt.

"For that shadow to be spatially accurate, the apple would have to be partially *inside* the teapot." He glanced at Tammy, who quickly blinked and shifted her focus.

"That makes perfect sense," she said.

Catching the flicker of a smirk at the corner of Nick's lips, Lark had a startling realization.

He knew *exactly* where Tammy's attention had been focused.

"May I?" he asked, holding out his hand for Tammy's pencil.

"Of course."

"To fix it, we just need to adjust the angle of this shadow." Lark stared, transfixed by the sight of his strong, graceful hands. Surprised by the warm, heavy sensation settling in her middle.

She realized she was no longer watching Tammy watch Nick. She was watching him herself.

Feeling the intense, magnetic pull of attraction.

When was the last time she'd experienced it? The early, early days with Reese?

It couldn't have been that long.

Could it?

"Make sense?" Nick asked, handing the pencil back to Tammy.

As Nick stood, Lark didn't miss his subtle glance at the pathetic tangle of lines on her own page.

Doing okay? he mouthed, a crease appearing on his forehead beside a dark lock of hair.

Lark nodded quickly, the idea of him crouched as close to her as he had been to Tammy thrilling and terrifying in equal measure.

Nick gave her an encouraging smile and returned to his seat. For a hellish period of time, Lark made more false starts, her frustration reaching crisis point when the lights blinked back on.

"All right," Nick said, scrubbing his hands together. "Should we take a look?"

Linda and Tammy sat back in their chairs, affording Lark a peek at what they had produced. Seeing their enthusiastic but amateurish efforts, she steeled herself for the critique they were about to receive.

Only Nick failed to deliver it. He offered only vague suggestions wrapped in patronizing compliments.

How were they supposed to improve if they didn't know what they were doing wrong?

Lark wondered if his refusal to offer them feedback was born out of pity or apathy.

The idea of being on the receiving end of either made her skin feel too small. Nick's storm-gray eyes missed nothing as they moved over her mess. Remembering the kinds of drawings she used to produce. Pitying her as he searched for something positive to say.

She couldn't bear it.

Not for a single second longer.

Without waiting for him to finish complimenting Linda on her use of crosshatching, Lark crumpled up her papers, grabbed her portfolio and bolted from the classroom.

She turned down several empty corridors until she came to a sitting area outside the administrative offices where a giant wall clock informed her there were twenty minutes before her mother would return to collect her. Texting her to come early would only create another conversation Lark didn't want to have, and anyway, twenty minutes of unsupervised doomscrolling sounded like heaven after nearly an hour in the presence of other humans.

Lark plopped into one of the chairs before pulling out her phone.

The screen remained stubbornly dark.

Dead.

She hadn't even thought to check the battery before she'd left the house, and she left the house so rarely that it hadn't occurred to her to bring a charger.

Treacherous tears blurred her vision. She hated that small oversights often had the power to unstitch her. One more piece of evidence that she was in no way ready to return to college.

Horrified at the idea of spending twenty minutes alone with her own thoughts, Lark reached for one of the magazines on the side table. The editor of *Campus Life* seemed to think students spent their time gathering on the lawn for picnics or listening as someone strummed a guitar.

Definitely not medical school, she thought bitterly.

At five minutes to nine, she heard voices echoing down the hallway as Tammy and Linda exited the building. Only after another set of solitary footsteps followed a few minutes later did Lark emerge from her hiding place and make her way to the parking lot.

A fine mist fell, cooling her cheeks and settling on her skin.

Her mother's SUV nowhere to be seen, she walked over to a waist-high brick border and set her portfolio down to wait.

And wait.

And wait.

Lark's lower back hurt from standing, her exercise regime over the last several months mostly shuffling from her bedroom to the bathroom and back again. Placing two hands on the cool brick, she boosted herself up to sit on the wall.

Her mother could be scattered, but given how hard she'd worked to convince Lark to go to this class, there was no way she would have forgotten Lark entirely. With a rare evening free of any social club or professional commitments, her mother would be coming from their home on the sprawling golf course. A fifteen-minute drive Diana Hockney had made hundreds of times.

Which left only two possibilities: a hideous accident or an emergency delivery.

Cold tendrils of worry curled around her stomach.

Even six months ago this wouldn't have been a big deal, but now, sitting in the rain on this brick wall like some kind of Dickensian urchin, Lark felt...lost. Alone.

Afraid.

Irrationally angry.

The doors banging closed behind her made her jump.

She glanced over her shoulder to see Nick Hoffman coming down the sidewalk.

Please just walk to your car, she silently willed him. *Please don't see me.*

Lark held her breath as he dug into the pocket of his jeans and came back with a key fob. Headlights flared from the lone car in the lot, bathing her in silvery light that made her shield her eyes.

Nick's face swung toward her movement, and their gazes locked.

He was coming straight toward her.

Two

He never should have come back here.

The thought had been playing on a loop in Nick Hoffman's head pretty much since the tires of his BMW had crossed the Spring Valley city limits almost a month ago.

Whatever madness had possessed him to think returning to a town he'd mostly hated would allow him to decompress from his hectic life in Manhattan had officially evaporated.

Even before his mother had guilted him into teaching a community art class for all of two—scratch that—*three* students.

One of them currently perched atop a parking lot wall like a princess turned stone gargoyle.

Nick had wanted her to be gone.

He had *needed* her to be gone.

He'd even spent an extra ten minutes futzing around in the classroom before venturing out to the parking lot for that very reason.

Because he'd known that if he ran into Lark Hockney out here wearing that stricken expression on her pale, heart-shaped face, he would do exactly what he was doing now.

Diving headfirst into drama that wasn't his goddamn business. Which was exactly the opposite of what this summer was supposed to be about.

What happened to not getting involved?

Nick heard his father's voice as clearly as if his old man were a cartoon devil perched on his shoulder.

Alarming, considering Pop had been dead for ten years.

And yet this had kept happening since Nick had taken up residence in his mother's home.

A dead man offering unsolicited advice on his career. His love life. His promise to himself to avoid anything resembling the entanglements he'd been attempting to unravel by leaving the city.

A promise he was about to break.

Nick cleared his throat. "Hey," he said.

"Hey."

"Are you waiting on someone?" he asked.

Lark hugged her oversized hoodie tighter around her. "Nope. Just like the view."

So she had enough fight in her to give a smart-ass answer. Good.

Not an assumption he'd necessarily have made based on what he'd seen earlier.

Seeing her had been the shock of a lifetime.

Lark Hockney. Queen of their entire fucking high school transformed into a pale, thin, shaky specter glaring at her sketch pad like it had betrayed her. The look she aimed at the deserted parking lot wasn't much friendlier.

"My ride will be along any minute now."

"Cool," he said, leaning back against the wall.

"I'm really fine," she said, gnawing an already ragged cuticle. "You don't have to stick around."

Nick gave her what he hoped was a reassuring smile. "I don't mind."

Lark drew herself into an even tighter ball, which he wouldn't have thought possible until that precise moment.

"Look, I'm not trying to be rude, but I'd really rather just be alone, okay?"

"No problem." Gathering his things, Nick walked a few paces down the sidewalk and set them down again.

Lark turned to look at him. "You're still here."

"I suppose that depends on how you define *here*," he said.

"I'm literally looking right at you," she insisted.

"Solipsism holds that knowledge of anything outside one's own mind is unsure. The external world and other minds cannot be known and might not exist. So technically—"

"That didn't get you out of our sixth-period Art History final, and it isn't going to work now."

Nick was mostly flattered that she remembered. If asked, he'd have bet the thing Lark Hockney remembered was him ruining their yearbook page by refusing to have his picture taken. Ensuring that her perfect photo would forever hover above a black void named Fenwick Hoffman.

Goddamn, but I'd been a pretentious little shit.

"Then how about this? I don't feel comfortable leaving until you meet up with your ride. Call it a moral obligation as your instructor."

Lark hopped down from the wall and snatched her portfolio from the sidewalk. "I'm not interested in being anyone's moral obligation."

There was enough venom in the words to confirm what he'd already suspected.

She hadn't signed up for his class by her own choice.

Nick jogged to catch up and fell in step beside her as she marched down the sidewalk toward the parking lot's exit. "Look, I'm not trying to be that guy, but you can't walk home."

"Why not?" she asked. "I like walking."

"Even under normal conditions, there's no way that would be a good idea."

Lark stopped abruptly, pinning him with an icy glare. "Normal conditions?"

Nick's heart pounded in his chest. "If it wasn't pitch dark, raining and far enough out of town that a marine would refuse to run it."

The tight smile failed to reach Lark's red-rimmed eyes. "I'm okay, Nick. I promise."

"No, you're fucking not." The words were out of his mouth, and now that they'd started, Nick couldn't seem to make them stop. "You sat in the back of my classroom for thirty minutes looking like you were about to cry and filled the wastebasket with half a dozen sketches. Now you're standing in the rain, getting soaked, waiting for a ride that has yet to materialize. Meanwhile, you look like you haven't slept in about a year, and there's no way in hell I'm leaving you alone in the dark on the outskirts of town."

To Nick's abject horror, Lark's chin wobbled. Without warning, she dropped the portfolio at his feet and took off in a run.

"*Lark!*" he called after her. "Wait."

Too late he remembered that once upon a time, she'd been a state-qualifying sprinter on the Spring Valley High track team.

He glanced back at the parking lot and swore under his breath. His chances of catching her on foot while dragging her portfolio were slim to none. Changing direction, he jogged to his car, slung the oversized folder into the back seat and threw the vehicle into Drive before he had even buckled his seat belt. He sent a mental apology to his mother and stepped on the gas.

Lark had gotten as far as the first stoplight when he pulled up to the curb next to her and rolled down the passenger-side window.

"You know, the SVPD still patrols this road all the time," he said, shouting to be heard through the window. "So unless you'd prefer a ride from one of Spring Valley's finest, I would urge you to get in the car."

The rain was coming down harder now, sheeting off the windshield and beating on the moonroof. At last, Lark slowed, then stopped entirely. She stood in the middle of the sidewalk, breathing hard, her eyes fixed on the stretch of road ahead. He could practically see the battle going on inside her head.

Not until that moment had it occurred to him that just because she knew his name didn't mean she knew *him*.

She hadn't known him then.

She didn't know him now.

"If it's a safety thing, you can call someone and leave it on speaker while we drive," he suggested.

"My phone is dead," Lark said in a flat voice.

"Then we can use mine." He reached into his pocket and pulled it out, swiping open the screen and holding it up for her to see.

Lark's shoulders slumped, and he felt a rush of relief when she pivoted on her sneaker and marched toward the curb.

Nick reached across to open the passenger-side door, and Lark slid in, yanking it closed behind her. He attempted to hand her his phone only to have her shake her head.

"It's fine," she said.

Nick didn't know whether he should be flattered or concerned at her lack of precaution.

Finding his gym bag by feel in the back seat, he pulled out a towel. "It's clean," he said holding it out to her. "I use fabric softener and everything."

At least when living pinching distance from his mother, who had accused him of forcing her to dry off with sandpaper the one time she'd stayed in his Manhattan rathole.

"Thanks." Lark dried her face before dragging the sodden hoodie over her head. The tank top beneath was damp as well, clinging to her breasts in a way that made Nick's jeans tight.

Lark blotted her shirt before reaching up to pull an elastic free from her hair. The rain-darkened chestnut skein fell to the bottom of her ribs, filling the sedan with a delicate floral scent. Leaning forward over her thighs, Lark wrapped the towel around the mass and wrung it out like a washcloth.

Nick cleared his throat and tore his eyes away. "Where to?" he asked.

A damp tendril brushed Nick's arm as Lark swung her hair over her shoulder to rub the towel over her scalp. "The Lakewood Estates."

"Seat belt," he said.

Lark complied as he pulled away from the curb.

In his peripheral vision, Nick tried—and failed—not to notice the way the strap snugged against the now sheer fabric of her top.

Slowing for a stop light, he sifted through his memory for a safe topic of conversation. "So, what brings you back to town?" he asked. "You're at Dartmouth if I remember right?"

The towel paused. "I was."

Hearing the catch in her voice, Nick glanced over to see fresh tears welling in her eyes.

Shit.

"I'm sorry," he said. "I didn't mean to upset you."

"You didn't," she said. "I'm the one who should be sorry."

"For what?" Nick pressed the small button on his console to clear the fogging windshield.

"For leaving class early. For making you chase me down in the rain. For dirtying your gym towel."

"The first two are no big deal, and the third is nothing that a wash cycle won't fix. Besides, the stuff we're working on you were already doing by the time we were sophomores." He slowed at the stoplight connecting Main Street with King James Avenue, on the edge of Spring Valley's quaint historic downtown.

Lark sagged back against the seat and stared out the window. "Believe me, whatever talent I once had is long gone."

"I highly doubt that," Nick said.

Lark's head rolled to face him on the headrest. "I couldn't even draw an *apple*."

Nick arched an eyebrow at her. "And is that inability something you're expecting to impact your future in a significant way?"

"It's not about that. It's knowing I can no longer do something I used to be good at."

"I used to be good at cartwheels," Nick said. "I could hop out and show you what that looks like now if it would make you feel better."

The corner of her mouth ticked up. "You'd do that?"

"Fuck no," he said. "But way to call my bluff. I'm also terrible at shuffling cards, if you want me to bring a deck next week to demonstrate. Providing you're planning on coming back to class, that is."

"Oh, my mom will make sure I get there. Whether I get home, on the other hand…" Lark trailed off.

Nick's pulse quickened with a flash of anger he had absolutely no right to feel. "Is that who you were waiting for?"

Lark nodded, her eyelids lowering as she sank down further in her seat. "Yep."

His grip on the steering wheel tightened. "And she didn't call or text or anything?"

"My phone died, remember?" Her mouth contorted on a yawn. "Probably in the middle of a delivery," she said in a sleepy voice.

"That's right," he said, her assertion having jogged his memory. "I forgot your parents run their own clinic."

Husband-and-wife doctors. A far more impressive pairing than his own household's high school teacher turned department head and NYPD officer turned small-town cop. Transplants, Nick's parents had met and married in upstate New York before bouncing around New England and finally settling in Spring Valley when his father had been nearing retirement. A town his father had idyllic memories of from a few childhood summers spent at his grandfather's place growing up.

Nick's experience of it had been...somewhat different.

Flipping on the turn signal, Nick hung a right into the upscale neighborhood attached to a sprawling golf course. Upper middle-class McMansions in every architectural flavor sprung up on either side of the secluded drive. Fun-sized French chateaus. Miniature Mediterranean villas. Tidy Tudor country houses. All of them artfully lit from below so they could be appreciated both day and night.

Like their East Coast accents, his parents' comparatively limited finances had been a source of friction during Nick's high school years. In Spring Valley's relatively affluent circle, he'd stuck out like a smashed thumb.

"So did you move back to Spring Valley after NYU?" Lark asked as if picking up his thoughts.

It was the first question she'd asked him about himself. "I'm still in New York City," he said. "I'm just here for the summer."

"Just to visit?" she asked.

"Something like that." The something in this case being hiding. Fleeing the increasingly uncomfortable knowledge that the career, the company, the life he'd built for himself in the city was beginning to chafe.

"And you decided to teach a community art class for fun?"

"More like my mother decided," he said. "This is normally her class, but she wanted to scale back and they haven't been able to find anyone."

That had been his mother's story anyway. Upon spending his first full week at home, he'd been surprised to learn his mother had offloaded not only this class but all her classes. In addition to her duties as department head. When asked why she'd taken a sabbatical, she'd only shrugged and said she wanted to spend more time gardening. A claim Nick believed about as much as he believed her assertion that he'd have the house to himself because she "wanted to respect his personal space."

Which she'd done exactly never.

For a woman who was unfailingly blunt, Julia could be surprisingly wily when it came to her motives.

"Is that what you've been doing in New York?" she asked. "Teaching?"

Failing, more like. Acid ate at his stomach, remembering the circumstances of his departure. A major blowout with his best friend and business partner, Marshall Graves. One of the many thorns in the bramble of problematic personal relationships that seemed to sprout around Nick wherever he landed.

He'd so wanted this summer to be different.

To clear his head. Catch his breath.

Figure out what the fuck you're actually doing.

Marshall's parting shot as Nick had marched out of the

trendy Flatiron District coworking space before he'd upended a desk.

Yet Marshall hadn't been wrong.

Somewhere after they'd launched their tech start-up, Nick had become…itchy. A low hum of malaise and irritation had made meetings seem endless and plans seem like prisons. Especially when Marshall's ambitions had outstripped their limited resources. They were always chasing. Hustling. Grinding. And a bunch of other bullshit words. Now they had come to a crossroads, and for the first time in his life, Nick's ego balked.

If he didn't figure out what the fuck he wanted—and soon—he was in danger of losing everything he and Marshall had started to build.

Noticing his T-shirt sticking to his back, Nick turned the AC down a couple degrees.

"I'm trying to get an AI art start-up off the ground. I'm sure you've heard the controversy surrounding that."

"I haven't exactly kept up with the news."

The rain had slowed, and the windshield wipers screeched before Nick turned them off. "I won't bore you with the details."

He hadn't realized it was an invitation for her to ask for more information until she didn't.

"It's that one up there on the right with the oak tree."

Slowing the car, Nick turned into the empty driveway. The edifice was clean and modern. Large windows. Spare decoration. To Nick, it looked more like a spa or a bank than a home. The kind of place whose furniture you were never really meant to sit on.

Lark stared at the second-story window revealing part of a chrome-and-glass staircase.

All the questions crowding Nick's mind felt impossible to

ask. *Do you think anyone's home? Will you be okay by yourself? Why do you look so sad?*

His cell phone chimed with a text message, breaking the immobilizing silence. He glanced at the glowing screen and saw her do the same.

Julia: Is everything okay? I thought we were having dinner together.

Lark unclipped her seat belt. "I'm sorry. I've kept you from your plans."

"You haven't," he said too quickly. "That's my mom."

She arched an eyebrow at him. "You call your mom Julia?"

"She was part of a women's aging workshop a while back and decided she was no longer energetically aligned with the mother phase of life. Reclaiming her first name is part of embracing her crone energy," Nick recited.

"She sounds like an interesting lady," Lark said, folding the damp towel in her lap.

"She's interesting, all right." Nick reached into the back seat and retrieved her portfolio. "Don't forget this."

"Thanks," she said. "You at least have to let me wash this towel and get it back to you." Lark held it close to her damp tank top.

Nick felt an absurd urge to reject her suggestion, hating himself for wondering if the towel would bear a trace of her intoxicating scent. This thought was quickly replaced with one even more problematic. If he let her take the towel, she would need to return it, which would make her more likely to come to another class.

"If you insist."

"I do." Lark opened the door. "Thank you again for the ride. I owe you."

"You're right," he blurted.

Her expression shifted from polite to wary. "What's that?"

"You owe me a drawing. You never turned in your assignment."

Her delicate brows lowered. "I didn't realize that was a requirement."

"I take my duties as an instructor very seriously," he said, attempting to inject levity into his voice. "I'm willing to accept a makeup, but on one condition."

"And that is?"

"Charcoal," he said. "You choose the subject matter and the size, but charcoal has to be the medium."

"That's it?" The dark fringe of her lashes lowered as she narrowed her eyes at him.

"That's it," he said.

"Don't expect much."

Their hands brushed as they both reached for the handle of the portfolio, and a strange tingle sizzled up Nick's arm. For the first time that evening, Lark's cheeks held a rosy flush.

The hint of a smile on her lips felt like winning the lottery.

"Thanks, *Mr. Hoffman*," she said in an alarmingly accurate rendition of Tammy's southern drawl. Nick's stomach floated in his rib cage as their eyes met and held. Then Lark slid out of the car and slammed the door.

He waited as she made her way to the front porch and punched a code into the glowing panel next to the door. Lark turned back and waved before disappearing inside. He caught a flash of dark hair at the top of the stairs as he pulled away into the night.

The modest three-bedroom Craftsman home in Spring Valley's suburb made for a stark contrast to the Hockneys' elegant property. Nick sat idling at the curb with the lights off, allowing the last of a Howlin' Wolf song to finish as he nerved himself up to go inside.

When he'd wrung the very last melancholy note from the Delta blues classic, he begrudgingly killed the engine, stalked up the driveway and slipped in through the carport entrance. The heavenly scent of Bolognese sauce hung on the air.

"Forty minutes your dinner has been in the oven. The pasta is going to be mush, and you have no one to blame but yourself," Julia Hoffman said. She stood at the sink washing dishes, an apron knotted behind her broad hips.

Nick unhitched his messenger bag and hung it on the same hook that had once held the keys to his very first car. A battered Mustang that had trailed engine oil and blue smoke all the way to high school every morning of his senior year.

"I'm sorry. I had to give someone a ride home."

Her yellow dish glove stopped, and her chin angled over a shoulder dappled with sun damage from decades of gardening. "Oh?"

"Yep." Nick bent to unlace his boots and kicked them off before settling at the kitchen table where a place had been set. A foil-covered plate landed in front of him, and Nick eagerly peeled it back.

"Not so fast," his mother said, snatching his fork and setting it back down on the napkin. "Salad first."

"*Mom*—"

"Julia," she corrected. "You need the roughage." She set a bowl of greens next to his plate.

Nick picked up his fork and began to stir the leaves.

"Dressing's at the bottom."

Nick grinned behind her back, amused that she felt the need to point this out despite the fact that she'd been arranging salads this way for years. But then, these recitations were part of their ritual. The elaborate and familiar pantomime where his mother pretended to be put out at having to fuss over him and he pretended not to enjoy it.

He speared a bite and chewed the peppery greens. Familiar flavors. Familiar surroundings.

Unfamiliar feelings.

Against the memory of the pristine all-white kitchen he'd noticed when dropping off Lark, the space he'd always considered homey felt close and cluttered. It wasn't that his mother was messy. Just that objects tended to…accumulate. Books. Bags. Bills.

He made a mental note to investigate the pile of unopened mail against the bread box.

His mother dragged out the chair across from his with a mud-flecked gardening clog and set down two wine glasses and an already-opened bottle of cabernet.

"So?"

His mother's ubiquitous one-syllable question. The ticket that entitled her to any new developments in his life.

Nick turned his attention to the manicotti. "So, I had a new student tonight."

"Oh?"

"Yep," he said around a mouthful. "I went to school with her."

"At NYU?"

"Spring Valley High."

"You're kidding," she said.

"One hundred percent not." Nick stuck his fork into the pasta and lifted the bite. "Lark Hockney. You remember her?"

"Do I remember her? She was only the valedictorian. Gave the most beautiful speech." Her hand landed on the shelf of her bosom.

Nick nodded. "That's her."

Her hazel eyes widened as she sat back in her chair. "I knew she was back in Spring Valley but hadn't heard a thing about her in months," she said, as if her not receiving regular updates was an oversight someone ought to be written up for.

"Heard how?" Nick set his fork aside to train his full attention on her.

"Oh, you know how people around here talk." She waved a hand as if this revelation could be dispelled as easily as a wisp of smoke.

He knew.

"Which people?" Nick asked.

His mother's eyes flicked to his abandoned fork. "You remember my friend Judy, who works at the country club?"

"You mean the Judy who taught me piano every Thursday from the time I was seven until I left for college?"

"Don't be smart." The crinkles at the corners of her eyes deepened as she gave him a look.

"I kind of thought that was the point."

"Keep this up, and I'll eat your tiramisu myself. See if I don't."

Checkmate.

"Yes, I remember Judy."

"Well, six months ago, she was finally promoted to general manager of the country club's restaurant. Of course, if that tight-assed tycoon who owned the place had two brain cells to rub together, he'd have done it years ago," she added.

"*Julia.*" His saying her name was the equivalent of a train conductor pulling the lever to send the engine back down the main track.

"All right, all right." Brushing crumbs from the table into the palm of her hand, she dropped them onto a napkin. "Anyway. Every year, they do this fancy Easter brunch, and this year, Lark comes in with her parents and that kid." She snapped her fingers as if this would dislodge his name from her memory. "The rich one who was always in the papers for breaking baseball records?"

The chicken and pasta congealed into a cold lump in Nick's stomach. The data he associated with the student in question was indexed rather differently.

"Reese Hudson."

"That's right." The table jiggled when she thumped it for emphasis, and Nick made a mental note to tighten the legs. "Anyway, everyone is enjoying their Easter lamb and mint jelly when Reese taps his champagne flute and raises a toast to Lark's parents. Talks about how they're pillars of the community and inspiration to anyone studying to be a doctor, blah blah blah, and that they raised the most amazing woman he's ever met." Ever the expert at heightening the tension, his mother paused and sipped her wine. "That's when he gets down on one knee and proposes."

Acid climbed Nick's throat.

"Everyone is clapping, cheering, carrying on—even some of the staff have come out to watch. Judy's trying to get them back in the kitchen when she notices that Lark is just kind of sitting there, staring at the ring."

"Yeah?"

His mother nodded sagely. "At first, Judy thought it was shock. I mean, *I* would be shocked if someone just up and offered me a diamond the size of a cat over brunch."

"Who wouldn't?" Nick asked with far more levity than he felt.

"But then her face goes white as a sheet." His mother's fingertips hovered near her cheekbones. "She breaks out in a sweat and starts yanking at her blouse, saying she can't breathe. Of course, her poor mother is frantic."

"Of course," Nick agreed.

"Judy is trained in CPR because she's a volunteer lifeguard at the YMCA, but she's not sure if Lark is having an allergic reaction or a stroke or something, so she calls 911. Before the paramedics could even get there, Lark stands up and runs right out of the room."

This response sounded familiar.

"Judy didn't see the next part, but one of the valets told her Lark and the Reese kid got into a screaming match in the parking lot before her parents came out and broke it up. Seeing as there haven't been any announcements in the newspaper, I'm gonna guess it was a no. Which is a shame because Judy said it really was beautiful ring."

His mother's eyes drifted to her own left hand where her wedding set still sat nestled in a crease below her reddened knuckles. Seven years his father had been gone, and she'd never taken it off.

"Those don't improve with age you know," his mother said, nudging the edge of his neglected plate.

Nick's appetite had vanished somewhere in the maze of his thoughts, but he made a token effort, sawing off another bite and chewing mechanically.

Lark Hockney and Reese Hudson. Spring Valley High's golden couple.

Together since sophomore year, they'd been predictably nominated to every court and won most of them. Their too-pretty-to-be-true faces splashed over every yearbook page. Leads in every school play and musical. Matching scholarships to Ivy League colleges. Comet tails of superlatives trailing both names. To hear that they'd continued dating after high school and that Reese had proposed surprised Nick not at all.

The fact that Lark had fled a country club brunch to refuse his proposal?

Fucking shocker, right there.

"Hey, space cadet, you want it or not?"

Nick had only vaguely registered his mother's voice in the background and guessed at her question mostly by context. "Sure, I want it."

Pushing back from the table, his mother went to the fridge and came back with two parfait glasses covered in plastic wrap. She slid his across the table to him and lifted the transparent covering from hers.

"How did she seem?" his mother asked, dipping her spoon into the cocoa-flecked pillow of cream.

"How did who seem?" he asked.

"*Lark*," his mother said, shaking her head at Nick's appalling lack of investment in the transfer of juicy tidbits.

"Quiet," he said.

"Quiet," she repeated.

Peeling back the plastic wrap from his own glass, Nick picked up his spoon. "Yeah. She sat in the back of the room. Didn't say much."

"Not even to the *harpies*?" She pronounced the word with poisonous relish.

His mother had harbored a dislike for the pretty, chatty divorcées since she'd come to evaluate his class on behalf of the humanities department. Their mild flirtation had barely registered on Nick's radar until his mother had pointed it out. And were it not for Spring Valley's relentless rumor mill, Nick might have taken them up on their interest. He'd dated older women almost exclusively since he'd left for college and lost his virginity to a teaching assistant in his first semester.

"Especially not to them," Nick said.

"How'd she look?"

Nick raised a *really, Mother?* eyebrow at her as he dug into his dessert.

"What? I just wanted to give Judy an update. She was very concerned."

Judy was concerned about *everyone*.

In Lark's case, it was actually warranted.

Nick's chest caught at the memory of her alone at the table at the back of the room. Her seawater-green eyes red rimmed, with dark hollows beneath. Too large in her narrow face. Pale lips drawn into a perpetual frown.

And for all that, still so goddamn beautiful she'd stolen the breath from his lungs.

"She looked…tired," Nick said, working over a mouthful of decadent, coffee-flavored sponge cake. "Left class early. I thought maybe she had plans until I ran into her in the parking lot."

Recognition spread over his mother's wholesome features like the dawn. "*She's* the one you gave a ride to?"

Christ, why hadn't he just left out that detail?

"Yeah," Nick said, spoon scraping the bottom of his glass.

"Did her car break down or something?"

Just dig yourself deeper, why don't you? "Her ride didn't show."

Nick could pinpoint almost down to the second when his mother got the full picture, her curiosity melting into compassion.

"Can I make you an espresso?" she asked, getting to her feet.

"Nah," Nick said, pushing back from the table to help clear it. "I'm just going to make a pot of coffee."

The wrinkles at the corners of his mother's eyes deepened as her eyebrows drew together. "But it's already nine thirty."

"Yeah, I know. I just need to get a little catch-up work done tonight."

"Nicky," she said. "I thought we agreed."

Technically, his mother had agreed. Nick had surrendered after months of badgering. Upon his arrival a few weeks back, she'd launched her campaign of reforming his sleep, nutrition and work schedules.

"We just have to get over the last hurdle." Relieving his mother of their dishes, Nick carried them to the sink and started rinsing. "The grant submission deadline is in three weeks, and Marshall and I still have to hammer out a few of the sections."

"Seems you're the one doing most of the hammering," she muttered under her breath, wiping her hands on the dishtowel.

Marshall and Nick's mother had only met once, when Julia had come to New York for a visit, and they'd mixed like oil and nitroglycerin.

Nick had been so eager to bring her into the city, to show off Moonshot's base of operations. But as he had marched Julia around the sleek, upscale coworking suites Marhsall had insisted on renting at great cost, she'd been uncharacteristically silent.

For his part, Marshall had done his usual song and dance, attempting to charm her with compliments and questions.

She'd received all this coolly, waiting until dinner to deliver her stinging rebuke.

Refusing a glass of the Chateau Petrus Marshall had ordered, Julia had asked for "plain old tap water," following that passive-aggressive move by commenting that she'd rather they didn't spend money on her account since it only meant her son would have to work harder to cover expenses.

And that had been the end of that.

"Division of labor," he said now. Opening the dishwasher, Nick began to load their wine glasses.

"Let me do this," his mother insisted, hip-checking him out of the way. "The sooner you get working, the sooner you can get to sleep."

"You're the boss." He bent to plant a kiss on his mother's soft, fragrant cheek and collected his messenger bag before heading down the hallway to his old room.

His mother hadn't quite made a mausoleum of it, but neither had she removed all traces of his presence. Martial arts trophies on the shelves. *Fortnite* fan art on the walls. The desk where he'd scratched words into the surface for the three weeks of summer he'd been grounded. A vast collection of space-and-robotics-related ephemera. Drawings. So many drawings. Each one a small rebellion.

Mostly against his father.

Avram Hoffman—Abe to his friends, Pop to Nick and Sergeant Hoffman to the Spring Valley Police Department.

The man who'd insisted Nick was wasting his time "studying cartoons"—i.e., obsessing over anime—when he ought to be figuring out a way to make a contribution to the world.

The man whose close-cropped crew cut was the reason for Nick's wild locks. The man whose love of baseball and dismissal of intellectualism was the reason Nick had boycotted sports and toted thick tomes of Proust and Sartre in his battered backpack.

The man whose negative spaces had described the shape of Nick's ambitions.

He'd simply wanted to be everything Avram Hoffman was not.

And in Marshall Graves, Nick had found his perfect template.

Effortlessly sophisticated, annoyingly handsome, silver-tongued and charismatic Marshall, who had cringed when Julia had cracked jokes about needing to play the numbers to afford an appetizer. Marshall, who had half-jokingly asked if Nick could hire a stunt-mom to accompany him to the Tech Trailblazers Awards ceremony at the end of summer.

New York Nick had briefly considered it.

Spring Valley Nick felt like the world's largest asshole.

How he was supposed to bring the divided halves of his existence together, he didn't have the first goddamn clue.

So, as he so frequently had done to disastrous effect, Nick distracted himself instead.

Flipping open his bag, he pulled out the folded sheet of sketch paper. He'd smoothed it from the crumpled ball he'd pulled out of the trash can. A graphite smudge bore a print of the side of her palm.

Having spent the better part of the year writing code that would teach an AI engine to recognize patterning, Nick could clearly see hers. The ethereal quality of her line work. Her exquisite sense of form and spatial positioning. The exact place where the beast had begun to bite into her.

Perfectionism.

Attempting to capture, with exacting verisimilitude, the object itself rather than her individual impression of it.

It had been this specific quality that had inspired his idea of requesting she do a makeup drawing using charcoals. The dark, soft medium dealt only in the boldest of lines. But more specifically than that, charcoal wouldn't allow her to erase her mistakes.

Three

Lark woke in the predawn with a familiar weight on her chest and a familiar scent in her nostrils.

The weight, their family cat, Muppet, who had appointed himself her emotional support animal.

The scent, her mother's perfume.

Lark stirred, igniting the engine of Muppet's purr.

"Sweetie, are you awake?" her mother whispered.

"If I say no, will you go away?" Lark asked in a sleep-fogged voice.

The mattress sank near Lark's left calf as her mother sat down. "I'm so sorry about last night, honey."

Lark buried her fingers into the cat's warm, soft fur. "It's fine, Mom."

A beat of silence.

"When you didn't respond, I just thought you might be… upset."

Upset didn't begin to cover it.

When the black hole of her phone had resurrected itself, she'd seen the text of profuse apology her mother had sent. By that point, she'd been too humiliated and wrung out to respond.

None of which it would help her mother to know.

"I wasn't," she said.

Drop it. Please.

"Did you have any trouble getting an Uber?"

No such luck.

As much as she'd hoped to talk around it, Lark couldn't bring herself to lie outright. "I didn't call an Uber."

A beat of silence. "A taxi?"

Muppet's paws dug into her shoulder as he pushed himself up for a stretch. "I got a ride with the instructor."

"You rode home with someone you'd only just met?"

"How is that different than an Uber?" Lark asked.

"For one thing, Uber drivers are registered with an app that tracks their name, address and vehicle registration. Unlike some stranger—"

"He wasn't a stranger," Lark said. "I went to high school with him."

"Oh?" her mother asked, smoothing the covers. "Anyone I would remember?"

"I doubt it."

Not technically a lie. Lark's mother would most likely recognize his last name, but for reasons that had nothing to do with Nick. And that wasn't a conversation Lark was willing to have without coffee on board.

"So not a classmate you knew well."

The implication couldn't be any clearer. If Lark had known him, her parents would have as well, seeing as they'd made a point of practically running a background check on anyone who'd so much as shared a bleacher with her at Homecoming.

Not because Spring Valley was the kind of place where any parent had to worry, but because as the lone victory in her parents' extensive battle with infertility, Lark represented the sum total of their staggering emotional and financial investments.

The walking, talking, overachieving proof that all their effort had been worth it.

And though it wasn't like they'd said as much directly, Lark had felt the weight of that expectation pretty much from the time she'd taken her first staggering steps.

"Correct," Lark said after an extended silence, hoping the one-word answer would give her mother the hint.

"Well, that was very kind of him," her mother said brightly.

"Mm-hmm." Muppet marched in a circle on her belly and settled back down on her chest.

"What did you think of the class?"

Translation: *Are you still angry at me for making you go?*

"Pretty basic," Lark said, keeping her eyelids firmly shut.

Translation: *Yes, but I'm too exhausted to talk about it.*

"Do you think—"

"Yes, Mom, I'm planning on going back on Thursday, so you can dispense with the subtle hints and inquiries." Lark hated herself a little for the stab of satisfaction she got from venting her frustration. Logically, she knew her mother was just trying to help.

"Honey, I wasn't—"

"I know, Mom," Lark said, cutting her off. "I just don't want to talk about the class anymore, okay?"

"Okay," her mother agreed. Another beat of silence. "Your father and I were thinking of going to Biaggio's for dinner tonight."

A family-owned Italian bistro with an operatic maître d', Biaggio's had long been the Hockneys' "place" of choice. Festive enough to feel celebratory, homey enough to ensure they were greeted by name. A combination of factors that made Lark's chest tighten.

"What's the occasion?" she asked.

"Does there have to be an occasion for us to want to have a dinner out with our daughter?" her mother asked.

"There doesn't *have to* be, no."

There just always was.

The mattress shifted with her mother's body weight. "We thought that maybe if we were somewhere you felt comfortable…"

Ah.

So, her mother was doubling down. Attempting to seize the momentum for the process of Lark's recovery. Now that she'd successfully coaxed Lark into attending a semipublic event with other humans, surely dinner in a restaurant wouldn't be a stretch.

And if a class *and* a restaurant dinner were possible, might that suggest Lark should entertain the idea of returning to medical school before her twenty-seven-day grace period ran out?

Scratch that.

Twenty-six.

Her heart began to thump dully beneath the down comforter. "I think I'll pass," Lark said. "The instructor gave me a solo assignment that's due Thursday, and I want to get started. But you and Dad should definitely go."

She could feel her mother's resistance to the idea of leaving her alone, especially the night after failing to give her a ride home.

"You guys haven't been out together since I came home." Lark managed to inject enough emotion into this plea to get her mother's attention. Most of her observations tended to fall as flat as she felt. "You guys are always on me to start getting back to my normal life. Don't you think you should too?"

Her mother turned her still-beautiful profile to the walk-out basement's bay window. Even in the dim light, Lark could make out the resemblance to her own features. Maybe that was part of what had made it so hard—proximity to a woman who was much like her but had managed to be more successful.

"I don't like the idea of you here all alone while your father and I are out at one of your favorite places."

The sheen of tears coating her mother's eyes stirred something in Lark. "Why don't you bring me back some penne rustica?" she suggested. Her appetite had been one the many casualties of her depression, and expressing a craving made her mother's eyes light up.

Her mother found Lark's hand atop the comforter and squeezed it. "We could do that."

Instant relief came from multiple sources: successfully evading potential plans and the prospect of an evening with the house to herself.

Apparently satisfied, her mother shifted to leave. "So, what's on the docket for today?"

She glanced toward her desk where the towel she had borrowed from Nick sat slung over her desk chair. "I'm going to do some laundry. Then I thought I might walk to the art store to get some charcoals."

Her mother's face creased in a frown. "Charcoals? But I didn't see those on the supply list."

"Because they weren't," Lark said. "You did fine, Mom. This was a special assignment from the instructor."

Calling Nick Hoffman *the instructor* still felt odd despite the quiet authority he'd radiated at the front of the classroom. Lark had spent the remainder of yesterday evening scouring social media for any information about Nick's life since high school and had come up with surprisingly little beyond his LinkedIn profile.

He'd attended NYU with a dual major in computer science and graphic design. Worked at a couple of Manhattan marketing firms. Founded Moonshot, an open-source AI tech start-up, a couple years back. Nowhere did she see evidence of his romantic leanings.

It was the first time she'd felt anything like curiosity since she could remember.

"Well, that sounds nice," her mother said. "How do you feel about taking George with you?"

How she felt was annoyed. Despite an impeccable pedigree, the black Lab her father had surprised her mother with last Christmas was one of the most stubborn, destructive and abominably behaved creatures Lark had ever encountered.

And those were his positive traits.

"I'm pretty sure they don't allow dogs in the art supply store," Lark said.

"You won't be in there for very long, will you?" her mother pressed. "And practically everywhere downtown they have dog hitches and watering posts."

About this her mother was correct. Spring Valley had recently undergone a tourist-friendly facelift complete with pet accommodations at most restaurants and social venues in the quaint town square.

"I'll think about it," Lark said.

"Okay, sweetie," her mother said. "There's coffee and bagels upstairs. Your father already left for work." This last addition was a courtesy on her mother's part—letting Lark know that she could safely venture upstairs without facing her father's questions about her plans for the day, the week, her life.

"Thanks, Mom."

Lark rolled back onto her side as her mother rose and fixed her with a beaming smile.

"I'm really proud of you for going last night, honey. I know that wasn't easy."

"You think Spring Valley Community College offers academic scholarships?" Lark asked around a yawn.

Her mother's smile plummeted as swiftly as a shot bird.

Too soon, it seemed.

For Lark, the loss of her prestigious fellowship had been just another brick of guilt in the wall that made resuming her former academic trajectory seem impossible. For her parents, it had been the source of a tense discussion at the kitchen table when they hadn't known Lark had been listening. Phrases like "pay out of pocket" and "can't guarantee this won't happen again" had been all she'd needed to decipher the content of the conversation.

"Sweet girl," her mother said, ruffling Lark's hair the same way she had since Lark had been a kindergartner. "Have a good day." She always pronounced the phrase tentatively, the last word curving up like a question.

"I'll try."

Lark lay in bed after her mom had left, the tightness in her chest easing when she heard the garage door open, her mother's car back out, then the door close again.

This had always proved to be Lark's least favorite part of waking up. Peeling back the warmth of the covers, forcing her feet to meet the carpet. Gathering momentum for the day. She had reached the phase of bargaining with herself for only ten minutes of TikTok—and she really meant it this time—when the phone buzzed in her hand.

A notification from the community college's class app.

Her heart skipped a beat when she scanned the banner and saw the sender's name.

HoffmanN.

Pushing herself up in bed, Lark quickly swiped it open and read.

HoffmanN: Hey there, just checking to see how you're doing.

Only as she was studying the words for the tenth time did Lark notice the checkmark next to his message marking it as read.

Shit.

She couldn't very well *not* reply to it now.

The question was *how?*

Should she go cool? *Fine, thanks.*

Casual? *Not too bad. Thanks again for the ride.*

Confident? *Doing great! Currently working on my assignment.*

Or maybe—

Three blinking dots appeared below his message.

Nick was typing *more.*

Her pulse picked up to a gallop as she waited, jumping a little when the phone buzzed again in her hand.

HoffmanN: Not to pressure you about the drawing or anything. I just meant in general.

Lark had just begun to type her reply—So far, so good—friendly, noncommittal, when the dots reappeared again.

HoffmanN: Promise I'm not trying to be intrusive.

And then, before she could stop herself, Lark was typing.

HockneyL: Actually, I'm surprisingly good this morning.

HoffmanN: What's surprising about it?

Hard to say, she typed. The air feels lighter, if that makes any sense.

The dots reappeared immediately.

Makes perfect sense, he replied.

HoffmanN: obviously, that's my doing.

Lark experienced a curiously tight feeling in her cheeks and realized she was smiling.

My therapist might take issue with that assessment, she shot back.

Dear God. Had she really just told him she had a therapist? Like it would be a great shocker after last night's performance.

Again, the dots appeared.

HoffmanN: Mine probably would too.

And just like that, a catch in her chest clicked open, and a tide of grateful warmth suffused her from her neck to her knees. Even if he was saying it out of a gracious need to normalize her admission, it had worked like a charm.

Still. The idea intrigued her. That Nick Hoffman's mild demeanor might be hiding psychological knots in need of untangling.

You too? she typed.

The fact that this made him even more intriguing was probably something she should add to this week's therapy agenda.

They issue you one the second you arrive in Grand Central, Nick replied.

Lark snorted loud enough to startle Muppet from her lap.

So you're saying if I had chosen NYU instead of Dartmouth, all of this could have been avoided? she answered.

HoffmanN: Probably. But then I wouldn't have had the pleasure of loaning you my favorite gym towel.

Lark bit her lower lip as she glanced at the towel again. Without even thinking, she sat up and peeled back the covers before crossing to her desk to retrieve it.

HockneyL: Speaking of which, I'd better get some laundry going so I can return it to you unharmed.

She watched the dots dance as she climbed the stairs, wincing as George broke into a cascade of barks at her approach. Lark shooed him outside before turning down the hallway to the laundry room.

For no reason she could think of, she lifted Nick's towel and sniffed.

A fainter version of the scent she remembered from his car last night filled her lungs. Subtle, clean cologne. Woodsy soap or shampoo. The barest hint of fabric softener.

Tossing it into the machine, she told herself it was only her lack of breakfast and coffee that made her head go all swimmy. An assertion not supported by the way her stomach somersaulted when her phone pinged.

HoffmanN: sports wash cool with like colors. 60-minute synthetic dry cycle. Fabric softener appreciated but not required. Synthetic dry cycle is essential. Cannot stress this enough

HockneyL: I'm glad you told me because I was about to take it out into the backyard, dip in the koi pond and beat it against a rock

HoffmanN: what kind of filter does the koi pond have? Are we talking granite or limestone?

HockneyL: Limestone?? With that pH? Do you hate koi or are you just basic?

Lark bit her lip, waiting to see if he'd get the joke.

HoffmanN: I've been known to walk on the alkaline side

HoffmanN: Kindly stop being so goddamn witty and making me helplessly reply to you. I have work to do

HoffmanN: See you tomorrow

HockneyL: See you then

It wasn't the subtle flare of disappointment Lark felt at the standard sign-off that surprised her.

It was how much she'd wanted their exchange to keep going.

"You are an absolute disgrace, you know that?"

Lark wound George's lead tighter around her wrist to avoid having her arm pulled from the socket as they rounded the final corner to City Center.

On the walk over, he'd attempted to eat no less than four squirrels, urinated on a mail truck—while the mail person was still in it—then nearly caused a retiree's heart attack when he'd snapped at her corgi.

It had been a mistake to bring him, but she'd also felt bad that he spent so much time cooped up in the house while her parents put in long hours at the clinic.

Lark knew the feeling.

And it was such a beautiful day.

Virginia in the full flush of summer—the perfume of flowers on the air and leaves in their deepest green coats.

She couldn't remember the last time she'd been outside at ten o'clock on a Wednesday morning.

Certainly not since *before*.

Lark slowed at the crosswalk and waited for the sign to turn, nearly pulled off balance when George lunged at a man who crossed the empty street despite the Don't Walk sign. The light turned, and she proceeded across the street, slowing in front of her destination.

Though Brilliant Brushes was one of the many stores that encouraged patrons to bring their pets, the idea of George knocking over a display—or worse, one of the other customers—filled Lark with dread.

Spotting the water bowl left out for four-legged guests, Lark walked George over to it and hitched his lead to the anchoring post provided. She squatted down before him, took his silky ears in her hands and looked him straight in his eerily intelligent golden-brown eyes.

"I just need to go in for a minute. If you stay here and be quiet like a good boy, we'll swing by the Sultry Sips and get you a Puppuccino."

George cocked his boxy head as if he was listening to her.

"*But*," she said, "if you so much as growl at another pedestrian or attempt to intimidate another toy-sized dog, it's straight home and you can forget about the whipped cream."

The dog gave low *woof* before sitting back on his haunches.

Which might have been why Lark went inside with more confidence than was entirely justified given the situation. A bell chimed as she pushed open the door, and she was immediately enveloped in a cloud of familiar scents.

Earthy clay and resiny linseed oil. Mineral-rich graphite and woodsy paper.

The smell of art.

Lark closed her eyes and breathed it in, letting it transport her back to when she'd been a teenager. When the heady bouquet had filled her with a sense of endless possibility. She could have spent hours poring over every soft sable brush and thick creamy pad, dreaming of what she might create.

Not that her schedule had ever allowed many large spates of unsupervised time.

Until now.

Lark found herself drifting over to the shelves, running her fingers over the feathery paintbrushes, tracing the boxes of pastels in their perfect rainbow rows. She'd just reached the cardboard sleeves of charcoals when the sound of a familiar voice jangled her nerves.

"Well, how the hell am I supposed to know what gouache is? Lloyd was always too busy pulling his boxers out of his butt crack to support any of my interests."

Tammy, the southern belle from class.

"If you'd ever come to the museum with me, you might have learned a thing or too by now," Linda's smooth, plummy voice replied.

"You're a volunteer, Linda. So don't get all uppity with me."

"Well, Dr. Blanton says they're going to create a paid week-end position for me just as soon as the museum gets that grant. He knows I'm still rebuilding my clientele."

"Of course he does." Tammy's voice swooped up like a sparrow. "He's a letch, not stupid. He's being all complimentary so you'll stay on for free and he can keep ogling your tits while you drag daycare kids around the joint on a rope. Me, I have better things to do with my weekends."

Judging by the husky dip in Tammy's voice, Lark could guess what those things might be.

"I'd personally rather remove every single one of my toenails with an ice pick before I try online dating again."

Lark caught a glimpse of Linda's tawny shoulder beneath the fluttery sleeve of an eggplant-purple blouse.

"That's because you're doing it wrong." One of Tammy's sandaled feet slid into view, tanned and recently pedicured.

Lark glanced down at her own feet, stuffed sockless into old tennis shoes. When was the last time she'd painted her toenails? Christmas?

"You just need to let me make you up a profile," Tammy continued. "I'll have 'em lined up at your door with their peckers pointing due north."

Lark clapped a hand over her mouth to keep from snorting.

"That is my literal nightmare," Linda replied. "I honestly think the last two years I stayed with Phil were because I just wasn't ready to deal with a new dick."

"Lord, do I hear that," Tammy agreed.

The voices were coming closer now.

Slipping past the shelves of markers and paint cans, Lark ducked around to the back aisle, usually stocked with canvases and premade frames, and peeked out into main part of the store. Linda was hovering near the checkout counter. Careful not to make any sudden movements or unnecessary noise, Lark slipped behind a display of oversized sketch pads, hoping the women would just check out and leave. Her fingers had begun to sweat against the pack of charcoals, the cardboard softening in her grip.

Of course, George chose precisely this moment to begin losing his mind. His barks seemed to bounce off the brick buildings, doubling and tripling in volume as he warned an unseen foe.

"Good Lord." Tammy leaned to see out the shop's front window. "What on earth is wrong with that creature?"

"Looks like he—" Linda's gasp made the blood drain from Lark's head in a prickling rush.

A black streak shot across the window.

The realization dawned with rippling horror. George had broken his harness.

Lark's stomach dropped into her shoes, and she took off, nearly knocking both women over as she sprinted out the front door and down the sidewalk.

"George!" Hearing the anguished panic in her own voice only made Lark's heart beat harder, outpacing her pounding footfalls as she ran flat out in the direction of the dog's glossy black retreating rear end.

Already, he had two blocks on her and was gaining.

"George, *stop!*"

George didn't stop.

Nor did the mail truck.

The intrusive thoughts that had been her unwelcome companions over the last several months began piping up.

What if he runs out in front of a car?

What if he turns the corner and disappears?

What's your mother going to say when you have to tell her you lost her dog?

Lark's thighs were on fire, her lungs screaming for air when a squeal of tires and a thunderous bang sent white-hot panic searing through her.

No.

No no no.

"Georgie!" a syrupy sweet voice sang out.

Seeing Tammy come around the corner at the end of the street made Lark stop so abruptly she nearly toppled face-first into a planter.

George's sprint slowed to a trot as he reached the cross street where a white BMW had swung into view. Linda's car, Lark surmised, seeing the dark head behind the wheel.

"Oh, has Aunt Tammy got something good for you." The plastic bag rustled as she slid open the zipper and wiggled it enticingly.

George had stopped in the center of the sidewalk, his nose twitching in Tammy's direction.

"That's a good boy." Tammy reached into the bag and came back with a tawny strip clutched in red-lacquered fingernails. "Does Georgie Boy want some bacon? Does he?" Her question held not one atom of concern.

Lark, meanwhile, was frozen. Too terrified to move for fear her scent might spur George back into a gallop.

His licorice whip of tail began to wag.

Tammy's flashy gold slingbacks clicked on the sidewalk as she took a cautious step in the dog's direction.

George's pink tongue swiped his black lips before the bacon disappeared into his maw.

Traitor.

"Good boy, Georgie," Tammy crowed, producing another slice. The second he leaned in to take it, Tammy grabbed his harness.

All the air exited Lark's lungs on a rush of relief. She wobbled up the sidewalk on jellied legs and sagged against another planter, heart hammering as Tammy towed George back to the curb.

"So sorry about that," Lark said when she was close enough.

Tammy waved her apology away with a flip of her hand and

bent to scratch George behind his ear. "This fella just wanted him some thick-cut, maple-cured turkey bacon is all, and I just happened to have some. Low-carb diet."

The look of bliss on the dog's face brought irrational tears to Lark's eyes. The reality of what could have happened if things had gone differently was still sinking in when the first hot drops slid down her cheeks.

"Thank you so much. I was so scared that—"

"It's all right. If I had to count the number of times my Precious had gotten out, I'd need a prosthetic."

Lark gave a congested snort as she took George's harness.

The white BMW rolled up to the curb. "Can I help with anything?" Linda asked.

"No, you just go ahead and sit right in that air-conditioning while Lark and I do all the work."

"I'll get the leash." The car's engine purred as Linda motored back toward the art store.

George flopped down between their feet, panting like he'd just run a marathon.

"Ain't that just like a man?" Tammy clucked, shaking her head. "Causin' all the trouble, then actin' like he's due a good long rest."

Linda returned ten seconds later, springing out of her car with the leash in hand and looping it through the nylon harness strap before pulling it snug.

George had managed to break the clip, but the configuration looked secure enough.

Freed from dog duty, Tammy dug into the pocket of her floral-print capris and came back with a tissue that she handed to Lark.

Only in reaching out to take it did Lark realize she was already holding something.

The charcoals.

She had officially just added *shoplifter* to her list of undesirable titles.

Flake.

Dropout.

Failure.

"I stole them." The tears came harder then.

"Oh, honey." Tammy clucked, dabbing at Lark's cheeks. "They're overpriced anyway. Any fool who's ever been to a bonfire knows you can make those for the price of a Bic lighter and a six pack of Pabst."

Lark's shoulders shook from an improbable mix of laughter and grief.

"You know what I think?" Tammy asked. "I think we should take George over to the dog park and let him off his leash, get him some real exercise, and then you should come to lunch with us."

Lark's throat tightened as she dabbed her nose. "I couldn't," she croaked. "Really. I need to get George home. And I've caused you enough trouble for one day."

"*Trouble* is Tammy's middle name," Linda chimed in.

"You hush your mouth, Linda," Tammy said, turning back to her. "What d'you say?"

"Really, I can't. But thank you so much for helping catch this rascal." Gripping George's lead, Lark aimed him toward home. "If there's ever anything I can do to repay you, please let me know."

Fixing Lark with a foxy look, Tammy smiled. "You could buy me margarita at lunch."

Lark wasn't sure how two strangers had managed to convince her to go to a Tex-Mex restaurant for lunch, but here she was, sitting with Tammy and Linda in the middle of a cozy patio. The weather was perfect, the sun felt warm on her shoulders and the laughter from other patrons provided an unexpected balm.

Tammy's eyes twinkled as she tipped back an enormous margarita glass. "I think you need one of these," she said, gesturing to Lark. "It'll help you forget about the shoplifting."

The frosty, salt-rimmed glasses with their cobalt stems looked so inviting. And she had at least a good five hours until her parents got home. Lark hesitated before finally giving in with a shrug of surrender. "All right."

"Atta girl." Linda motioned to their server, who promptly strutted over to their table. "Our friend here would like to join us in an afternoon libation."

Their server—Trent, according to his name tag—ducked his sleek head. "Coming right up."

Both women watched as he made his way to the indoor-outdoor bar.

"We're his favorites," Tammy informed Lark. "He knows he'll get a big tip."

"More like he wants to give *you* one," Linda teased.

As if on cue, Trent shot a dazzling smile at their table and gave a little wave that sent Tammy and Linda into a fit of girlish giggles.

Lark sipped her water with lemon, feeling an unfamiliar pang of jealousy over their obvious enjoyment.

"So," Tammy asked, getting down to business. "Where are you from?"

"Here," Lark reported. "Born and raised. How about you?"

"I was born and raised in Macon, Georgia," Tammy said, balling her straw wrapper between her fingers. "Miss Linda here moved there when she was in fifth grade. And we've followed each other around ever since."

"We just moved here from Orlando," Linda reported.

"Both of you?" Lark asked.

"Yep," they said in unison.

"Together?"

"Yep," they said again.

"We do everything together," Tammy reported, licking salt from her glass before taking a sip. "Dancing, drinking, divorcing our husbands…"

"Thank God," they said in unison and clinked their glasses just as Trent returned with Lark's drink.

Somehow, the margarita looked even larger now it was set in front of her. A soup bowl of bad decisions.

"Is there anything else I can bring you ladies right now?" he asked, his eyes lingering on Tammy's for a beat longer than necessary.

"Not right this second," she said. "But we'll sure let you know when we need you."

Twin spots of pink appeared on Trent's chiseled cheekbones. If she trusted her assessments at all, Lark might've been tempted to say their waiter was enjoying the attention.

"You're going to scar that young man," Linda said with a hint of bitterness.

"Only if he's lucky." Tammy's lips curled in a sensual grin. "Cheers," she said, lifting her glass.

"What are we drinking to?" Linda asked.

Tammy tapped the table with a fingernail. "To Hottie Hoffman's art hussies," she said.

Lark's cheeks heated at the mention of Nick's name, the memory of their text exchange earlier that day making her flush with unexpected pleasure. In the hours since, she'd found herself rereading the thread more than once, appreciating Nick's sense of humor more each time.

He was just so…so…charming? Disarming?

It was the only explanation she could come up with for why she'd so readily mentioned her therapist.

Kindly stop being so goddamn witty and making me helplessly reply to you.

Nick Hoffman thought she was witty.

Lark quickly sipped her margarita to cool herself.

The tartness and the hint of lime tickled her taste buds. When had she last sipped a margarita in the sunshine at— she quickly checked her phone—2:27 p.m. on a Wednesday?

Never?

The question gave Lark pause.

Her public unraveling had become a convenient line for dividing her life into *before* and *after*. But the truth was that even before Reese's proposal at the country club had sent her into a screeching panic attack, the cracks had already begun to show.

Days and nights running together as she'd sat in her dorm with the blinds drawn, willing her brain to retain information as it once had. Missed classes. Skipped meals. Clusters of apologetic emails sent to her professors.

From the vantage of this sunny patio, Lark was far enough removed to see the gradual skid that had led to her sudden crash. In the months following, her parents' basement had become her own personal purgatory. Neither heaven nor hell, but a dull, gray den where she could hide while the depression sanded away what was left.

And yet now, here she was.

Out in the daylight. Listening as two women who had

been total strangers to her only last night brainstormed names for the various looks Nick sported to class. *Lonely Lumberjack* being the top contender so far.

"I went to high school with him," Lark blurted.

Both Linda and Tammy paused with margarita glasses halfway to their mouths.

"Seriously?" Linda asked.

Lark nodded, taking a healthy sip before setting the glass down in front of her. "We were in the same graduating class."

"Tell us everything," Tammy said, reaching across the table to clutch Lark's hand. "What was he like? What did he wear?"

Lark paused, allowing the sharp-faced young man Nick had been to drift into her mind. "Kind of a loner, lots of black and graphic tees."

"I could see that," Tammy said, sighing. "All melancholy and artistic."

"Actually...yeah," Lark said. "Kind of. It was sort of like he didn't see the point of having friends. Or at least, not the kind of friends on offer at Spring Valley High. We only ever had one class together."

"Which one?" Linda asked.

"Art, oddly enough," Lark said.

She paused, recounting the memory of Nick bent over a drawing—earbuds always plugged into his head, his long, curly hair falling in his face.

"Please tell me you have a yearbook picture," Tammy said.

"There isn't one."

"Did he miss picture day or something?" Linda asked, scooping a chip through fresh salsa.

"Boycotted it, more like," Lark said. "He actually had to appear before the student council to make his argument."

Which Lark knew because she and Reese had both been on the council. Treasurer and president, respectively.

"Something about phenomenology and the fact that since his body belonged only to itself and not to his consciousness, a photo wasn't an accurate representation of him as an entity?"

Tammy blinked at her with tequila-glazed eyes. "You just said a whole lot of words."

"That's about how the student council reacted," Lark said. She remembered their discussion well. Until the proposal, it had been the only argument she and Reese ever had.

Hers had been the tie-breaking vote.

In Nick's favor.

"Anyway, his drawings were incredible," Lark continued, taking another sip of her drink. "He had this kind of raw style that was really captivating."

"Still does, from what I hear." The sly twist of Tammy's lips was enough to set Lark's antennae twitching.

"What do you mean?" she asked.

Linda plucked the lime wedge from the rim of her glass and squeezed it into the pale green contents. "She means gossip."

Lark felt herself stiffen.

Discovering that it was possible to go from congratulatory triumph to cautionary tale over one measly brunch had left Lark with the uncomfortable knowledge that gossip had always been part of their community's social economy.

She'd just been on the beneficial side of it up to her public implosion.

To know that Nick, too, had been sucked into its vortex brought her a measure of comfort.

Tammy's voice dropped to a whisper as she leaned in. "Word around the office is that Mr. Hoffman had an ongoing arrangement with a certain prominent Spring Valley woman that ended recently."

Linda plunged another chip into the salsa. "One, you know it creeps me out when you call him Mr. Hoffman, and two, which woman? Do I know her?"

"A friend of one of my coworkers at Fisher and Fogelman." Tammy fanned herself dramatically with a drink menu, then added, "Apparently they met at some high-end fundraiser in New York City and sparks flew."

Lark told herself it was definitely the acid of the lime juice, not jealousy at the idea of Nick with a glamorous attorney, causing her throat to tighten.

"You're a lawyer?" she asked.

"A paralegal," Tammy said.

"Tammy's studying for the LSATs," Linda explained. "She's applying to law schools this fall."

"Oh, wow," Lark said, hoping her face didn't betray her surprise that a woman in her maybe midthirties had up and decided to become an attorney. "That's amazing."

Tammy shrugged. "We'll see. I've got to finish my bachelor's and get accepted somewhere first."

"You're going to get accepted." The fervent conviction in Linda's statement gave Lark a sympathetic jolt. "Once this last fine arts elective credit is knocked off the list, it's in the bag."

So *that* was what they were doing in Nick's class.

"Is that why you moved to Spring Valley?" she asked. "Because it's closer to one of the law schools you're hoping to apply to?"

"Yes, ma'am." Tammy nodded.

"How about you?" Linda asked. "Does your family live in Spring Valley?"

"My parents do," Lark answered as tension creeped back into her limbs.

"Brothers and sisters?" Tammy asked.

Another frosty swallow. "Only child."

Thankfully, Trent arrived to take their orders, momentarily distracting Tammy and Linda from their friendly interrogation. Lark ordered the fajita shrimp salad, mostly because salads were easier to pick at without anyone noticing she didn't have much of an appetite. Once he'd departed, Tammy got down to the question Lark had felt her working up to from the beginning.

"You have a boyfriend?"

Two slugs. "I did. We broke up a couple months ago."

"I'm so sorry," Linda said, her dark head of natural curls cocked at a sympathetic angle. "What happened?"

A simple question with a not-so-simple answer.

Whether it was the half margarita or the convivial company, Lark told them.

All of it.

The proposal. The panic attacks. The depression.

Tammy and Linda listened in rapt silence, only interrupting her to motion to Trent for a second round.

"It's weird," Lark said, pushing flakes of sea salt around the table as she came to the end of her story. "Seven years, and then one day, it's like the person you know best in the world, you don't even know at all."

Tammy and Linda shared a look that spoke volumes.

"You ever hear from him?" Linda asked.

Taking a sip of her fresh drink, Lark offered up the part she'd not shared with her parents. That, for the last month, Reese had been texting her.

"What all does he say?" Tammy asked.

Lark took a deep breath and looked up at the ceiling, where a fan spun slowly above their heads. "Mostly that he misses me," she said. "That he still loves me," she said, her throat tightening. "He's even sent me some pictures of his new house in Charleston."

Tammy and Linda both raised their eyebrows in surprise. "He bought a house?"

"*His parents' trust* bought a house," Lark explained. "He's been very clear about the fact that it was supposed to be our wedding present."

"His parents were going to give you whole house?" Tammy's glossed lips hung agape.

Lark had always found it difficult to explain the Hudsons to people who'd never been around that kind of wealth. They'd take a private plane to Telluride for a ski weekend on a whim but demand a refund on a seventy-five-dollar snowmobile rental fee if it wasn't the model they'd asked for.

Having been raised in an upper-middle-class home in a modestly upscale neighborhood, Lark knew what privilege her upbringing afforded her. But imagining a life where the process of falling in love necessitated trustees and a prenup had always set her teeth on edge.

"A whole house," Lark said. "I just wish I knew what to say to him."

"May I?" Linda held her hand out.

"She's really good at this." Tammy rested a hand on Lark's forearm. "She's the one who finally got my worthless ex-husband, Lloyd, to agree to the divorce settlement."

Taking a deep breath, Lark opened the text thread and handed her phone over.

Linda's golden-brown eyes moved over the screen as she scrolled through the messages with her thumb.

She nodded slowly when she reached the bottom, her lips pressed together in concentration before her thumbs began to fly. After several seconds of furious typing, she handed the phone back for Lark to read.

Reese, thanks so much for reaching out. While I appreciate your kind words, my therapist has advised me that it's best for my recovery if I create some space to sort out my feelings around the end of our relationship. I appreciate your willingness to respect my wishes during this process.

"This is amazing," Lark said. "But I can't lie to him."

"About what?" Linda asked.

"My therapist didn't say that."

"She's a licensed marriage-and-family therapist," Tammy said, poking her friend's toned arm. "So technically..." She trailed off.

Glancing down at the screen, Lark took a deep breath and pressed Send just as their food arrived. She was surprised when she felt a gnawing hunger in her stomach, something she hadn't experienced in a long while. She took her time savoring the spicy, succulent shrimp. The cool, crisp lettuce and creamy dressing. Even the thinly sliced radishes, which normally she hated. Lark had finished her second giant margarita, her entire salad and all the leftover chips and salsa when her phone pinged.

The food she'd eaten with such gusto shrank to a stone in her stomach when she saw her father's name. She reached for the device with clammy palms and opened his text. Lark stared at the two words before quickly dropping the phone onto the table as if it had burned her.

Call me.

Her face prickled with panic as she pushed away from the table.

"I—I need to make a call really quick. I'll be back," she stammered before grabbing her purse and fast-walking away from the outdoor seating area. Lark's mind was a tangle of hastily conceived excuses as she pressed the button for her father's number. He answered on the first ring.

"Where are you?" His question was all hard edges and closed doors.

Lark hesitated, her mind spinning as she tried to think of a response that would satisfy him. "I just ran into some friends, and we decided to grab lunch," she said.

"Are you forgetting something?"

This was, by far, one of Lark's least favorite games, and the reason she'd always insisted her mother be the one to quiz her for tests. To teach her to drive.

Her father's methods were largely shame-based.

Or so her therapist had told her.

"Not that I can recall," she said, nothing from the family's shared iPhone calendar coming to mind.

"Mrs. Hudson?" he prompted.

Realization flooded her margarita-addled mind. Her ex-boyfriend's mother was supposed to stop by this afternoon to drop off the birthday gift she'd brought to that fateful Easter luncheon.

This had been one of the complications of her having broken up with Reese. Their parents had been best friends since before Lark and Reese had been born. Mr. and Mrs. Hudson were Lark's godparents. That she and Reese would someday become a couple too had felt inescapable. The final link to seal their families' joint future.

"Oh, shoot," Lark said, her heart descending into her guts. "I'm so sorry, Dad. I completely forgot."

"Did you not get a calendar reminder?"

She couldn't bring herself to tell her father she hadn't even looked at her phone since she'd gotten George home safely. She pressed a hand to her forehead, willing her thoughts to sort themselves into some kind of order. "I must have had my volume turned down."

Her father's heavy sigh was a brick dropped directly on her chest. "How soon can you be home? She's been waiting in her car for twenty minutes."

Lark wilted against the wall and closed her eyes, feeling like a child as she marinated in her father's disappointment. "Ten minutes?" she said, knowing damn well she was shaving off five.

"I'll let her know."

The sudden silence stung her ear.

Taking a deep breath, she straightened her shoulders and walked back to the table with heavy steps. Her throat constricted when she saw that Tammy and Linda had already boxed up what was left of the food and beverages and taken care of the check. Neither of them asked if she was okay, and meeting their eyes, Lark realized it was because they already knew.

"Ready to roll?" Tammy asked, looping an arm through hers.

Lark nodded, not trusting her voice.

She'd only just slid into the back seat when her phone pinged. *Not* the notification of a text message, she realized with gratitude, but the cheerful chime from the SVCC app.

HoffmanN: how's the drawing coming?

HockneyL: what happened to not pressuring me? ☺

HoffmanN: okay, you got me. I'm on a boring conference call and needed an excuse to message you

HoffmanN: I feel like it's still too soon to talk about the koi

Lark's stomach fizzed with excitement at the idea of Nick wanting to message her.

HockneyL: This may be a good time to tell you I don't actually have a koi pond

HoffmanN: !!!

HoffmanN: then I guess it's also a good time to tell you that I do, in fact, hate koi

HoffmanN: they're duckling-eating assholes

HockneyL: I've personally always thought they were carp with fancier outfits

"And who's that you're texting with back there, Miss Lark?"

Lark glanced up from her phone and caught the reflection of her flushed face in the visor mirror Tammy was using to reapply her lipstick.

"Just a friend from school," Lark said, returning her attention to her chat.

"I sure do miss those kinds of friends." Tammy's eyes crinkled at the corners when Lark met them in the mirror.

HoffmanN: Okay, leaving you alone now I promise

HockneyL: Solipsism holds that only one's mind is sure to exist.

HockneyL: Pretty sure I'm always alone already

HoffmanN: What pretentious bastard came up with that bullshit?

HoffmanN: Before I forget, any chance you could come early tomorrow?

Lark's heart knocked against her ribs.

HockneyL: probably. Why?

HoffmanN: I'm going to need to inspect my towel

Lark bit the inside of her cheek to hold back a dopey grin. I'll be there, she typed back.

The heady rush of anticipation almost made her forget about what waited for her at home.

Four

Nick arrived just in time to watch the sun set over the horizon, painting the sky a brilliant orange pink. He inhaled deeply, letting the sweet scent of summer blooms from the campus landscaping calm his buzzing nerves.

Nick took his time getting to the humanities building, scrolling through his email as he walked.

Marshall had bombed his inbox again in the twelve minutes it had taken him to drive from his mother's house to campus, Marshall's customary stream of consciousness broken into eight separate messages with No Subject titles.

He was, after all, the idea guy.

The familiar smell of floor polish and art supplies greeted Nick as he pushed through the door to the humanities building and waved to Arthur, the gray-uniformed custodian, who stopped his large chrome buffing machine.

"One of your students got here early, so I went ahead and let her into the room," he said. "I hope that's okay."

Nick's heart leapt at the words. "More than okay."

He hurried down the hallway to where the cracked door spilled light onto the freshly polished linoleum. Clearing his throat to alert Lark to his presence, he took a moment to get rid of his idiotic grin before pushing the door open.

Only it wasn't Lark.

Tammy sat at her usual table, her tanned skin glowing

against a floral pink sundress, her shoulder-length blond hair freshly curled.

"Hey, Tammy," he said, walking to the front to set down his messenger bag. "You're here early."

"Oh, I just had a practice brief to finish up, and I thought I'd borrow the campus Wi-Fi," she said with a smile. A laptop sat open before her, an empty notepad and a pen at her elbow.

Staged scene if I ever saw one, Pop's voice diagnosed.

"If I won't be botherin' you, that is," Tammy added, kicking a strappy-sandaled foot beneath the table.

Nick had been aware of her frank appreciation of him pretty much from minute one by the way her big blue eyes played connect the dots between his mouth, hands and forearms every time he was up in front of the class. But he'd taken one look at the pretty divorcée and known she had *entanglement* stamped all over her. And if ever there was a summer that needed to be entanglement free, it was this one.

Then what was all that texting about yesterday afternoon? Pop added rather annoyingly.

"Be my guest," Nick said, opening his bag to pull out the notepad with his lesson outline. "I just need to get a few things set up for class."

"You go right ahead, sugar," Tammy said, her husky accent sweet as a Georgia peach. "It'll be like I'm not even here."

Doubtful, Nick thought, as the room was already tinged with the lemony-floral scent of her perfume and the sound of her manicured nails clicking away on her keyboard.

Grabbing the small keyring to the supply cupboard, he began pulling out the materials he'd need for his lesson. He'd planned to delve into color theory tonight. Well, color theory lite.

What he had in mind would divert from the college-approved curriculum, but he hadn't had a surprise department observer in a month. Remembering how unenthusiastic the last one had been, Nick had concluded the primary objective was to make sure he was actually showing up to teach the bi-weekly evening class.

"So, I heard a rumor you went to school with our new classmate."

"Oh yeah?" Nick asked, pulling down an ancient color wheel and blowing the dust away. "Where'd you hear that?"

"Oh, all right," Tammy said as if he'd been hectoring her for answers for the better part of an hour. "It wasn't really a rumor at all. Miss Lark told me herself over five-dollar margaritas down at the Blue Goose Cantina."

Nick might have been less surprised if Tammy had told him she'd seen it written in the sky by a witch on smoking broomstick. He set his armful of visual aids on the table. "You had margaritas with Lark Hockney?"

"I sure did," Tammy reported. "Me and Linda ran into her down at Brilliant Brushes. Her dog took off, and the poor little thing looked like she was about to have a fit. Lark. Not the dog."

"She caught him, yeah?" he asked, his tone casual considering his investment in the outcome.

"*I* did, technically," she said, "but not until after Lark tore up Main Street like an Olympic sprinter."

"She ran track," Nick said. "Still holds some records at Spring Valley High, if I'm not mistaken."

A frequent visitor to the principal's office, Nick had spent an inordinate amount of time staring at the glass case designed to show off SVH's finest. He remembered seeing Lark's name etched on various plaques, her yearbook picture shellacked next to a never-ending list of accomplishments and designations.

"I'm not one bit surprised," Tammy said. "George must have inherited some of his mama's athletic aptitude because there was no catching him until I pulled out the turkey bacon."

Nick couldn't help but smile at Tammy's dramatic account. "That was really nice of you," he said.

Tammy gave a wholesome shrug. "Anyway, after we got that rascal back home, we talked Miss Lark into coming to lunch with us, and a couple margaritas in—"

"A couple?" Nick asked.

Tammy's wide eyes took on a mischievous gleam. "Like you've never had a Wednesday that needed a few margaritas to make tolerable."

In fact, he had.

With increasing frequency since Marshall's vision had steered Moonshot further and further away from the art that, for Nick, had always been at the core of his reasons for starting the company in the first place. To make the aesthetic output AI could produce more accessible using ethically sourced input. Not, as Marshall seemed obsessed with as of late, to leverage the technology to bury their competitors.

"Anyhow, she was telling us all about growing up in Spring Valley, her parents, y'all's high school. Miss Lark was saying *you* were a troublemaker."

Nick's eyebrows lifted in surprise. Not at the idea of anyone describing him as a troublemaker, but that Lark had actually *noticed*.

"I told her I thought she had to be pullin' my leg," Tammy said, nudging his shin with her perfectly polished toes. "Nice, clean-cut guy like you."

Nick was only half listening. The other half imagining Lark, flushed and mildly day drunk, with his name on her salt-flecked lips.

"—true?"

He glanced down at Tammy, who had obviously asked him a question and was awaiting the answer.

"Is it true that I was a troublemaker?" A context-based guess.

Tammy nodded.

"More like an easily distractible underachiever with a robust mistrust of authority figures and a pretentious teenage fixation on philosophy."

"But I bet you got good grades," she said, glancing sideways at him as she swiped gloss across her pouted lips.

"Nope." Noting the clock at the back of the room, he began arranging supplemental materials. "Solid C student. And then only because computer programing and art kept me out of the D bucket."

"Oh!" Tammy snapped her fingers. "That reminds me of the other reason I came early." She rifled through the oversized tote and handed him a slim, russet-colored case. "Will these work, you think?"

"Oh, wow," he said, flipping open the lid. "You got the good ones." Nick handed them back to her. "You didn't have to spend so much just for this one lesson."

Tammy waved away his concern. "My ex-husband was so cheap, he wouldn't give a nickel to see Jesus ridin' a unicycle," she said, emphasis on the *ex*. "Every time I buy something Lloyd would've pissed and moaned about, I feel like I've just had a three-hour massage."

"That's got to be—"

Nick's words died away as he caught sight of Lark Hockney in the doorway.

And damn near lost his breath.

He would never have believed a couple of days could make

such a drastic difference in someone's appearance. In place of the baggy hoodie, Lark wore a cardigan and camisole. The dark olive skirt she'd selected instead of Tuesday's yoga pants hit her at mid-thigh, revealing legs still muscular from years of running. Her chestnut hair was pulled away from her face in a high ponytail, showing off prominent cheekbones, an elegant jawline and a graceful neck.

The effect made her look more like the version of her he'd known in high school. And made him more like the kid he had been in those days. Butterflies swarming his rib cage. Palms blooming with sweat. Heart threatening to pump blood to parts of him that would make it exceedingly difficult to teach class.

"Hey there." Nick knocked over the can of paintbrushes as he reached for his lecture notes.

"Oh goodness," Tammy said, jumping out of her chair to help him.

"It's all right," Nick said. "I've got it." His eyes flitted toward Lark, who glowed with a secret smile—confirmation she hadn't missed how flustered he was.

"Hey, darlin'." Tammy waved Lark over like they were old friends, patting the chair next to hers. "Don't you look cute," she said, giving Lark's ponytail a little flip.

"Linda's idea," Lark explained. "This is my *I'm responsible and together enough to borrow the family car* outfit."

"Didn't I tell you she was amazing?" Tammy asked, turning to Nick with a strangely beatific expression before picking up her phone and tapping away at it.

Lark leaned in and whispered something to Tammy that summoned a wide smile. "I knew there was a reason I loved that woman," she said.

Linda appeared in the doorway as if summoned by the compliment. In her hands, a cardboard drink carrier containing four plastic cups of what looked to be frozen pink lemonade.

"Frosé anyone?" She whisked into the room and set frosty cups down in front of Lark and Tammy before bringing the last up to him.

"I'm, uh, not actually sure alcohol is allowed in the building," Nick said, actively hating how nerdy he sounded.

"Don't you try to fool us, mister," Linda said. "We've heard all about you and alcohol in the classroom."

Nick's brows drew together as she shot Lark a questioning look.

Two spots of rosy color appeared in her cheeks, and her sheepish smile nearly unmanned him.

Apparently their lunchtime conversation about him had covered wide ground.

"It's a good thing this is only a summer gig," Nick said, lifting his frosted cup. Seeing as Tammy and Linda were already sipping their drinks, Nick didn't see much point in protesting. "You guys are going to get me fired."

"Okay, folks," he said, pushing his glasses up his nose after one sip. "We better at least pretend to have a class."

He typically tried to keep the lecture to a minimum—interacting with the medium was by far the most important aspect of learning any kind of art form. Tonight he intended to break with his usual modus operandi, for experimental purposes.

He began by holding up the ancient cardboard color wheel with the metal brad in the center that allowed him to spin primary and secondary colors to demonstrate the concept of contrast.

"So, according to the curriculum, I'm supposed to teach you about simultaneous contrast, the difference between primary, secondary and tertiary color schemes, hue versus chroma—" Nick paused to take another sip of his frosé, which earned him a smile from Tammy and Linda "—and all that fancy color-theory stuff."

He strolled over and turned off the room lights, eliciting a surprised squeak from his students.

"But I think the best way to learn about color compositions is to see them in action."

Walking back to the table, Nick booted up his laptop, and the projection screen lit up a vibrant yellow that deepened into marigold and orange before reaching vermillion. The room had fallen silent.

Nick cleared his throat and moved through his notes about each color as it filled the screen. Its symbolic associations; its psychological capacity to evoke hunger, comfort, fear or stress; its ability to create an atmosphere of warmth or hostility.

As he spoke, Nick found himself stealing glances at Lark as she sat in rapt attention at the front table. Her chin rested in her hand as she listened intently. When the colors had made a complete cycle, they faded into a montage of various paintings from art history's most prominent colorists. Giotto. Da Vinci. Turner. Matisse. Monet. Van Gogh. Picasso. Pollock. Klein. Rothko. When the lights came up, Nick noticed the sheen in Lark's eyes about the same time he saw Tammy and Linda's drinks were mostly gone, and Lark's had barely been touched.

She stared blankly ahead, her cheeks almost the exact shade of pink he'd seen in the sunset earlier. Nick could have sworn he felt Lark's eyes burn into him as he busied himself with his laptop.

"So that's what I've been doing wrong," Tammy began

slyly. "All this time, I thought my dating app was full of duds when really, I just shouldn't have painted my bedroom blue."

"I'll never be able to pass a McDonald's again without thinking about the yellow-red hunger quotient," Linda added.

Nick took a deep breath and lifted his head to find Lark raising her hand.

"Yes, Lark?"

Her eyes had been fixed on the empty screen, but now she glanced up at him. "You forgot gray."

But he hadn't.

He had purposely avoided it for this very reason. Because when he'd seen her in class earlier this week, Lark Hockney had *been* gray. The walking embodiment of fog. The last thing he'd wanted to do was push her further into it.

"So I did," he said. An email notification from Marshall lit the fuse of inspiration. Pulling up his AI engine, Nick typed in a command. **Create an immersive exhibit of things on Earth that are gray.** While it compiled, he hit the lights again.

"I think people like me tend to take gray for granted."

Dolphins. Ashes. African parrots.

"At least in popular culture, it's often synonymous with *boredom*, *sameness*, *blandness* and *depression*."

Koalas. Storm clouds. Greyhounds.

"But I think it's because gray is so subtle."

Basalt. Lizards. Silver sage. Sandhill cranes.

"You have to look at it more carefully to see the changes."

Agate. Andalusians. African elephants.

"How infinite the variations are."

Doves. Concrete. Great gray owls. Geese.

"Red is associated with passion. Blue with serenity. But gray can be peaceful, serene, stately, imposing, foreboding, reserved, venerable."

Granite. Quail. Gray whales. Thunderclouds.

"It all depends on the mood of the observer."

The moon.

The series ended there.

"How on earth did you do that?" Tammy asked, looking at him like he'd been personally responsible for hanging the giant orb hovering on the screen behind him.

"I'm afraid that's proprietary information," Nick said, raising an eyebrow at her. He looked over to Lark. When she met his eyes, her expression was impossible to read. Was she interested? Bored? Relieved?

Beautiful.

And then, the most miraculous thing.

By degrees it would take a glacial scientist to measure, the corners of her lips tilted upward. Lark smiled as if she was remembering how.

It wasn't the first time he'd seen it. Just the first time she'd ever smiled *at him*.

Though their locked gaze lasted only a few seconds, Nick felt a wave of nostalgia washing him backward in time.

The first day of school during junior year. When, arriving ten minutes late to art class, he had looked out over his fellow students and seen her face. Even now, he could remember it exactly as it had been that day. How during his explanation to Mrs. Keil that time was a relative and arbitrary invention based on industrial standardization, Lark alone had sat forward like she was actually listening. After Mrs. Keil had told him she wouldn't give him a tardy slip if he would just shut up and sit down, Nick had made his way to his seat, dumped his backpack onto the floor and stolen a second look at Lark.

And she had smiled at him.

Nick's heart had felt like it'd expanded about five times in his rib cage, spreading warmth to the center of his chest.

Just like now.

Glancing at the clock in the back of the room, he was shocked to see they had only fifteen minutes of class remaining. Nick picked up his neglected frosé and perched on the edge of the table.

"I see what this was about now." Droplets of condensation fell from the bottom of the glass as he jiggled it. "This was a cooperative effort. You all just wanted to derail me from my lesson plans."

As if reminding Lark she had one too, she picked up her drink and took a healthy slurp.

Something tightened low and deep within Nick at the sight of her perfect pink lips wrapped around the straw, and he forced himself to tear his attention away.

"I think he's onto us," Linda said, nudging Lark with an elbow.

"Don't you lump me in with those miscreants," Tammy

said, batting her eyelashes at him. "I came prepared." She tapped a nail on the case of her expensive gouache set.

"Suck-up," Linda accused.

"Squealer," Tammy fired back.

Seated between them, Lark didn't seem to mind their good-natured back and forth. If anything, it deepened the rosy glow in her cheeks. Widened the grin that he never wanted to leave her face.

"All right, you two," Nick said, setting his cup aside. "We'll do an abbreviated version of tonight's assignment." Working quickly, he outfitted them each with a plastic palette, paint-brushes, water and a five-by-seven watercolor paper. "Between now and the end of class, I want each of you to pick one emotion and express it through a color that isn't usually attributed to it."

Even though they were short on time, Nick pulled out his Bluetooth speaker and turned on the music he'd planned to accompany the lesson. Chills rose on Nick's forearms as the first twangy notes of Robert Johnson's "I Believe I'll Dust My Broom" filled the classroom.

Lark glanced up from her paper, catching Nick's eye. "The *blues*?" she asked with a smirk that made his ears feel hot.

Nick shrugged and held out his hands in a gesture of help-lessness. "Can't resist a theme."

Typically, Tammy and Linda carried on a running dialogue of jokes, jibes and news from their respective days while they worked. Tonight they were oddly silent. Contemplative, even.

Nick let them go about five minutes past time before suggesting they get cleaned up and compare notes. Lark seemed not to have heard him. She stared down as if she was looking not at a paper but into an abyss. Which was exactly what she had created in miniature.

Nick gazed at her work, transfixed.

The edges of her composition were bright, cheery lemon yellow, deepening slightly into the golden color a child might choose for the sun. Had he stopped there, he'd be tempted to describe the piece's emotion as happiness or joy. But that would mean missing the most important part. Dead center, a mottled clot of muddy umber ate into the brightness like a cancer.

Staring down into it, Nick felt unsteady on his feet. As if it had a gravity of its own, capable of pulling him off-balance.

Tammy had chosen a scribbly erratic green to represent rage.

Linda, a frenetic blue to communicate excitement.

"Damn, girl." Tammy shivered and rubbed her bare arms as she looked at Lark's piece. "Someone understood the assignment."

Speaking of, Nick had nearly forgotten about the charcoal. Shit.

"That's it for tonight," he said, a little more urgently than intended.

Tammy and Linda chattered while they packed their supplies and filed out, each giving Lark a hug before departing.

"See you next week, troublemaker," Tammy called, shooting him a saucy wink before she and Linda slipped through the door.

Leaving him and Lark alone with the blues.

She still hadn't moved from where she was standing, gazing thoughtfully at her painting like it was a question she needed to answer.

"Great work tonight," Nick said.

Lark glanced up at him as if just remembering he was still in the room. "What? Oh, thanks." She picked up the painting and shoved it into a folder in her bag. "I really enjoyed your lesson."

The contrast between the stiff superficiality of their face-to-face interaction with the wit of their online conversations was strangely delicious. The same slow negotiation he often felt during foreplay.

"Don't think flattery is going to make me forget you owe me a drawing," Nick said, zipping his laptop into its protective sleeve.

"Was that Moonshot software you used to create the visuals?" she asked.

His hand froze. He didn't remember having mentioned the name of his and Marshall's company specifically.

Lark answered his question before he had the chance to ask it, holding up the towel with the Moonshot logo he and Marshall had spent entirely too much money on for ByteCon last year. "I googled."

The back of Nick's neck felt hot. "So now you know my dirty little secret."

"That's what you do in Manhattan?" Lark asked, rinsing out the plastic palette without his having asked.

"Try to," he said. "We're currently in our ten-thousandth grant application process."

Lark's silky ponytail ticked past her slim neck like a pendulum every time she turned her head. Nick's eyes kept landing on the fine hairs at her nape, his unhelpful brain informing him he knew exactly how they would feel beneath his fingers as he anchored a hand there to draw her mouth toward his.

"—surprising?"

"I'm sorry?" he said, hoping she would assume it was the faucet, not his fantasizing that prevented him from hearing the question.

"I was just saying that's a little surprising that you're having trouble finding funding. Seems like just about every industry is looking to plug in these days."

Nick shrugged. "I guess ethical AI just isn't as sexy."

Jesus. Fuck.

Had he just said *sexy* to Lark Hockney?

After patting the palettes dry with a paper towel, Lark handed the stack over to him. Nick returned them to the supply closet and locked the door.

"Let's see that drawing of yours."

"Do we have to?" she asked.

"We don't *have* to," he said, seeing the way she twisted a lock of hair around and around her finger. "But I'd like to."

"I mean, it's pretty rough," she said. Opening her bag, Lark hesitated before finally pulling out a large sketchpad with a charcoal drawing of an old-fashioned ship set against a stormy night sky.

Nick stepped closer to get a better look, careful not to crowd Lark as he studied the details. He felt his chest swell with admiration at how perfectly she'd captured the sense of impending doom of this lone vessel on dark waters.

"Wow," Nick said sincerely, lightly hovering his finger above the stern of the ship. "This is amazing."

Lark glanced up at him quickly, then back down at her hands clasped in front of her. "I kind of cheated."

"Cheated?" he repeated with mock dismay.

"It's a ship in a bottle that my grandpa gave me, but I didn't want to mess with trying to make charcoal pretend to be glass, so I just added the sea and sky."

"That's not cheating," he said, closing the sketchpad and handing it back to her. "That's artistic improvisation."

"So, you're not going to send me to the principal's office?"

Nick picked up the towel she'd returned and tucked it into his bag. "Not this time."

"Oh! I was going to say, if you're into Picasso, you should check out Françoise Gilot," she said. "The only woman to ever leave him. Picasso went around to every gallery in Paris afterward and made sure they wouldn't show her work. Kind of a dick move."

Nick glanced at the clock, willing the minute hand to slow. He didn't want to leave, didn't want this easy exchange to end.

Lark's smile faltered. "I'm sorry," she said. "I'm just rambling on, and you need to go."

"Not at all," Nick insisted a little too eagerly. "I mean, I do, but you're not rambling. I just have this standing appointment on Thursday nights."

"Hot date?" she asked.

"With my dad's old cop buddies." He scrubbed at the back of his neck. "I don't suppose you'd want to come have coffee and pie and listen to a bunch of sixty-year-old men talk joint replacements?"

Even more surprising than Nick having invited her was Lark's answer.

"I'd love to."

Five

Lark really hated it when her mother was right.

For the last several months, she'd been pastor at Our Lady of Dress Better and You'll Feel Better, to which Lark had become a recent and reluctant convert.

Of course, this wouldn't necessarily have been the outfit her mother chose, but it did make Lark feel a little more…solid?

Not that her actions followed suit. Accepting Nick's invitation had been pure impulse. A desperate attempt to hold on to the tenuous sense of normalcy she felt in his presence. Rare moments of ease where she forgot to be worried.

It hadn't even occurred to her to be nervous about her decision to join him until they had pulled into a parking lot near the diner. There, she'd killed the engine of her mother's Land Rover and shot a quick text to her about being a little later than she'd planned and almost immediately received back a painfully obvious attempt at not sounding concerned.

No worries, sweetie. You remember that your father turns on the security alarm at 10:00 p.m., right?

As if he hadn't done it every single night of Lark's life.

Lark's **Sure do** was met with a thumbs-up. A sign her mother wasn't happy about this diversion from the original plan of Lark coming straight home from class.

She knew she was pressing her luck.

Convincing her mother that she was ready for the all-important step of driving when it had been one of the activities Lark had relinquished after the panic attacks started had required significant finesse. Finesse mostly supplied by Linda, who had been Lark's digital Cyrano de Bergerac when she had sat her parents down to make her pitch. It had been Linda's brilliant suggestion that she lean into rather than away from the countdown. After all, if she planned on returning to college, surely resuming basic adult activities could only help.

Shockingly, the angle had worked.

And though her palms had been slicked in sweat as she'd backed out of the driveway under her mother's watchful eye, Lark had been pleasantly surprised by how quickly muscle memory had taken over.

Even a trip somewhere completely unplanned had proved a pleasant experiment.

And now, strolling down the sidewalk alongside Nick Hoffman, everything just felt…okay.

"You're sure you feel up to this?" Nick asked. A night breeze ruffled his dark curls, his earnest expression making him look boyish as they slowed beneath the faded red steel awning of Happy Jack's Diner.

Lark glanced through the plate-glass window at the scattering of patrons inside. There was a surprising amount of traffic for a Thursday night. The happy clatter of dishes and cutlery, snippets of conversation and laughter drifted out as a couple exited arm in arm.

"Would you mind walking in first?" she asked.

She saw the understanding soften his eyes. "Not at all," he said. "But just so you know, the guys are going to give me shit for not opening the door for you."

"Duly noted," she said, ducking behind him as pushed inside.

The walls were lined with framed vintage photos of miners, loggers and railroad workers who had called this area home for centuries. Booths upholstered in cracked black vinyl lined one side of the room, while red leather barstools flanked a long wooden counter. At the back end of the restaurant was an old-fashioned jukebox stocked with fifties classics like Elvis and Chuck Berry.

Nick glanced around, lifted his hand in greeting to someone at the far end of the dining area and turned back to Lark. "Ready?"

Lark nodded, hanging a step back so she could disappear behind him. She concentrated on slowing her breathing and was surprised by Nick's warm, dry hand swinging back to find hers. Lark gripped his fingers as he anchored their clasped hands against the small of his back while he led her through the maze of tables to a booth in the far corner where three men already sat.

"Is this okay?" Nick asked. "We can move to a table if—"

"It's fine," she said quickly. The idea of all the restaurant patrons looking on as the men shuffled and reseated themselves was far more intimidating than being wedged in a booth.

As if picking up on that exact thought, Nick slid into the booth first, on the side where one man sat, leaving Lark the seat closest to the end.

As she settled in, Lark became aware of Nick's body, of the places where it met hers. The hard press of his thigh. The warm brush of his rounded shoulder. She instantly knew how it would feel to have that arm around her, to be neatly tucked up against his side.

"It's about goddamn time," the man across from Nick said.

"You going to make the introductions or sit there looking like you just won the lottery?"

Nick cleared his throat, shifting to make sure she could see everyone. "Lark, this is Mike," he said, gesturing to a barrel-chested, stocky man with dark skin, close-cropped hair, and a wide, easy smile.

"Craig," Nick said, indicating the silver-mustached man next to Mike.

"And David," he finished, leaning out of the way so Lark could see the man seated next to him, his brown eyes twinkling.

"Guys, this is Lark," Nick said. "She had the misfortune of signing up for my community art class, but we've known each other since high school."

They offered an assortment of masculine grunts and greetings as they reached across to shake her hand. They'd made it the whole way around the table when a waitress clad in an iconic pink dress approached their table and smiled at Nick.

"Hey, Nick," she said. "Want your usual?"

"Yes, thank you," he said appreciatively.

"What's the usual?" Lark asked him quietly.

"Coffee, Dutch apple pie and chocolate ice cream," he replied with a smile.

"I'm sorry," she said. "Did you say *chocolate* ice cream?"

"Thank you," Mike replied as his meaty fist thumped the table. "Someone gets it."

Warmth bloomed in Lark's chest at receiving such positive accolades.

"What'll you have, honey?" the waitress asked.

Glancing down at the laminated menu smudged with probably several days' worth of fingerprints, Lark's eyes widened. In her mind the loop had already started.

Coconut cream pie—hydrogenated coconut oils.

Grasshopper pie—artificial coloring.

Pecan pie—high-fructose corn syrup.

Caramel pie—processed sugar.

Nutrition, like so many other details affecting her aptitude, had been a point of considerable emphasis in her upbringing. Not that her parents had been health zealots of any kind, but they had always instilled in her the importance of being mindful of what she put into her body.

And now she found it impossible not to be.

On the rare occasions she'd tried to cast caution aside, Lark's mind had refused to cooperate, worrying over the potential consequences of her irresponsible choices like a dog with a bone.

"I think they'll just have some coffee," she said. "And do you have almond milk?"

"We should," the waitress said—Ruby on her name tag. "But I'll double-check."

After taking the remainder of their orders, Ruby disappeared toward the kitchen.

"All right, Nicky, make with the details," Mike urged. "How long have you been holding out on us?"

Nick's throat bobbed with a swallow as red invaded his cheeks. "Holding out?"

"Yeah," Craig said. "You two have obviously been together for a while, and you're just *now* introducing her to us?"

"To think," David said, stroking the salt and pepper goatee braking up his fleshy face, "this is the same kid who wouldn't even change his socks for his bar mitzvah, and now he's dating way out of his league."

"Guys," Nick said, leaning his elbows on the table. "We're not—"

"I mean, they *have* to have been together for a while because I can't think of any other reason Nick completely neglected the manners we hammered into that thick skull, am I right?"

The men murmured their assent.

"Guys—"

Lark placed a hand on Nick's arm, cutting him off. "I asked him to come in first," she said with a reassuring smile. "I was a little nervous."

Admitting this out loud to actual humans was something of a revolution. Under normal circumstances, Lark would have done her level best to keep a smile plastered on her face regardless of how she was feeling.

"And can you blame her?" Nick's shoulder brushed Lark's as he reached for one of the water glasses Ruby had left. "I didn't have a chance to prepare Lark for you guys. We barely even sit down and you're halfway up my ass." His affection was apparent despite the crude language.

"Sorry, Nicky," Mike grumbled. "We didn't mean to embarrass you."

"That's right," Craig agreed. "If we'd meant to embarrass you, we could have told her about the time you time you pissed your pants on the hiking trip."

"Or the time you got carsick on the way back from Disneyland and threw up in your Mickey hat," David added.

"Or the time you—" Mike began.

"All right, all right," Nick interrupted. "Now that you've made sure Lark is gonna drop my class immediately, you think we could talk about something else?"

"How's your mom?" Mike asked.

"It's Julia now," Nick reminded them, and Lark felt oddly touched that he would insist on holding this line even when his mother wasn't there to require it. "And you sure there isn't something *else* we can talk about?"

Despite the protest, Lark felt the tension in his body ease and his thigh relax against hers. "She's good," he said when the men offered no other topics. "Keeping busy with the garden and her clubs."

"She seeing anyone?" Mike asked.

As quickly as the tension had released, it was back again. "Not at the moment," Nick said.

Ruby returned with a carafe of coffee and set mugs down in front of Lark and Nick.

"Here's that almond milk," she said, parking a small cream pitcher shaped like a cow in front of Lark.

"Kind of ironic, no?" Nick asked, nudging the creamer with a knuckle.

Lark's heart fluttered as he gave her a sideways grin. The warmth of his body radiated through his clothing, creating a layer of sensation that made it hard to concentrate.

"Hard to make almonds into kitsch," she said.

The coffee was strong and surprisingly good. But then, this seemed like the kind of establishment where patrons might abide stale doughnuts but never bad coffee.

"So," Craig said, stealing the carafe to refresh his coffee, "you from Spring Valley originally?"

"Born and raised," Lark admitted.

A deep crease furrowed Craig's formidable brow. "I thought I knew everyone in this town."

"You mean your *wife* knows everyone in this town," David muttered, drawing a chuckle from the other two men.

"How is Judy?" Nick asked. "Still teaching piano?"

The smile wilted from Craig's ruddy face. "The rheumatoid arthritis doesn't let her do much of that anymore, I'm afraid."

His mustache disappeared into the brim of his cup. "But she's still working at the country club part time."

Lark's throat turned to parchment. She set her mug down on the saucer just as her hand began to shake. Beneath the table, Nick captured it, moving it to his knee.

It was such an intimate gesture, but done so casually it seemed like the most natural thing in the world. The combined warmth of his palm and thigh radiated up her arm, finding its way into her chest, where gradually, it coaxed her heart to slow.

"Julia was telling me that Judy's having you add a conservatory onto the house?" Nick prompted.

Craig uttered a belabored groan. "Three contractors we've been through now. This most recent clown…"

His monologue of discontent melted into the background as she and Nick snagged gazes.

Did he know the specifics of what had happened at the country club, or had he just picked up the hum of anxiety she assumed crackled around her like a downed power line?

Searching the depths of his gray eyes, Lark was surprised to realize the answer didn't really matter. The surge of gratitude for his presence and the peace it bought her trumped any concerns she had about what had motivated it.

"Here we are." Ruby arrived with a giant tray containing four slices of pie.

Nick angled his shoulders toward Lark, and she felt herself leaning into him ever so slightly, as if her body was drawn to him like a magnet. The intensity of her physical reaction left her feeling dizzy and overwhelmed.

"One bite?" he said, angling the fork's handle toward her.

Lark's stomach growled conspicuously. Despite the chocolate sludge forming around the base of the pie, the golden-brown, flaky crust and spicy apple filling looked delicious.

The hopeful look in his slate-gray eyes proved irresistible. Taking the fork, she shaved off a bite.

Nick's eyes flicked to her mouth as she chewed. "Verdict?"

"I can see the allure," she said, handing the fork back to him. "In a spicy Mexican-chocolate kind of way."

This seemed to please him. "You sure you don't want any more?"

In fact, she wasn't sure. She felt…hungry. As if that single bite had woken something more primal than just the basic human need for food.

"Positive," she said. "You go ahead."

It took the men all of five minutes to wolf down their pies and another ten to finish their coffee. Lark sat there with her hands wrapped around her warm mug, adrift on a sea of convivial chatter and friendly shit-giving.

Mike was the first to signal the end of their gathering. Patting his stomach and pushing his coffee cup away, he waved to Ruby for the check. Which then resulted in a five-minute argument about whose turn it was to pay.

They made their way out to the sidewalk, where Nick was bear-hugged by all three men in succession and received a bonus hair-ruffling from Mike, who also informed Lark that she now had a standing invite to join them whenever she'd like.

"I'll have to take you up on that," she said, surprised to discover she actually meant it.

Nick and Lark walked to the parking lot together, neither of them seeming in a great hurry to get there.

"I hope that wasn't too painful for you."

"Quite the contrary," Lark said. "I really enjoyed their company."

"They kind of became my unofficial uncles after my pop died," Nick explained. "They took turns doing the dad stuff. Coming to my games. Taking me camping. Kicking my ass when I stepped out of line."

The air seemed to change as he spoke, a sudden heaviness weighing it down. Lark looked up into his eyes. There was something so heartbreakingly vulnerable in his expression, it made her want to reach out and take his hand. She'd known he had lost his father at sixteen, but it hadn't occurred to her how devastating a loss that must have been until this very moment.

"That makes me like them even more," Lark said. "And not just because I have excellent lunch fodder to bring back to the ladies."

"Which reminds me." Nick slowed and faced her. "How did you hear about me having alcohol in the classroom, back in high school? I never got busted for that."

Lark had wondered if this might come up after Linda and Tammy had mentioned it.

"I was sitting in Principal Gregson's waiting area one time, and I saw you at your locker filling your water bottle with gin in between classes."

Nick raised an eyebrow. "My first question is what you were doing in the principal's office."

"I forged my parents' signature."

Now Nick stopped in his tracks. "Forgery? You?"

Hugging her cardigan tighter, Lark nodded. "I was trying to drop Honors Anatomy and Physiology."

"And they wouldn't sign the schedule change form?" Nick asked.

She turned to face him. "I didn't want to ask them." It felt like the lamest of admissions. "I thought if I just did it, they'd have to deal with it, and it wouldn't have to be a huge discussion for once. I know it's stupid—"

"It's not." Nick's voice held a vehemence that surprised her. "If you wanted to drop it, I'm sure you had a good reason."

A night breeze whispered across the back of Lark's neck. "A *lack of confidence in my ability to perform under pressure* seemed to be the general consensus."

Nick's jaw flexed. "Or they were just pushing you way too hard."

"They were right, though," she said. "I did get through it."

"And with an A, I'd wager," Nick said.

"Of course."

They turned into the parking lot.

The scent of warm asphalt clung to the air, mingling with the honeysuckle from the tangle that had taken over the bordering chain-link fence. Overgrown grasses at its base sighed as a breeze moved through them. The crickets and tree frogs were at their peak now, filling the air with a chorus of trills and chirps.

"Thanks for coming," Nick said, stuffing his hands back into his pockets.

Lark hugged her arms around her rib cage. "Thanks for asking me."

"Just out of curiosity, would it be weird if I were to ask you to go somewhere sometime where one of my late father's former coworkers wasn't paying?"

A swarm of butterflies took flight in Lark's middle. "It would only be weird if you invited Dave to come along," she said.

"That definitely wasn't part of the plan."

"So, there's a plan?"

Splotches of color appeared over his high cheekbones. "A very loose one." He dug his phone out of the back pocket of his jeans. "I will need an alternative method of contact. I'm afraid if I'm caught messaging students about personal matters on the campus app, my tenure could be at stake."

He punctuated his joke with a sheepish grin as he handed the phone over to her with the contacts screen open. Lark quickly typed in her name and cell phone number as well as her Instagram handle. Not that she'd used it in forever, but at least part of her wanted him to see the version of herself she'd been when she'd at least appeared to have her shit together. Lark handed the phone back to him without saving the contact so he would see the extra information in the notes.

When she glanced up at him through her lashes, she saw his mouth twitch into a small smile. "Imagine how scandalized SVH would have been if we'd have followed each other back in high school."

They resumed strolling toward their vehicles. "I wish we had."

"You don't, I assure you. My feed was nothing but *Fortnite* porn, Heidegger quotes and Twitch streams."

"At least yours had a recreational component. My parents didn't approve of games or extracurricular activities that weren't educational and meritorious."

"What about this?" Nick asked, turning his phone screen back to face her. "This looks pretty recreational."

It was a picture of her and her three closest sorority sisters all dressed up for the spring formal. Perfect white smiles and flashy little gowns. Makeup on point. A pang of sadness rose up as long-forgotten faces swam to the surface of her memory.

The tearful hugs. The commitments of everlasting friendship and sisterhood.

It all felt so foolish now. So hopelessly naive.

Like her high school friends, all that had bound them was shared social expectations and similar economic background. Even her sorority sisters, with whom she'd taken actual vows, had peeled away one by one. They'd made an effort early on, sending occasional check-ins and texts of support. But Lark had been unable to return the effort. Especially since they were all so preoccupied with things she just couldn't relate to anymore. What did you even say to someone stressing about tenths of a GPA point when you hadn't changed out of the same pair of sweats in three days?

"So, I'll text you, then?"

"I'll look forward to it."

And then, to Lark's absolute amazement, Nick grabbed her hand and squeezed, running his thumb lightly across her knuckles before letting go.

A wave of warmth washed through her, and she walked to her borrowed Land Rover on legs made of jelly. She'd been so distracted by the feeling of his thumb grazing her skin that she didn't realize he'd pressed something into her hand until she went to put the key into the ignition.

Glancing through her driver's-side window, she saw him watching her with a mischievous grin. Opening her palm, Lark saw a rolled-up scroll of paper napkin. Her fingertips tingled as she unfurled it.

The pen sketch was quick but incredibly effective.

A squat, surly koi fish standing erect on its tail fins. Poking from one corner of its wide, downturned mouth like a cigar was a tiny webbed duck foot. Above its head, a dialogue bubble read *I'm basically an asshole.*

Lark stared at it for several beats before bursting out in belly-shaking, face-crumpling laughter. Nick had drawn the fish with such detail, from its beady eyes to its raised gills. She was still trying to recover her composure when her phone pinged with a text message.

You have dimples when you laugh.

Glancing out the window again, she saw Nick grinning at her. Lark quickly saved his number into her contacts and buckled her seat belt before putting the car in gear. He waved as she pulled away, her stomach aching and her eyes in danger of spilling over as she steered her mother's car home on streets made of air. The high lasted until Lark stepped into the kitchen via the garage door to be greeted by the sight of her parents at the dining room table.

Her father sat stiffly at the head, his handsome face creased and his hands wrapped around a coffee mug. Her mother sat to his right, nervously wringing a tissue that had started to shred.

Like a loyal mutt, anxiety came trotting to Lark's side. Sweat bloomed on her palms and beneath her armpits. Her stomach tightened into a knot. And then, in a completely new development, anger showed up on its heels. Fiery and pure. The few times in her teenaged years when her parents had felt a sit-down lecture necessary, Lark had felt only a scalding mix of fear and disappointment in herself for having let them down.

Now the pageantry of this staged confrontation struck her as not only unnecessary but unfair. Hadn't they been the ones practically driving her out of the house with a stick all this time? Insisting it would do her good to socialize?

"Hey," Lark said cautiously, folding her arms across her chest. "What are you guys still doing up?"

Her mother's mouth opened, but her father spoke first.

"You said you'd be home by nine thirty at the latest." Her father's eyes lifted from his well-groomed hands to fix on Lark's face. "Can you tell me what that clock says?"

Lark didn't need to look at it to know. She'd felt a ripple of panic move through her when she'd started the engine and seen *12:33 a.m.* on the Land Rover's console. Their time in the coffee shop had seemed like less than an hour, but two had elapsed.

"I texted to say I'd be late," she reminded them.

"A little late is fifteen minutes. Half an hour, tops. You couldn't even be bothered to answer your mother's call?" her father demanded.

"I didn't realize my phone was on Silent. I didn't even know she had called." The truth, not that it would help. Lark had gotten into the habit of quieting her phone to avoid the jet of anxiety she felt whenever she received a notification.

"You didn't check your phone *once* while you were…wherever you were?" her father asked, scooping the air with his hands.

Lark shifted on the soles of her sandals, sticky now with sweat from being on the receiving end of her father's scrutiny. "I was with friends at a coffee shop."

"And that's fine, honey," her mother quickly inserted. "We'd like you to go out with friends. We were just concerned that—"

"Which friends?" her father asked.

Here.

The core of her father's "concern." Not that she'd been out, but that he hadn't know who she'd been out *with*.

Why she'd expected this to have changed just because she'd been to college in between stints living under his roof, Lark didn't know. But never had a single unsupervised outing elapsed in her younger days that her father hadn't known exactly who would be in attendance.

Lark's half-hearted protests that she could be trusted regardless of the company were usually met with her mother's equivocation. *It's not you he doesn't trust.*

"Friends from my art class," Lark answered.

Her father pushed his chair back from the table. "Are these the same friends you went to the Blue Goose Cantina with the other day?"

Lark's mouth fell open, her pulse rushing in her ears. "How did you know I was at the Blue Goose?"

Her mother's eyes slid guiltily to her twisting hands.

"How did you know I was at the Blue Goose?" Lark repeated. "Have you been tracking my phone?"

"It was your first time out in so long," her mother said, eyes brimming with tears. "We just wanted to make sure you were okay."

Lark's cheeks burned as blood rushed into her face, her insides roiling with embarrassment and outrage. "How is that even remotely okay?"

Her father calmly sipped his coffee. "There's no need to be so dramatic. All our phones are on the same family tracking plan."

Yet another reminder of her dependence.

Lark was living under their roof. Eating the food they provided. Using internet they paid for. Sleeping in a bed they'd bought. Receiving medical care through their health insurance. Without a scholarship subsidizing her daily life, every single element of her existence bore her parents' golden fingerprints.

In the weeks immediately following her initial implosion, they'd seemed more than willing to provide her a sanctuary where she could recoup and regroup. But having failed to do either several months on, Lark increasingly felt their kindness had passed an expiration date she hadn't known existed. That her failure to smoothly step back into the life they'd both approved of had ended their patience with her.

For Lark, the money awarded for her scholastic achievements hadn't just given her a sense of pride at being able to cover the majority of her own expenses. It had given her a sense of self-determination. The right to make decisions. And though she had no idea how, she knew she had to find a way to get that independence back. In the meantime, she'd assume the penitent posture she'd mastered so long ago.

Hanging her head, Lark swallowed her anger and fixed a mildly regretful expression on her face. "You're right, Dad," she said. "That was very inconsiderate of me. I'm really sorry."

At that moment, she would have said anything to retreat safely to her basement hideaway.

Her father cleared his throat. "We're not trying to be hard on you, Lark. These past few months have been tough for all of us. We just don't want your—" her father's green eyes searched the polished wood floor "—condition to affect your future options."

Though Lark was tempted to argue, she suppressed the impulse and simply nodded, placing the key fob on the counter. "I understand. It won't happen again."

Stealing a quick glance at her father's face, Lark saw that the rigid set of his jaw had faded. "I think I'll head to bed," she said.

"Good night, sweetheart." Her mother rose and hugged her, enveloping her in the same lavender scent she had been using since Lark had been young.

Her father stayed seated but gave her hand a gentle squeeze as she passed. "'Night, honey."

Finally, Lark released a breath of relief once the door to the basement closed behind her.

The air was cooler as she descended the stairs, tinged with an earthy depth she'd never noticed before. Stopping by the bathroom, Lark flipped on the light and turned on the tub's faucet before heading to her bedroom to undress. Taking Nick's drawing from the pocket of her cardigan, she set it on her nightstand and kicked off her shoes.

Lark wasn't sure if it was just that she hadn't worn sandals in so long, but the carpet beneath her bare feet felt thicker, more luxurious as she crossed to her closet and hamper.

Back in the bathroom, she set her phone on the counter and checked the bathwater. Finding it perfect, she unclasped her bra and had just hooked her thumbs into her panties when her phone began to ring.

Forked lightning tingled through her veins when she saw the name on the screen.

Nick was *calling* her?

With not so much as a warning text? Was that even allowed?

Hugging her arms to her chest, she grabbed it and answered before she could chicken out.

"Hello?"

A beat of silence. "Hey."

"Hey," she said back.

"I just wanted to make sure you got home okay."

Fresh from her parents' mini lecture, Lark stiffened at the implication. "Because you were worried about my ability to safely navigate the whole ten minutes home?"

"Because I kept you out so late."

Something in Lark's middle went warm and soft at the sincerity in his voice. "Well, I made it home just fine," she said.

"Good. What are you up to now?" he asked.

Was it possible to sound even sexier by phone? If so, Nick had that nailed.

"Oh, umm, just getting settled in for the night. How about you?"

"What do I hear in the background?" he asked without answering her question.

Shit.

In her rush to answer his call, she hadn't even thought about him hearing the tub filling.

If she turned it off now, he'd know exactly what it was. If she didn't, she was in danger of flooding the basement. And after how her night had already gone, she had no desire for any further drama.

"Could you excuse me for just a second?" she asked.

"Sure."

She pulled the phone away from her face to press the Mute button before walking over to turn off the faucet, grabbing a towel to wrap around herself on the way. "I'm back."

"Your bath is going to get cold." Something in the quality of his voice suggested he was both lying down *and* smiling.

"I guess I'd better let you go, then," she said, dearly hoping he wouldn't take her up on it.

"Or you could just get in."

"I can't do that," Lark said, her cheeks burning.

"Why not?" Nick asked. "It's not like we're on FaceTime or anything."

Now, why did he have to go and put a thing like that in her head? Better yet, why did her mind so eagerly supply images of that very scenario? For the last several months, her

body had been a millstone whose needs she'd alternately neglected or resented. Now every square inch of it thrummed
with awareness. As if Nick was already there. Could already
see the towel slipping down to reveal the curve of her—

"Still there?" Nick asked.

Lark nearly dropped her phone at the intrusion of his voice
into her feverish thoughts. "Yep," she said.

"And?"

"And I can't talk to you while I'm… I'm—"

"Naked?"

The flush in Lark's cheeks spilled down her neck. "Yes."

"How do you know *I'm* not naked?" He said it not like a
come-on but with the same light, playful tone he'd employed
when joking about needing her number to avoid losing his
nonexistent tenure.

"I don't, I guess." *Smiling, and lying down.* Some people
slept naked. Nick could be one of those people. Right this
second, he could be lying down in bed, nothing but a sheet
covering his—

"See, the funny thing about my asking that is now you're
picturing me naked. It's the Pink Elephant Paradox. The mind
is a mighty suggestible engine."

Air from the overhead vent felt arctic on Lark's fiery skin.
She didn't bother with a denial.

"As for you, I'm guessing a towel. Probably one of those
super-fluffy white ones," he said.

In her peripheral vision, Lark glanced down at the fluffy
cotton swathing her body.

"I'm right, aren't I?" Nick asked.

"What you are is irritating," she huffed.

"Then why are you smiling?"

Her eyes flicked to the mirror. Sure enough. "Listen, sir—"

"I can hear it in your voice." And now she could hear it in his.

"You don't know me well enough to know what I sound like when I'm smiling."

"You're forgetting that I sat three feet away from you twice a week for nine months."

"You always had your earbuds in," she pointed out.

"But the question is did I always have them *on*?" Nick asked. "It's amazing the things people will say about you when they don't think you can hear."

Like the guilt-fueled animal the last several months had trained her to be, Lark began to mine her memories for anything resembling criticism that he might have overhead.

"You're not one of the people I'm talking about."

"Stop doing that!"

"Get in the tub." His low, raspy, presleep voice stirred something deep inside her, sending heat pooling in her belly.

"Fine." Turning away from the mirror, she let the towel drop and quickly stepped into the water. The resulting splash was satisfyingly unsexy. "Happy now?"

"Yes," he said. And there was such conviction, such bedrock truth infused in that one syllable that Lark felt her eyes begin to sting. "But," he added, "I'm about to embarrass myself by asking if you're free this Sunday night, so it's unlikely to last."

"Why would that be embarrassing?" she asked.

"Because all the rulebooks dictate it's way too soon to even be having this conversation." He paused, and she heard rustling on the other end of the line. "But seeing as we're both only here for the summer, I don't really have the time to jump through the usual social hoops."

We're both only here for the summer.

That he took her departure from Spring Valley as a given

somehow made her feel lighter. Like just his words were enough to hack away the roots that threatened to hold her in this basement forever.

Lark sat back, allowing the water to climb to the base of her neck. "Then I guess I don't have the time to pretend to check my completely empty calendar."

"Excellent," Nick said. "Pick you up at seven?"

"That works," she said, biting a knuckle to keep the gigantic grin from warping her words.

Another silence.

"Still got that ponytail in?" It was close to an admission that he was attracted to her too. Lark was surprised when it set off a swarm of manic butterflies in her stomach.

She reached up and fingered the damp tips of hair brushing her shoulder. "Yes," she said, her breathing suddenly shallow.

The sound he made was neither a moan nor a grunt but some mysterious hybrid that had her nipples peaking.

What was even happening?

Nick was quiet on the other line.

"Still there?" she asked.

"Very." His breathing had changed too. It whispered over the line faster than before.

Her hand rose from the water, tracing a path down her throat and between her breasts. Warm and alive.

"Lark." Her name was heavy with the unspoken question she desperately wanted him to ask.

"Yes?"

She waited through several more cycles of his shallow breaths. "Good night."

Six

Nick woke to the scent of cinnamon and his mother not-so-subtly rattling pans in the kitchen. Under normal circumstances, he'd be delighted at the prospect of his favorite breakfast. Given the dream he'd been woken *from*, challah French toast was a poor substitute.

Closing his eyes, he let his head fall back on the pillow. Maybe if he just stayed in the darkness behind his eyes long enough, the back seat of his car would reassemble itself. Maybe Lark would reappear in his lap, her khaki skirt riding up her thighs as her bare breasts pressed against his naked chest. Her hands inching toward his hard, aching—

"*Niiiick?* You awake?"

Hissing a curse into his pillow, Nick threw back the covers. "I'm awake," he called back. Rubbing his sleep-fogged eyes, he grabbed his glasses from the nightstand and checked his phone.

9:15 a.m.

Jesus.

When was the last time he'd slept past 7:00 a.m.?

Already Spring Valley was making him soft.

"Breakfast will be ready in fifteen minutes," his mother warbled just on the other side of his door. "I have an in-service meeting at the college at eleven."

Truly, if Nick had known how much time his mother would be spending *not* teaching this summer, he might have reevaluated his plans to come home. In summers past, she'd not only taught at SVCC but at several other universities with online offerings. She'd slowed down considerably for reasons she still hadn't shared with him.

Nick quickly grabbed his covers and dragged them over his lap despite knowing his mother did not, in fact, have X-ray vision as he had believed when he'd been a teenager.

"Thanks, M—Julia. I'm going to grab a quick shower," he said.

"Don't be too long, or the challah French toast will go all soggy."

"I know," Nick said, digging through his drawers for clean underthings. He held the bundle to his crotch as he crossed the hall and forced himself into a shower just shy of arctic.

Unsurprisingly, he wrapped it up in record time. His mother seemed inordinately pleased to see him filling his coffee mug eight minutes later, his hair wet-combed back from his face.

"Your hair's getting so long," she said, tugging a damp almost-curl at his nape.

Nick blew on the steaming brew before taking a sip. "Hence why I'm getting it cut this afternoon."

"People pay for hair like yours, you know," she said, moving turkey sausage from a pan onto a plate lined with paper towels.

"You've been telling me that since I was five." Nick splashed some half-and-half into his coffee and sat down at the table.

"So how was last night?" she asked over her shoulder. "Did you have fun?"

Nick stretched his legs under the table as he began scrolling through his overflowing inbox on his phone. "It was good."

"Just good?" she asked, sliding thick slices of golden French toast onto their plates.

"Yeah," he said. "The guys are as cantankerous as ever. Mike said to tell you hi."

"He did, did he?"

It might have been Nick's imagination, but he thought he heard the hint of pleasure in her voice.

"Yep. He asked when you were going to bring some of your pastitsio by the Elks Lodge." Nick glanced up from his phone. "Since when have you been bringing food by the Elks Lodge?"

"Since they had the winning bid on my cheesecake cannoli at the annual Spring Valley Civic Society bake sale. They liked them so much, I just started bringing a treat by for them every now and then." His mother wiped her hands on a dish towel and opened the fridge to pull out a container of homemade strawberry jam. "Don't change the subject."

"What subject?" Nick asked.

His mother turned from the counter and pinned him with a knowing gaze. "About the extra guest you brought to the coffee shop."

Nick felt heat creep from beneath the collar of his T-shirt. "Did that make the front page already, or do you have spies around town I ought to know about?"

"Judy texted me this morning. She said Craig said that Lark was lovely. Quiet, but lovely," she added.

Nick should have known. "Uh-huh," he said.

The dream was still too near for him to comfortably think about just how lovely she had been. How the thought of her thigh pressed up against his beneath the table had made his breath hard to catch. How discovering her scent on the sleeve of his shirt had caused him to hang it over his desk chair instead of tossing it into the hamper.

"It was nice of you to invite her," his mother hedged, clearly fishing for information.

Nick indulged in a long exhale. "We ended up chatting about color theory after class, and I was running late. I didn't want to be rude, so I asked her to come with, fully expecting she would decline."

The last part was true at least.

He hadn't expected Lark to accept his invitation. Much less nestle into his side while the three men who'd taken over looking after him and his mom after his father's death laughed at her jokes.

His mother's slippers scuffed against the wood floor as she carried their plates to the table. "You thinking of seeing her again?"

Nick gratefully accepted his, spooning on the bright red jam. "I'm sure I will. Class doesn't end for another eight weeks."

His mother drizzled syrup over her single slice. "I mean *outside* of class."

Nick chewed the sweet, eggy bite, temporarily losing himself in a wave of nostalgia. Maybe it was his abiding love of breakfast foods. Maybe the effervescent excitement he'd felt remembering his call with Lark from the evening before. Either way, he elected to tell his mother the truth. "I'm seeing her Sunday."

Julia's fork paused on the way to her mouth.

"Don't make a big deal about it, okay?" Nick stabbed a sausage and bit into it.

His mother set her utensil aside, her brown eyes fixed on his face as she placed her hands on the table.

Oh boy, Pop's voice piped up in his head. *You've done it now.*

"I know it's none of my business—"

"You're aware that's a full sentence, right?" Nick interrupted.

His mother's coral lips flattened into a tense line. "I know it's none of my business," she began again, "*but* I do you really think it's a good idea getting involved with a girl who's been through so much lately?"

"Who said anything about getting involved?"

His mother arched a dark brow at him in a well-worn *Who you trying to kid?* expression.

"I'm not trying to criticize, Nicky, I'm really not. I just can't watch you go through it again."

"Go through *what* again?"

Plump, sun-spotted arms folded over the shelf of her bosom. "You really wanna do this?"

He didn't, in fact, but he'd come too far to turn back now. Nick put down his own fork by way of a gauntlet.

"Every *single* time you've got a good thing going in your career, you get involved with someone who desperately needs your help and all the sudden, *poof!*" She shot out her fingers with a magician's flourish. "Up in smoke it goes."

"You think *Marshall* is a good thing?"

Her eyes narrowed. "Marshall is one of the someones. You had a 4.0 average and could have joined any animation studio you wanted, and instead you dropped out of college because he needed help getting his *start-up* off the ground." Julia hissed the word like it was a contagious disease.

Nick scrubbed a hand over his not-yet-shaven jaw. "So what do I have going for me now that you're afraid my high school classmate is going to ruin?"

"The chance to figure out what you really want to do with

your life." His mother's coffee mug jumped as she slapped a palm on the table.

Taken aback by the force of her statement, Nick blinked at her. "Weird—I thought I already had."

Red rose to the surface of his mother's cheeks, a sure sign she was fighting back anger. "You've figured out what *Marshall* wants you to do with your life."

Nick's face stung as if he'd been slapped. Words refused to climb his suddenly parched throat.

"If I thought you were happy doing that, I would hold my peace," his mother continued.

Nick bit the inside of his cheek to keep from breaking out into a laugh despite the tension crackling in the air around them. The idea of his mother holding her peace was almost as preposterous as her belief that Marshall was running his life.

"I've heard you talk about the tech and the ethics and the investors and the goddamn grants," she ticked off on her fingers. "But you know what I haven't heard you talk about?"

Nick resisted the urge to fire back a smart-ass answer, this house conjuring the spirit of his younger self into the discussion. "What's that?"

"The *art*," she said, leaning toward him over her plate. "The *art*, Nick. You remember how we sat at this very table and you told me it's what you were born to do? That it was the reason why you *had* to go to NYU in the first place?"

He did remember.

Only it hadn't just been the two of them.

The third chair where his father had sat that morning now lived in the garden—a makeshift receptacle for his mother's gloves, spade, and hand rake. The now empty space where it had been reverberated like an echo between them.

So that was why his mother had badgered him into teaching the art class. Why she'd left all his old drawings on the walls. She'd been hoping it would wake the old hunger in him.

Instead it was waking brand new ones.

Like the desire to see Lark Hockney again.

To see how many times he could make the asymmetrical dimple flash above the left corner of her lips. To feel any part of her brush against him.

For that, he would surrender an entire summer's worth of plans.

His mother's hand landed on his arm, her expression softening. "I just want you to be smart, okay? To look out for yourself for once."

Nick lifted his eyes from the table's surface. "I will, Mom."

She snatched her hand back in mock outrage. "That's Julia to you, Fenwick Avram Hoffman.

"Now, eat your French toast."

"We boring you, Nick?" Marshall's annoyingly perfect face hung in the topmost box of their video call, the other participants glancing around uncomfortably at the introduction of this new dynamic into their discussion.

A discussion that was, admittedly, boring the shit out of him.

Not because Nick wasn't invested in the branching of their code tree prior to the next design phase of Titan3, but because he'd just received a text from Lark.

They'd been going back and forth over the last several days, with Lark making witty comment after witty comment and Nick compulsively replying to prove he'd picked up her every reference.

Even the ones he'd had to google.

This one was pretty straightforward, but he made himself

wait to answer it until after he'd dealt with Marshall's passive-aggressive comment.

"Sorry, guys. I had a time-sensitive message to respond to. Please continue."

Marshall made a point of clearing his throat to express his exasperation before continuing. No sooner had they'd started than Nick tuned them out again.

Glancing down at his phone, Nick considered how to answer Lark's latest text.

Optimal wardrobe for this evening?

For what he had planned, she'd need to be able to move freely and be outside where it would likely be sweltering.

Shorts and a shirt of your choosing

Her answer winged back almost immediately. Brunch shorts, or baseball game shorts?

There's a difference?

Length, fabric and the presence or absence of pockets.

Nick considered the options. Whatever you'd feel most comfortable in.

Shoes?

"Nick?"

Now it wasn't just Marshall looking at him pointedly but pretty much everyone on the call, including a team of West

Coast investors Marshall had been courting since January. He and Marshall had flown out to Silicon Valley to wine and dine them, hiring a stretch SUV to ferry them to Napa for a winery crawl that had nearly caused a fist fight between Nick and Marshall once they'd returned to their hotel that night.

Exhausted from a long day of pretending to laugh at jokes his business partner had made at his expense, Nick couldn't restrain himself from telling Marshall to fuck off when he'd informed Nick that he'd signed them up to play eighteen holes of golf with the elitist assholes the following morning. Still lit, Marshall had stopped Nick from walking out with hard with a heel to the sternum.

Do you want the kind of investors that can launch Moonshot to the stratosphere, or don't you?

Nick no longer knew the answer to that question. And had nearly rendered it obsolete by plowing his fist into Marshall's chiseled features.

Those features now glowered from the screen of Nick's laptop.

"Can you repeat the question?" Nick asked, wrenching himself from the memory.

"Gentlemen, I think it's better if we just revert offline," Marshall suggested, cutting off one of the investors. "Nick, do you want to hang back for a few?"

In fact, he didn't.

"Sure."

One by one, the other participants dropped off until his laptop screen held only his and Marshall's faces.

"Bro. Want to tell me what the deal is?"

Nick felt his eyelid tick. He *hated* Marshall's faux-friendly solicitude.

"The deal is it's totally fucked up that you called me out

like that when I dialed into the call even though I told you I didn't have time today."

"Look, I understand you felt the need to drop everything to take care of your mother, but that doesn't mean Moonshot's operations can stop." A white cardboard cup floated into view in Marshall's hand. "I can't expect you to show up for our business the way you do everyone else, but the least you can do is stay engaged for a thirty-minute call."

Competing waves of guilt and irritation crashed through Nick. Wanting to avoid a confrontation, he'd leaned heavily into his mother's health woes, citing a need to go home for the summer to help out when he'd announced he'd needed to leave the city for an extended period.

Not that the excuse had helped.

"I was up until two o'clock this morning revising our grant proposal—which I still don't have your notes on, by the way," Nick pointed out.

"If we land the Hyperion Group, we won't *need* the grant."

"As long as we don't mind letting them completely remap our business plan." Nick was livid now, the words spilling out of him in an angry tirade.

Marshall held up his hands in a placating gesture. "Look, let's just table this for tonight. I think we could both use a break."

Nick let out a breath. "Fine. Talk to you soon."

He watched Marshall's image disappear from his screen, a sudden wave of regret washing over him. It was hard to believe it had been almost three years since he and Marshall had first met in college. It had been a time of hope and possibility for them, of dreaming about the kind of ethical AI company they wanted to build together.

In those days, Nick had provided the vision, Marshall, the

business know-how. They'd been an electric, dynamic al-
chemy of dreams and drive, complementing each other in
their respective fields. Leaning into, instead of away from,
new frontiers. Friends first, business partners second.

But the realities of running a business left little room for
the angels of their better natures, and Nick had naively un-
derestimated the power money had to carve away any remaining good will

Sitting at the desk where he'd once dreamed of getting out
of Spring Valley, Nick found himself missing those early days
when they'd had all the time in the world to talk, debate and
plan their future.

Insistent tapping startled him out of his reverie.

"*Nick*," his mother stage-whispered near the cracked door.
"Are you still on your call?"

"No, Julia," he called. "I'm off."

His mother widened the crack enough to poke her head
through. "Were you going to eat anything before you go? I
just pulled some beautiful heirloom tomatoes from the garden, and there's leftover bacon. I could make you one of those
BLTs you like."

"I'm fine," he said, glancing over his shoulder. "Thanks,
though."

"Do you want to take some to Lark?" she asked, holding
up a brown paper bag she clearly already intended he use for
that purpose.

"I'm not showing up to the Hockneys' house with produce."

"I'm just saying, a bouquet of flowers may be pretty, but
what are they going to do? Wilt and die, that's what."

"I'm not bringing flowers either," Nick said.

"Not bringing—" In his peripheral vision, Nick saw his

mother's hand float to her mouth. "You can't just show up for a date—"

"It's not a date." Nick pushed back from his chair and walked over to the closet. "It's a hangout."

"*Hangout?*" she asked.

"A casual gathering of two or more people who enjoy each other's company," Nick explained.

"That reminds me," she said, fishing in the pocket of her gardening apron. "This was in your jeans pocket."

When the overhead light caught the foil condom packet, Nick's soul briefly left his body.

"*Ma,*" he barked, shock causing him to slip back into their well-worn nomenclature as he snatched it. "Why are you going through my jeans pockets?"

"I'm sorry. I needed to do a load of darks, and I was short. I didn't want to waste water."

Only then did Nick noticed the neat stack in the laundry basket next to her dirt-flecked gardening clogs. Opening his door wider, he stepped back to grant her entrance. She set the neat stack on his bed and stood there expectantly.

"I haven't worn these jeans since I came home from Manhattan." Nick tossed the dryer-beaten packet into the trash beneath his desk. "But thanks for washing my stuff."

His mother cleared her throat. "I guess I didn't know you were dating anyone in the city," she said, her laundry basket perched on her hip.

Tell her the truth? That his dissatisfaction with the way things were going in his professional life had led to a string of impulsive and mostly disastrous dating decisions that had created a mess he was still attempting to clean up?

Nope.

Definitely not.

"Yeah, you did. Jessica?"

Her eyes widened. "You haven't worn these jeans since you were with Jessica?"

"Nope." Nick opened the folding doors to his closet and began putting the clothes away. "Not since the New Year's Eve party right before we broke up."

Mentioning the breakup had been a strategic move on his part.

His mother had hated Jessica.

He hated lying to his her, but there were certain aspects of his life in the city she would never comfortably understand.

Aspects he wasn't especially proud of.

"Well, at least you were smart enough to use protection," his mother clucked.

"All right," Nick said, shooing her toward the door. "As much as I'm enjoying this little heart-to-heart, I need to get ready."

"He's getting ready," his mother said, waggling her dark brows. "I didn't know *hangouts* were the kind of thing a man needed to get ready for."

"They are when you haven't showered since the gym this morning."

Lie number two.

He'd told his mother that was where he was headed after he'd wolfed down his breakfast, but his errands had taken him somewhere altogether different. In short, some necessary preparations for his non-date with Lark.

"What time are you leaving?" she asked, switching the basket to the opposite hip.

Nick glanced at his phone. "Half an hour. Why?"

"Can you make sure you lock up? I'm headed out to my bridge game a little early."

"Of course." Nick stripped off his T-shirt and pitched it into the hamper, feeling a pop of gratitude that his favorite black band T-shirt was an option after all since his mother had co-opted his laundry. After an embarrassing amount of consideration, he'd opted to go with jeans and a pair of Chuck Taylors, given what he had planned.

What that plan hadn't included was Lark *also* opting for Chuck Taylors.

"Well, one of us has to go change."

She stood in the open doorway off the front porch, one hand planted on her hip as her eyes moved over him scalp to sneakers.

Seeing her for the first time since their call while she'd been in the bath followed by his vivid dream about her on Friday morning, Nick experienced a punch of need low in the gut. In denim cutoffs, a crisp white tank top and with her hair a loose, dark cloud around her shoulders, she looked like summer itself. His every adolescent fantasy. And several very adult ones.

Somewhere in the sprawling space beyond the Hockneys' house, a dog barked and bayed.

"George!" Lark shouted over her shoulder. "Hush."

George did not hush.

"Oh well." Lark sighed. "I guess we're just going to risk people thinking we're disgustingly precious." Turning toward the inside of the house, she armed a security system and closed the door after her.

"Parents out?" he asked.

"Black-tie benefit," Lark reported, walking down the front steps beside him. "Do I get to know where we're going yet?"

Nick loped ahead to open her car door. "You'll know in exactly thirteen minutes."

The floral scent of her shampoo warmed by a blast of the muggy summer evening air rose into his nostrils, bringing with it a flash of his dream.

Nick's hand buried in the silky hair at her nape. Drawing her head backward to bring his lips to her even silkier neck.

His heart beat harder in his chest, the blood threatening to pool elsewhere if he didn't get his mind under control.

He walked around to the driver's-side door and got in, paying extra attention to the back-up camera. "Feel free to adjust the AC if you're too hot or cool or whatever," Nick said.

"I'm fine," Lark said. Judging by the ripple of worry on her face as she took in the golf course's serene green expanse, Nick guessed this wasn't entirely true.

"The guys really loved meeting you the other night," he reported in hopes of offsetting her anxiety.

"Oh yeah?" she asked distractedly.

"Yeah," Nick said. "So much so that Craig went right home and told his wife, Judy, who then informed my mom."

Lark turned to him. "And what did she think about you bringing a girl to the coffee shop?"

"She wanted me to woo you with her prize heirloom tomatoes."

"Your mother takes an active interest in your love life, then?" Lark shifted in her seat and crossed her leg toward him.

"She's been trying to get me settled down from about the day she brought me home from the hospital," he reported, turning onto the highway that would lead them out of town. Not long after, flipping on his turn signal, Nick exited the freeway and pulled up to the last light before their destination.

He wondered if she'd figured it out yet.

The light turned green, and he maneuvered into the parking lot of a long, two-story stucco-and-brick building with gigantic tiles lined out on either side of the large glowing marquis.

Eat. Drink. Play.

"Here we are," Nick announced.

Lark glanced out her window. "ArcadeLand?"

"Yep," Nick said, killing the engine and unbuckling his seat belt. "It's time we rectified your appalling lack of gaming experience."

From the muggy parking lot, they entered a strange, cool twilight populated with soft beeps, pings, dings and whirrs. The front desk was large, brightly lit and manned by an exceedingly bored-looking teenager with her eyes glued to her phone.

"Welcome to ArcadeLand, where it's never too late to get in the game," she drawled without looking up. "Can I interest you in our Galaxy Pack? You get four hundred play credits, two beverages of your choice and a free appetizer at the Centauri Shack. It's the best bang for your space bucks." She bit one of her cuticles.

"That sounds great," Nick said, reaching for his wallet. "Can we do that and a bonus Rocket Booster Pack?"

Lark laid a hand on his wrist, sending a tingle all the way up Nick's arm. "You don't have to do that," she insisted. "I don't even know what I'm doing."

"Which is exactly why you'll need so many credits." Nick grinned at her and accepted the small plastic cards and bronze drink tokens. "So," he asked, leading Lark toward the main midway. "Where to first?"

Lark's eyes were wide as she took in the sprawling carnival-scape of blinking lights and glowing black-lit carpet. "I have no idea."

Nick flipped one of the tokens into the air with his thumb

and was surprised when she caught it. "All things being equal, drinks first."

They settled on a beer—Nick—and a margarita—Lark. Drinks in hand, they migrated through the billiards area, where clusters of college kids shot pool and played darts.

Lark's eyes were giant and luminous, reflecting the colorful lights as they entered the area containing retro games. Nick had figured this might be the easiest introduction given her unfamiliarity with all things gaming.

"How are you with first-person shooters?" Nick asked, spotting one of his high school favorites.

"Seeing as I've never played before, I'm going to say terrible."

"Only one way to find out," he said.

They both stuck their cards into their respective slots and took hold of the oversized laser guns.

"We'll start with clay-pigeon mode just so you can get used to this…thing," he said.

Lark raised an eyebrow at him. "The 'thing'?"

"Next time you can teach me something and I'll make fun of your terminology," he said, grinning slightly.

"You can count on it," she said.

Nick felt a bit sheepish for the brief flicker of excitement at the thought of another evening with her.

After they went through a basic tutorial, they selected a simple skeet-shoot course.

"Ready?" Nick asked as the screen counted down to one.

Lark's eyes were locked onto the game. "Ready," she said, her voice firm.

The first small clay disc flew across their field of vision. Nick waited, to give her an edge. She pulled the trigger several times, but each time the disc kept soaring. Finally, Nick fired off a shot and watched as it exploded into pieces on the screen.

"It takes a minute to get used to it," he said.

Lark nodded but didn't look at him, already waiting for the next one to come along. Nick could see the problem, but as she hadn't asked for help, he didn't want to dump advice on her. She was holding the gun too hard and jerking it at the last second.

By this point, Lark's jaw had hardened and her shoulders tensed toward her ears.

"We can play something else," Nick suggested.

"Because I'm embarrassing myself?" she shot back with more irritation than he would have expected. Light from the screen caught the sheen in her eyes, and only then did Nick realize she was about to cry.

He sensed she would be even more frustrated if he didn't finish the round, so he quickly completed the challenge and pressed the button not to continue, watching as Lark walked off. Nick jogged to catch up. "Hey," he said gently. "Are you okay?"

She shook her head and sat down on a bench next to a gigantic crane toy machine. "I thought I could do this, but I can't."

"Do what?" Nick asked, sitting down beside her.

"This," she said, gesturing around. "The people. The lights. The sounds."

"The pressure you put on yourself to do everything perfectly the first time you try it?" Nick added.

If he hadn't fully understood the depth and intensity of that pressure, he definitely did now. Lark swiped the tears away before they could fall.

"It's okay," he said. "We don't have to do this. It was just a dumb idea I had because you said you'd never played."

"It wasn't dumb," she insisted, looking at him through the screen of her hair. "It was really thoughtful." Her mouth contorted on the word as she fought to regain her composure. "It's just wasted on someone like me."

"Someone like you *how*?" Nick asked, handing Lark her drink.

She took it and sipped. "I have no idea how to do anything just for fun."

Nick blinked at her, his chest and throat tight. He'd heard of type A before, but this was on a whole other level. "Not one thing?"

Lark looked down at her lap, thinking. "Art, I guess. It was kind of the only thing that was just for me. The only hobby my dad didn't try to make into a competitive sport."

Nick snorted. "Meanwhile, my pop couldn't stand the kind of art I was into. He always said if I was going to spend so much time drawing, I might as well put it to good use doing something like graphic design."

"I guess that's every parent's worry, right?" Lark tucked dark strands of hair behind her ear. "That their kids are going to end up starving artists who can never support themselves."

Nick experienced one of those rare shifts that abruptly rearranged the entire mental landscape. He thought of the nights when his parents' bickering had woken him out of a dead sleep. His father's heavy sighs every time he'd come home from work to see the herd of grocery bags on their kitchen counter. The way he'd always hold up at least one thing Nick had personally chosen and ask the dreaded question.

Did we really need this?

Could his father's constant mocking of art really have been that simple?

He hadn't wanted Nick to struggle financially like they always had?

"I guess that's a valid fear," Nick said. "But there's a pretty big gap between being good enough at something to earn a living and being the best at every single thing you do."

It was an invitation.

How could she not see how talented she was? How intuitively gifted?

How had she become so self-critical that anything other than complete triumph looked like total failure?

"Try being the only child of husband-wife doctors whose battle for the valedictory chair at an Ivy League university is an integral part of their love story." She gave him a mirthless smile. "Excellence was practically part of their wedding vows."

"Wow," Nick said, sipping his lukewarm beer. "This is starting to make more sense."

"I can remember how excited I was when they'd bring me into the living room after my bath so I could recite the bones of the human body in front of their dinner party guests." Sitting back against the wall, she shook her head. "I'm making them sound like monsters, but the thing is I liked making them proud. I guess I just got into the habit and never really got out of it."

"Thus the lack of experience with non-life-enriching recreational activities like blasting space aliens into oblivion," Nick said.

"Correct," Lark said. Her eyes sheened anew. "And now I can't seem to be who I was when I made them proud, and they have no idea how to feel about who I am now."

Nick desperately wished he could gather her into his arms,

bring her any kind of comfort for the frustration he'd inadvertently triggered. He'd wanted to create an atmosphere where she could relax. Cut loose. Play, even.

Instead, he'd only compounded the pressure.

"Maybe I'm just a terrible sport," she added with a sigh. "I never learned how to lose."

Nick scooted to face her on the bench. "It just so happens I know the perfect activity for people who never learned how to lose."

"What's that?" she asked, curiosity in her voice.

"Follow me," he said, rising from the bench. Lark did as he asked, trailing him up the stairs to the area where the rides were stationed.

Nick looked to Lark. "Cave of Wonders, High Seas Pirate Adventure, roller coaster or Space Odyssey?"

"Space Odyssey," she said. "Of course."

"Excellent choice." Nick handed the attendant his gaming card and received two VR headsets and two pairs of gloves in return.

"You'll be in number eleven." He pointed them to a pair of side-by-side recliners at the end of the unoccupied virtual-reality viewing area.

Nick helped Lark get situated before settling into his own seat. His headset hadn't quite booted up yet when Lark's kicked in.

"Whoa."

Nick glanced over to see her reaching out in space before her, her head swiveling as she touched things he couldn't yet see.

"How have you never done this?" he asked.

Lark shrugged, lifting her breasts beneath the fabric of her tank top. He felt a bit like a creep watching her while she was blissfully hovering on the edge of some distant galaxy.

Patting the table beside her, she located her drink and lifted it toward her face, missing her mouth with the straw several times before successfully making contact. Nick bit his lip to keep from chuckling at the pure fucking cuteness of this completely unselfconscious performance.

"You seriously going to leave me here in a rocket ship bound for the Tarantula Nebula all by myself?" she asked, swiveling her headset toward him as if she could see him.

"Almost ready." Leaning back, Nick pulled on the gloves and adjusted the headset so it didn't crush his glasses against his face. He blinked several times to allow his eyes to adjust, and there they were. Sitting side by side in the cockpit of a rocket ship.

They broke through the atmosphere just as the speakers emitted the now iconic lines from "Space Oddity."

Without warning, the rocket ship fell away entirely and the curved screen filled with the breadth of the cosmos. Lark gasped as the stars rushed by them. Whether she meant to grab her chair or something else, Nick couldn't be sure. What she got instead was his hand.

She didn't let go.

"What do you think?" he asked, adjusting the volume on his headset.

"Oh, wow," Lark breathed. "It's so beautiful."

"This was one of the things that drew me to AI in terms of art," he said as they passed through a giant, sparkling star cluster. "It's a truly limitless medium. Or it will be, I think, when ethics catches up with the technology."

"Could it teach me how to play *Space Laser Five*?" Lark suggested with less bitterness in her tone.

"Absolutely," he said.

They were accelerating again with the swell of the music. Lark's hand tightened on his, and for a moment their clasped palms were visible on his screen.

"Want to dance?" he asked.

Her avatar turned to look at him. "What?"

"Want to dance?" he repeated.

"Is that possible with this thing on?" she asked.

"As long as we stay in the sensor boundaries," he reported, swinging his legs over the side of the lounger.

Lark pushed herself into an upright position. "How do I do this, exactly?"

Nick pulled his headset away just enough to see her sitting up. "Just turn toward me and put your feet on the floor, and I'll do the rest."

He kept hold of her hand as she scooted into position, then reached across to take the other one to help her up. They managed to find their footing, only bumping headsets once in the process. The beeping and chirping of the games died away, and it was only them, somewhere in the distant reaches of the galaxy, slowly swaying together inside a misty red-gold nebula.

"Do you know what it's doing?" Nick asked, turning so her avatar faced the cluster of brilliant, glowing blue-white lights.

"Making stars," she answered, a little breathless.

The hand that had sat stiffly atop his shoulder softened, migrating toward the back of his neck.

Fierce tenderness clutched at Nick's chest as the warmth of her palm settled against his nape. He leaned into her touch, breathing in her sweet floral scent and holding it in his lungs as the canopy of stars wheeled around them.

"I don't know how you're going to top this for our next

date." Her fingers flexed against his knuckles as he spun them in a slow circle.

"Is this a date?" Nick asked. "I thought we were just hanging out."

"Drinking coffee with your cop friends is hanging out," she said. "Dancing through the stars is a date."

Lark stepped on his toe and nearly lost her footing, her hand tightening in his T-shirt and her breasts flattening against his chest in her attempt to catch herself.

Nick sucked in a breath that Lark luckily interpreted as pain.

"I'm so sorry," she apologized. "I can't tell where the hell I even am." She moved as if to pull away, but Nick anchored her with a hand at the small of her back.

"One hundred seventy thousand light-years away from Earth," he said. "And I'm afraid I can't allow you to make your descent just yet."

"No?" she asked.

"Nope. We haven't yet discussed the details of this mission." If he was doomed to reach for dad humor to make Lark comfortable, he might as well lean all the way in.

"What mission?" she asked.

Nick paused to collect his thoughts. He wanted to say this right, and her proximity made being articulate a significant challenge. "You want everyone to stop expecting you to morph back into the valedictorian prom queen, right?" he asked.

"Yes."

Lark's breasts brushed Nick's chest again, and he was glad her headset prevented her from seeing his hard swallow. "And you're tired of constantly doing what everyone expects you to do but have no idea how to stop?"

"Yes," she repeated, with even more emphasis.

"Well, the solution is clear. You need to learn how to rebel. And what better way to start than to make all the irresponsible mistakes you missed out on in high school?"

Lark made an unimpressed sound. "What exactly is that supposed to help?"

"For starters, it will help you develop a healthy disrespect for authority," Nick said. "Which, as we both know, was a specialty of mine in high school."

"True," Lark admitted.

The song was winding down to the final stanzas. The rocket ship's interior reappeared around them as they began to sink back toward Earth's blue atmosphere.

"What do you say?" Nick asked. "Should we get into some trouble?"

Seven

Trouble.

The word alone sent a ripple of alarm through her.

But surprisingly, the alarm didn't stay.

There was no room for it when her body was full to brimming with the delicious sensory cocktail of her dance with Nick.

The firm but gentle grip of his strong hand on hers. The warmth of his fingers at the small of her back through the thin fabric of her shirt. His remarkably solid body, alive and near enough to emit intoxicating scents that made her want to burrow into him nose-first. Woodsy soap. Fabric softener. Green-apple shampoo. His warm, clean skin.

All forming a reminder that even though this was a virtual experience, it was still very, *very* real.

"What kind of trouble did you have in mind exactly?" she asked.

A throat conspicuously being cleared in their vicinity preceded Nick releasing her hand. Lark found herself missing the warmth.

"I'm going to need those headsets back," a voice she recognized as the attendant's said.

Lark reached up and slid hers off, blinking as the arcade reassembled itself around them.

Nick handed his over before passing Lark's along. As they strolled toward the stairs, he answered her. "We'd start by hitting some of the traditional high school hotspots for delinquents. The old rope swing, the drive-in movies, sneaking out of the house, co-opting a neighbor's pool."

"What if we get caught?"

Nick waved away her concern. "How good are you are lying? Because that's an invaluable skill for a delinquent."

"To myself, I'm a ninja. To anyone else, absolutely terrible." Lark gathered her hair into a bun at the base of her neck.

"So, what do you say?"

Lark was silent, debating the offer in her mind. The idea of jeopardizing her tenuous truce with her parents appealed to her not at all. But it wasn't like Nick was suggesting they go rob a bank or anything. In the end, it wasn't her desire to break free from her former identity that determined the answer to Nick's question.

It was how much she wanted to say yes.

Without weighing the costs. Without trying to predict every possible negative outcome. Without fear or apology. Without counting consequences or regrets.

"I say lead the way."

Nick gave her a roguish grin. "Atta girl. Let's get outta here." They headed out of the game lounge. "Where are we going?" she asked, scrambling down the stairs after him.

"Summer won't last forever," he said. "There's no time to waste."

They walked out of the arcade and across the parking lot to where Nick's car was parked. He opened the door for her and slid into the driver's seat before igniting the engine.

"Where are we headed?" she asked, fastening her seat belt.

Nick only gave her an enigmatic smile. "You'll see."

They drove out of town in companionable silence, lulled by the winding ribbon of road carrying them into the night.

Lark sat forward when the car began to slow, recognizing the gate at the mouth of an old dirt road she and her parents must have passed a thousand times over the years.

"I'll be right back," Nick said, unbuckling his seat belt.

Seeing the signs declaring *Private Property* and *No Trespassing* in bright orange block letters, Lark's pulse began to thrum in her ears.

"What are you going to do?" she asked.

He gave her an uneven smirk. "Open the gate."

She opened her mouth to protest but quickly snapped it shut again.

Was she really going to chicken out at the very first challenge?

Nick's lean form was haloed by dust in the headlights as he jogged over to the gate and opened it, flattening a thick swath of overgrown grass in the process.

He brought the scent of the summer night in with him as he slid back behind the whell. Lark gave him a shaky smile as they bumped over a cattle guard and stopped again so Nick could close the gate behind them. The tires crunched as they rolled forward, the rutted earth jostling them as they wound through the countryside seeing only as far as the headlights would allow. At last, they came to a small clearing. Squinting through the settling dust, Lark made out the reflection of a pond.

Nick cut the engine, and the two of them just sat there for a moment, taking in the serene beauty of their surroundings.

"Welcome to Hoffman Pond," Nick said, pushing open his car door.

Lark followed suit, reveling in the silky air on her skin. The night was alive around them, pungent and heavy with the chorus of cicadas and croaking frogs. A light breeze sighed through the fronds of an old willow tree tickling the water's surface. Above the dark border of trees, the lights of downtown sent up a corona of pale gold. Enough to see by once her eyes adjusted.

"Hoffman Pond?" Lark asked, her anxiety easing a little. "Does your family own this land?"

"Used to," Nick said. "Bank owns it now, I'm assuming."

Lark wanted to ask for more information but was afraid of seeming like she was trying to determine the degree of their infraction. Which—of course—she was.

"This would be more authentic if we had some stolen beer," Nick said, "but this will have to do."

In the flashlight beam from his cell phone, Lark saw a glint of brushed silver in a shape she recognized. "Excuse me," she said. "Is that an insulated water bottle?"

"Not *an* insulated water bottle. *The* insulated water bottle." Nick's mouth curled in a sheepish grin. "When you're coming home to live at your mother's house for the first time in five years, covert preparations become a necessity."

Mother's.

Not *parents'.*

Another reminder of the tragic way he'd lost his father.

Lark felt a pang of guilt as she remembered the unkind thoughts she'd had about her own father the other night. Even with his suffocating concern, his micromanaging and lofty expectations, losing her father would devastate her.

The metallic sound of a cap unscrewing interrupted her reverie. "Ladies first," Nick said.

Lark looked up at him, anticipation coursing through her in a heady rush. She'd had plenty of wine, mixed drinks and even the occasional lemon drop or martini but had never sipped straight alcohol.

Nick held out the bottle and, gingerly, she took it. At first, she was tentative, letting the tiniest fraction trickle through her lips. The whiskey was smooth and smoky, with a hint of sweetness as it ran down her throat. She coughed and gasped, caught between surprise and embarrassment.

Nick's chuckle was warm and amused. "You all right?"

Lark nodded, still wheezing a little. Her next swallow went down much easier. Smoky and fiery, a slow burn that made her eyes water but spread warmth through her veins.

She passed it back to Nick, who flashed her a wicked grin as he took a swig. "Not bad, right?"

"Not bad at all," she said, and meant it.

Nick smiled and, setting the bottle aside, leaned in the open driver's window to flip on the car's headlights. Seconds later, Billie Holiday's sultry voice sang from the speakers about summertime.

"Ready to swim?" he asked.

Lark looked out over the pond and the glimmering, moonlit surface of the water. She'd never gone swimming in anything but properly chlorinated water before, and the thought was both thrilling and daunting. Having heard her father's lurid tales of the people whose spines had been snapped by diving into such dark water, she hesitated.

"I… I didn't bring a swimsuit."

"You're in luck," Nick said, turning on the flashlight setting on his phone. "I didn't bring my contacts, and I can't see a damn thing without my glasses. You could be wearing a ski suit and I wouldn't know the difference."

"I didn't bring a towel."

He arched an eyebrow at her. "Guess who happens to have a freshly laundered one in the back seat of his car?"

Why was it that hearing Nick say the words "back seat"

made Lark want to drag him into it? Thoughts like this had deserted her long before depression had tranquilized her libido. Together for seven years, her occasional college reunions with Reese had been enthusiastic and affectionate, but he'd lit no fires in her. She'd all but given up on the idea of ever experiencing that kind of physical craving again.

Until now.

Until Nick.

There was something in his voice, his face, his body that dug the tender green shoots of curiosity deeper into in her belly.

And it made her strangely brave.

He was waiting for her, ready to follow her lead—whether it meant abandoning the idea or plunging full steam ahead.

"Okay, then," she said.

Nick opened the back door of the car and retrieved the towel, setting it on the hood before stripping off his T-shirt. The casualness of his gesture was a stark contrast to its effect on her. Nick was one of those men with sneaky muscles. The kind that looked merely solid and fit when in clothes, but blindsided you with pecs, abs and dangerous hip ridges once the shirt came off.

His pale chest was covered in a light sprinkling of freckles and a faint trail of dark hair that tapered down to his tight abdominals and narrow hips. The arms she'd been admiring since he'd showed up on her doorstep in a bicep-hugging black T-shirt flexed as he moved to undo his belt buckle and unbutton his jeans.

Lark's cheeks flamed, and still, she couldn't tear her eyes away.

Her greedy gaze drifted down his torso to his flat belly button. To the place where the black elastic band of his gray boxers met the smooth skin of his stomach. She found herself imagining how he would taste at that exact spot. Clean, naked, intoxicating skin tinged faintly with soap and the same fabric softener she'd breathed from the borrowed towel.

Lush heat coursed through her body.

She'd seen men in various stages of undress before. Mowing their lawns. Jogging through her neighborhood. Hell, in sponsored ads on Instagram. But somehow this seemed different.

Intimate. Private.

"Okay," he said, plucking his glasses from his face and setting them atop his jeans. "Legally blind."

Her turn.

The very thought made her heart bang against her rib cage as Lark toed off her shoes and slipped out of her socks. Reaching for the hem of her shirt, she hesitated.

Maybe it was the whiskey, maybe the moonlight, but instead of turning away, something compelled her to keep looking at him. To maintain eye contact as she gave back to him what she had taken.

The air was thick with quiet expectation, as if he knew what she was going to do next—and wanted it just as badly as she did.

With hands trembling in time with her racing heart, Lark pulled off her shirt, followed by her shorts until she stood there in nothing but her bra and panties. Far from feeling exposed or ashamed, she felt held by his gaze. Covered by it.

Warmed by its heat and intensity.

Nick out held his hand, and she took it without hesitation. Her pulse quickened with every step they took toward the water.

"You ready?" he asked when they reached the shore's edge,

"How deep is it?" Lark asked, feeling a pleasant shiver of anticipation.

Nick glanced out toward the water. "At the center, fifteen feet maybe. But you should be able to touch bottom for a good five yards in at least."

"You're not going to..." She shifted her eyes toward the silhouette of the rope, listing in the gentle breeze.

"I was going to escort you in first so you'd be in the optimal position to appreciate my athletic prowess."

"Oh, well, in that case," she said. "Lead the way."

Together, they waded in up to their knees. The water lapping at her skin felt deliciously cool and carried a faintly mossy, freshwater scent. Looking down at the lacy white bra she'd chosen earlier this evening, Lark turned to Nick.

"Exactly how bad is your vision?" Lark raised an eyebrow at him.

"Terrible," he reported. "Bad enough that you can totally lose your bra so you don't ruin it and I won't see a thing."

"I was actually going to ask you to help me with the clasp." Truly, Lark hadn't intended to ask that at all. In fact, nowhere in her conscious mind had she formed these words before they'd fallen from her lips.

"You ask me to do this *after* I take off my glasses?" She felt his knuckles skim her back as his fingers worked beneath the bra strap. "That's just mean."

"I'd assumed muscle memory would win the day."

His exhale tickled the back of her neck. "You're giving me way more credit than I deserve on that score."

"That's not what I heard," Lark teased.

His hands paused in their work. "How's that?"

Lark angled her chin over her shoulder. "According to my sources, you have quite the reputation."

She felt the familiar release of the strap going slack, and hugged the cups to her chest as Nick skimmed the straps down her arms.

He was still and silent behind her.

"It's okay, you know," she said, breaking the silence. "I'm not here to judge. And really, it's none of my business."

"I'll tell you anything you want to know," he said.

What she wanted to know was everything. Who had been his first. His most recent. Who'd been the kinkiest. Whose body he had liked best. Who he still thought about. How and where he met women. What a typical seduction looked like.

But he just didn't give off the kind of energy she associated with men on the make. She couldn't reconcile the charming and goofy exterior with the smooth, purposeful pursuit she assumed would be required to accumulate that kind of body count. No matter how staggeringly beautiful Nick's own was to look at.

"Think you could get this back to dry land first?" she asked, covering her breasts with her forearm and holding her bra out to him.

Lark watched as he hooked one shoulder strap with his index finger and pulled the chest band back like a bow. Squinting one eye, he aimed it in the general direction of the car and released it. The white scrap sailed through the night and landed neatly atop Nick's jeans.

"This whole 'blind without my glasses' thing is a scam, isn't it?" she accused jokingly. "You just lure women out to this pond and convince them to strip down so you can ogle them. I bet those aren't even real lenses."

In the semidarkness, Lark could still see his cheeks color. "I used to have to hang my mother's bras up on a clothesline. It felt less weird if I pretended it was a sport."

Lark laughed, the sound echoing over the water.

"Shall we?" he asked. Without waiting for her response, he waded deeper, the water rising to his waist.

Lark took a bracing breath and followed, keeping her arms crossed over her chest as she waded in.

Nick glanced back at her just as she got to the middle. "Ready?"

Lark nodded.

They both pushed off.

She muffled a squeak as the water hit the sensitive flesh of her breasts but was surprised at how quickly she grew accustomed to the temperature. Together, they swam farther out into the center. Lark couldn't help but be in awe of Nick's effortless strokes. At the deepest point, they paused and tread water, hovering in the dark depths. Nick turned to her, his eyes glittering in the moonlight.

"So?" he asked, providing her an opportunity to resume their previous conversation about his sexual past.

"We really don't have to talk about this," she said.

"I know," Nick said. "But since you brought it up, I'm guessing it might be on your mind."

About that, he was correct. "How many?" she blurted.

"Well—" he began.

"Wait, no. Never mind." Lark paddled more furiously. "I really shouldn't know that."

"Because you're afraid it might change what you think of me?"

Lark hadn't expected him to hit the nail quite so hard on the head.

Nick was quiet a moment before meeting her eyes. "It might."

Lark's heart felt like a lead weight in her chest, threatening to drag her toward the dark depths beneath her.

"Swim this way," Nick said, already kicking off. "I can touch bottom over here." They'd traveled a few yards when Nick turned and planted his feet. His neck and head rose above the water's surface. "Come here."

Lark let him tow her closer until random points of their bodies brushed below the water's surface. Her knee against his abdominals. Her foot against his thigh. He anchored her hands on his shoulders, his own gripping the backs of her knees to balance her weight.

They bobbed there together with water rippling between them, the awareness more intoxicating than the fiery whiskey already fading from her bloodstream.

And Nick was close.

So close, she could see each dark flecks of stubble on his chin and jaw. Close enough to count every eyelash if she had a mind to. Close enough to imagine how those angular, sensitive lips would feel slanted across hers.

"About your question—"

"Really," Lark said. "You don't have to tell me."

Please don't tell me.

"In high school, I was kind of pissed off at my parents. Then my dad died, and I was kind of pissed off at the world. At God. At everything. Shockingly, this didn't have romantic prospects lining up at the door."

"I could see that," Lark said.

"But when I got to college and none of the bullshit small-town social dynamics were there, all of the sudden I could be someone other than the angry kid."

Lark blinked at him.

Four years of undergrad studies and one semester of medical school, and not once had it occurred to her not to drag the role of overachieving academic superstar with her.

"All of a sudden, I was meeting all these people—"

"Female people?" she asked.

Nick's gaze grew serious. "Both, actually."

"Oh," she said, unsure.

"For the first time in my life, I just let myself be. I did what I wanted with who I wanted, when I wanted."

"That sounds very…liberating." Jealousy shot through her.

"It was," he said. "But these days I pretty much eat, sleep and breathe Moonshot."

"Except for when you're teaching adult-education art classes and helping former prom queens discover their inner delinquent?"

That goddamned uneven grin slashed across his face.

"Except for then. On a related topic," he said, glancing back toward the giant willow. "You want to try the swing?"

Lark's throat went dry. "Swing?"

"Yeah." Nick bobbed slightly as he rotated them to face back toward the shore. "The rope swing. Attached to that old beast of a willow."

"Oh," Lark said. "I thought—"

"You thought the trespassing was the point?"

She hated that she was so easy to read. "Something like that."

"It's part of the point. But I thought we could—"

"Nope," she said decisively. "But I'm happy to watch you."

"I'm going to need you to do that from a place where you can reach bottom," he said, already beginning to kick toward the shore.

"So that you won't have to worry about rescuing me?" she asked, cutting through the water in his wake.

Water droplets flew from his hair as he shook his head. "So that your hands will be free to applaud."

Lark swam after him, and soon her toes were digging into the soft sand beneath them.

Once on the shore, Nick took two giant strides before climbing up the wooden ladder attached to the willow and heaving himself onto the platform. He stood there for a moment, silhouetted against the night sky. She found herself wondering what he was thinking in the seconds before he grabbed the rope, pushed himself backward and launched.

Nick whooped as he swung through the air.

Releasing the rope at the apex of the arc, he seemed to hang suspended for longer than gravity should allow. Lark's breath caught in her throat as he flipped and twisted, breaking the water with a huge splash. When he finally surfaced, she was clapping, the sound echoing into the night. Nick made his way back to her amid the applause, a victorious smile on his face.

"Well, that was impressive," Lark said.

Nick shrugged, his face ruddy with the adrenaline and aerobic activity. "I try."

"I'm guessing you did this a lot during high school?" she asked, digging her toes deeper into the cool mud.

"Just for a summer."

Lark frowned.

"We only owned it for a year," Nick explained. "My dad bought it when we first moved down to Spring Valley from New York but couldn't afford to pay the property taxes after a while." The ghost of bitterness haunted his words. "But for that summer, Dad and I would drive out here late in the evening and he'd teach me how to swing like his grandpa had when he was a kid."

Lark listened intently as Nick's voice grew softer, a distant look in his eyes. "He'd always critique my form like some kind of Olympic sport. *The most important thing to know about a rope swing is when to let go.*"

By the shift into a vaguely East Coast accent, she guessed the last bit was advice he'd received courtesy of his father.

"If I held on too long, it was *Don't try to kill it.* If I let go at the right time, it was *Good swing, buddy.*"

They floated together for a few more moments, the sound of crickets and lapping water providing a gentle backdrop.

Finally, Nick turned to her, an impish glint in his eye. "Ready to try it yet?"

Lark's stomach clenched at the thought. "Me? Absolutely not. Out of the question."

Nick bobbed a couple of steps away from her. "I only ask because you keep looking at it."

"Because I'm trying to calculate exactly how insane you'd have to be to do something like that voluntarily," she said.

"Really?" He raised a dark eyebrow at her. "Because I could swear it looked like you were imagining yourself up there on that platform. Holding on tight to the rope with your knees bent and your weight pulling backward."

Lark nudged what she dearly hoped was a tree branch away from her calf. "You must be mistaken."

Nick rubbed his chin and narrowed his eyes at her in mock scrutiny. "I'm almost positive you had the look of a woman imagining herself letting go before she hits a forty-five-degree angle because she aced physics and knows all about pendulums and momentum."

"So, I guess you really do need those glasses after all." Lark pushed off to swim away from him but yelped when something warm wrapped around her ankle.

Nick towed her backward and spun her around to face him.

"On a scale of one to ten, what are the odds you're going to spend a good portion of the evening angry at yourself for not having tried the swing?"

Lark's gaze skated toward the shoreline. "I'm mad at myself already," she admitted.

"So, you want to try it, but what?"

That *what* might as well have been a mile long. "I'm terrified I'll freeze once I get up there and will just have to come down twice as angry at myself after spending half an hour with you saying encouraging things while I try to convince myself to jump. Or I'll jump, but I won't be able to hold on to the rope and face-plant right into the water. Or I'll hold on to the rope too hard and not let go at the right time and end up either tearing my arms out of the sockets or pulping my face against the tree, both of which would be a significant impediment to my going back to medical school."

"Is *that* all?" he teased.

"Also, jumping now would mean either ruining a good bra or potentially enduring any of the things I mentioned while topless and in front of a former high school classmate."

One corner of Nick's mouth curled upward.

"What?" she asked. "What's so funny?"

"I'm just honored that you consider me good-bra material," he said. "Anything else?"

Returning to the cartoonishly vivid scenarios her mind had unhelpfully churned out, she met his eyes. "If either of the last two things happened, everyone in Spring Valley would know that I was swimming mostly naked with the adult-education art teacher."

"Could be worse." Nick shrugged.

"How do you figure?"

"We could be all-the-way naked."

Just by saying it, he'd made the possibility a living, breathing thing. A scenario she could imagine in endless detail.

"I suppose this would be a popular spot for it." She knew she was fishing. Both wanting and not wanting to know if Nick himself might have skinny-dipped before and with who.

"The way Dad used to tell it, about half of Spring Valley's resident population was conceived at this pond."

Lark looked down at the water. "Should I be worried?"

She'd meant it to be a joke, but the flare of heat in Nick's eyes turned it into something else. Something that thickened her blood and heated her skin beneath the pond's silvered surface.

All at once, she wished he would kiss her.

Whether thoughts truly did have the power to shape reality or Nick simply sensed a shift in the air, he moved toward her. Lark's breath froze in her lungs as slowly, so slowly, he brushed a strand of hair away from her cheek. He searched her face, the scar below his eye tugging the corner of one eye slightly downward he tried to bring her into focus. She wondered what she looked like, the blurry version of what the mirror showed.

A sketch of what she might yet be.

Her heart raced as he leaned in closer, his thumb pressed against her cheekbone and his breath warm against her skin.

"I never want you to worry again."

It wasn't a response to her flippant comment. It was a wish. A blessing. An invocation that he sealed by bringing his mouth to hers.

Their kiss was tentative. Shy. As intoxicatingly awkward as they might have been had they arrived in this same moment in high school. Brushing, seeking, landing and drawing back again. His hand found her waist beneath the water, tethering them by this one additional point but allowing her to remain exactly where she was. Her toes planted like roots in the pond's silky silt.

Nick pulled back, and in that moment, she saw him as he'd been all those years ago. The uncertain, eager, ambitious, intense teenager inside the man. And he spoke to the girl in her. The girl she might have been had she been allowed the same liberties as other kids her age.

A girl who had fiercely wanted to be free.

Lark pushed off before the second-guessing could set in, propelling herself through the water with big, splashy strokes.

"Are you okay?" Nick called after her.

She couldn't answer him. Couldn't allow words to become part of this moment, or they'd trap her. Contain her. Demand she make sense of her decisions, her feelings, her failings. Movement was the thing. Letting her body ride the wave of adrenaline all the way onto the shore. Doing this the only way she seemed to be able to do anything anymore.

Recklessly.

Sprinting across the bank, Lark finally outran her thoughts. She registered only rough wood handholds beneath her palms. The well-worn planks beneath the soles of her bare feet. The fibrous rope in her fingers. The primal pulse drumming in her ears as she shuffled backward until the rope was taut in her grip. Dragging in one giant gulp of air, Lark didn't just step off the platform.

She leapt.

Using all the strength she once would have to clear a hurdle, she propelled herself into oblivion. Her stomach lifted as gravity took over and she was falling, then flying, her hair trailing out behind her like the tail of a comet as she climbed the sky.

"Let go!" Nick shouted.

Lark let go.

A triumphant whoop of pure, potent glee tore from her as she hung suspended for a split second between the water and sky. Her arms flapped out of reflex, and she plummeted straight down into the inky water with an unceremonious splash.

Below the surface, the world was quiet. Comfortingly muffled. Peaceful.

Lark lingered there, content to be alone with the sound of her own pulse as her heart galloped like a wild horse.

Someone was calling her name from a realm that felt far distant. She kicked toward it and surfaced with an exhale.

Nick was there, waiting for her with genuine fear in his eyes. "Jesus," he said, paddling over to her. "You scared the shit out of me."

Like the baptism that had promised to wash believers clean, she'd emerged a new creature.

And a hungry one.

Desire, dormant for years, roared to life with a fierceness that shook her, refusing to be contained, controlled, denied for even a second longer.

She wanted. Needed. Craved.

Her hands came up to grip Nick's shoulders, the feeling of his skin beneath her palms only adding heat to the blaze that welded her mouth to his. His lips were soft, his body hard. Forked lightning lit up her nerves as they moved together in an exquisite harmony of tongue, teeth and breath.

Nick's arms tightened around her waist, his hands pressing into the small of her back before sliding down to cup her ass and drag her up his body. A strangled groan rumbled from his chest as her breasts flattened against it. Lark brought one hand up to grip the back of Nick's neck and melted against him, letting him anchor her amid the waves of heat.

She'd forgotten how good it felt to be kissed.

Or maybe she'd just never been kissed like *this*. Thoroughly. Generously. Feverishly.

It was happening too fast and too slow all at the same time.

She was drowning in him but somehow couldn't get enough.

They broke apart, gasping for breath, their bodies still pressed together. Nick's hands trailed down Lark's back before settling on her hips.

"Want to get out of here?" His voice landed heavy in her middle.

"To your place?" she asked.

"Completely unsexy honesty first?" he asked.

"Always."

"I'm staying at my mom's house this summer. But she's out with her Puzzling Puzzlers group tonight and won't be home until midnight."

Truthfully, the thought of peeling herself away from Nick's body sounded like the very last thing she wanted to do. But the promise of a shower proved too tempting to ignore.

"Sure," she said.

She moved to disentangle herself so they could make their way back to shore, but Nick held her fast.

"Don't want to let go of you yet," he said, walking them toward the car.

These words paired with the hungry way he looked at her made her pelvis feel heavy and tight.

"I don't want you to either." She tucked her head into the crook of his neck and breathed him in, reveling in the feeling of his hip bones between her thighs. His strong, steely forearms and big hands.

When they reached the shore, he set her down on top of her shoes and handed her the towel. Lark wrapped it around her naked torso and did the best she could to remove the silt coating her bare feet. Beneath her towel, she removed her wet panties and pulled on her shorts before reaching for her tank top. This, too, she put on beneath the towel's cover before handing it back to Nick.

He used it to dry his hair and torso and pulled his jeans on over his boxers. He didn't bother with a shirt. Nick walked over to the driver's side and got in, starting the engine with a low rumble.

The air inside the car was thick with tension and anticipation as they drove toward his mother's house, the two of them saying little until they reached a neighborhood of Craftsman-style houses in earthy colors.

"How'd you like to check off a second item on the list?" he asked, pulling to a curb.

"What did you have in mind?"

"We could sneak into my room via the window."

"I thought you said your mom was at her puzzle club," Lark said.

"She is," Nick said. "But it's the principle of the thing."

Lark folded her arms across her still damp chest. "What happens when your neighbors call the cops?"

"Mrs. Zuppo is eighty-seven and has even worse eyesight than I do," Nick said, turning off the radio and unbuckling his seat belt. "My mom's house is just a block over. My bedroom window opens to the backyard."

Nick exited the car and hustled around to open Lark's door for her. Taking her hand, he held a finger to his lips and stooped as they made their way through a fenceless backyard and around the side of the house and through the gate into his mother's yard.

Funny how even pretended mischief could produce a tingling adrenaline she was acquiring a taste for.

The second Lark stepped into the backyard, she felt as if she'd wandered into a secret garden. The air was filled with the heady scent of lavender, sweet pea and mock orange blossoms. Moonlight illuminated beds of bright yellow daffodils, tufts of daisies and carefully pruned rose bushes. Toward the center, raised beds bearing tomato plants, bell peppers, squash vines and climbing cucumbers were haphazardly wedged into available real estate. Wandering over to a patch of herbs, Lark rubbed her hand over the resiny rosemary and bent to sniff the basil and lemon balm.

"Your mother planted all this?" she asked.

Nick nodded. "Has every year for as long as I can remember."

He plucked a cherry tomato from the vine and held it out for her to take. It was still warm from the summer heat. Lark popped it into her mouth and closed her eyes to savor the earthy sweetness.

"This way." Nick took her hand again and pulled her toward a darkened window at the back of the house. After pushing up the glass pane, he bent to give her a boost.

"Don't judge me," he said, hesitating right before he lifted her. "Julia left my room pretty much like it was in high school."

But his fears were groundless, as it turned out. Lark took one look at the cozy room and decided she liked Nick Hoffman.

Really, *really* liked him.

The shelves were stacked full of books about coding, software development and game design. An array of gadgets, from gaming consoles to 3D printers, crowded the desk while models of satellites, spaceships and hovercrafts hung from the ceiling on transparent fishing line. In the corner there was a soft chair piled with cushions and a blanket. By his bedside there were art books, a sketch pad, pencils and an old-fashioned alarm clock. And on the walls, his drawings.

They were even better than she'd remembered. Graphic novel–like illustrations in a surprising variety of styles.

Nick ducked his dark head to get through the window and spun to fold his long legs through.

"And here I was expecting at least a centerfold," she teased, lifting one of his books. *The Artist in the Machine.*

"I kept those beneath the mattress."

Lark wandered over to a bookshelf and picked up a robotic toy with large eyes, bent forks for hands and wheels for feet. "What's this?" she asked, examining the intricate joints and articulated limbs.

Nick nodded, looking pleased with himself. "It was my science project in the eighth grade. Kitchen kinetics."

He showed her how to turn it on, and the little robot spun around on its wheeled feet, emitting a series of squeaks and whistles that sounded like laughter.

Lark laughed along with it, charmed. "This is amazing."

"My dad was less than impressed. I stole some of the parts from his electric drill for the motor," Nick said, turning off the machine and setting it back on the shelf. "You can shower first, if you want. There's soap and an impressive array of hair-care products."

Lark hesitated for only a moment before nodding in agreement. They exited his room and walked down a narrow hallway bordered on either side by constellations of family photos.

Lark paused in front of one, her finger tracing the glass. A tall man with a dark, curly mop and a petite, round-hipped, red-haired woman stood in the middle of an apple orchard. Between them, a tiny boy in overalls with a gap-toothed smile proudly held out a bright orange leaf like it was a prize.

"That was taken in Connecticut," Nick said softly. "My dad's family was from Stamford."

Only in examining the rest of the pictures had Lark made the connection.

Nick was an only child as well. Subjected to the same close scrutiny she had been, and whose enthusiasms had probably received a similar occasional dismissal. Her heart ached then. For the boy who had loved art and robots but couldn't manage to make his father see the value of either. For the girl who understood the feeling.

"Here we are."

The bathroom was —tiny but comfy. Barely large enough to house the claw-footed tub fitted with a modern shower attachment, fluffy pink towels and a plethora of trial-size shampoos and body washes. Lark stood beneath the spray and let the hot water cascade over her, washing away the dirt and pond water.

She felt strange about using someone else's brush, so she elected to towel dry and finger comb her long tresses. Wiping away the steam, Lark looked at herself in the old-fashioned cabinet-style mirror. She'd had the same hairstyle since she'd been in sixth grade. Long, straight, frequently pulled up in a ponytail or hasty bun. Reese had loved her hair long. As if her staying exactly the same as she had always been could be counted on.

And hadn't she done exactly that?

Lark ran her fingers through her hair, feeling the wet strands. Lately, it had begun to feel…heavy. It was a lot to manage. A pain to take care of.

What might she look like with shorter hair, she wondered. She imagined what it would feel like to snip away inches until it only brushed the top of her shoulders. The thought put a wistful smile on her face as she changed back into her bra, tank top and jean shorts.

She didn't love going commando, but it was better than sitting around in clammy panties.

When she had finished, she hung her towel over the rack, opened the bathroom door and screamed.

Eight

Nick's heart flew into his throat as he bolted from his room.

A Ferris wheel of terrible scenarios spun through his mind.

And yet none of them quite matched the horror of what he found.

His mother, standing outside the bathroom, his father's baseball bat clutched overhead and her mud-mask-covered face frozen in an expression of shock.

Lark stood opposite, ghost white and with her hand pressed to her chest.

"Julia? What the hell is going on?" Nick asked.

"I… I thought I was home alone, and then I heard the shower going," she said, not taking her eyes away from Lark. "I didn't see your car, so—"

"I'm parked down the street," Nick said. "Jesus. What the hell did you think you were going to do with that thing?"

His mother glanced up at her hands like she just now remembered she was holding a bat. "Oh, goodness," she said, setting the impromptu weapon down with a flustered smile. "I can only imagine what you must think of me. Julia Hoffman. I'm Nick's mother." She held out her hand to Lark, who took it and shook tentatively.

"Lark Hockney," she said. "I'm Nick's…friend."

He hadn't missed the subtle delay before landing on an appropriate label.

Because there wasn't one.

Not one that would make sense to his mother anyway.

Even now, in Julia's libido-wilting presence, all he could think about was how badly he wanted to get Lark back into his room. To get his hands, his mouth, his *anything* on her.

"Pleasure to meet you, Lark." His mother pumped Lark's hand enthusiastically.

Don't say it. Don't say it. Please God, don't—

"I've heard so much about you."

Nick cringed.

"Only good things I hope," Lark said.

"Are you two hungry?" his mother asked. "I have some leftover pastitsio in the fridge."

Nick and Lark exchanged a look. They had sort of forgotten to eat dinner between the dancing in space, jumping from rope swings and making out in the pond.

"I could eat a little something," Lark said.

"Same," Nick agreed.

"After you." His mother motioned down the hallway and let Lark get a head start, drilling Nick with a questioning look the second Lark's back was turned.

"I took Lark to the rope swing," Nick said quietly. "We stopped by to shower because it's on the way."

His mother's arched eyebrow informed Nick she wasn't sold on this story. To her credit, it had been heavily edited.

"Why don't you go ahead and shower while I get the food ready," his mother suggested.

"So, you can grill Lark without my running interference?" Nick asked. "Not a chance in hell."

Her mouth tugged up in a smile, both of them knowing she'd been busted.

Julia scuffed into the kitchen after Lark, opening the fridge and pulling out a foil-covered casserole dish that she set on the counter. Reaching for clean forks from the dish drainer, his mother gasped at the sight of her reflection in the window over the sink. "Why didn't you tell me I still had this gunk on?" she asked, giving Nick's arm a light pinch as she breezed by. "I won't be a minute, dear."

This last was said for Lark's benefit.

Nick waited for his mother's retreating footsteps before heaving a sigh. "I'm sorry about that," he said. "She can be a bit...much sometimes."

Lark shrugged with a smile, her gaze on the floor. "It's all right," she answered softly.

Nick stepped closer and tilted his head so she had no choice but to meet his gaze. "No," he said firmly, running a gentle finger down her arm. "It's not all right at all. I'd planned to move on to phase three of tonight's operation by now."

"And which phase would that be?"

"So far, there's a very important item on the list of high school rebellion we've overlooked."

Lark's lips twisted to the side. "Stealing the Spring Valley High badger mascot costume?"

Nick hooked a finger in the waistband of her shorts and tugged her toward him. "Getting to second base."

Hearing the whapping of house slippers down the hallway, they leapt apart.

"There now." His mother reemerged into the kitchen, her cheeks glowing a rosy pink. "Where was I? That's right. The pastitsio."

They shared a long look behind her back.

Minutes later, his mother set steaming plates of the casserole on the table and took the seat at the head. "Well, sit down. The food's not going to come to you."

Nick and Lark joined her at the table, and true to his mother's word, the pastitsio was delicious. The creamy cheese sauce coated every bite of macaroni noodles, topped with flavorful ground beef in a rich tomato sauce spiced with red pepper flakes. Nick savored each bite as his mom shared stories from when he'd been a kid. When they were done, Lark helped clear the dishes while his mother ran a sink full of water.

"You two get on out of here," his mother clucked. "These will wait until morning."

At that moment, Lark looked like someone had informed her that the earth was, in fact, flat. "But..." she began.

"I insist. And take some of that baklava in the fridge home with you. The Puzzling Puzzlers didn't even get to try it before Annemarie got a migraine that sent everyone home."

Nick opened the fridge and lifted a couple wedges of the flaky dessert onto a plate. Another of his mother's specialties. Layered phyllo dough filled with honey-soaked walnuts and cinnamon, then drizzled in syrup made from freshly pressed oranges.

His taste buds contracted painfully at the prospect.

Swinging by the sink, he planted a kiss atop his mother's head. "Night."

"G'night, sweetie."

They'd successfully made it back to his room when Nick remembered he hadn't yet showered. "I'll be back in ten." Quickly gathering a shirt, clean boxers and gym shorts, Nick slipped across the hallway and cleaned off in record time.

When he returned, Lark lay curled up in the center of his bed, her chest rising and falling in a steady rhythm. One arm draped across her face to block out the lamp light, the soft curves of her body stretched against his bedspread.

He grabbed a blanket from the foot of the bed and gently tucked it around Lark's shoulders before leaning down to press a featherlight kiss upon her forehead. He lingered for what felt like an eternity before finally stepping back, grabbing an extra blanket from the closet and turning off the lights. Using the beanbag in the corner as a headboard, he covered himself with the extra comforter. Nick let out a contented breath and drifted into an exhausted sleep.

He awoke after an interval he could only measure by the stiffness in his back.

Among other places.

The familiar heated throb forced his eyes open. Blinking in the bleary dark, he could just make out the bed…which was empty. He'd barely begun to register alarm when he felt her behind him. Warm and close, moving beneath the blanket.

"So…phase three?" she murmured against the back of his neck. Shivers chased down his spine as she trailed fingertips lightly over his rib cage and lower.

Nick sucked in a breath as her nails grazed the skin next to the waistband of his basketball shorts. This was not *at all* how he'd thought this was going to go. He felt ambushed in the best way possible. Thrown completely off guard. Nick patted around on the floor next to him and found his glasses before rolling over to face her.

The moonlight made her a silver specter. Nick molded a hand to her downy cheek, as much to confirm she was really there as to satisfy a bone deep-urge to touch her.

Lark leaned into his palm, eyelids lowering as Nick's thumb traced the fullness of her lower lip. They held a steady gaze, neither speaking. Her irises flicked subtly side to side as she looked from his eyes to his nose to mouth. The air between them thickened with an invisible charge, all thought escaping Nick's mind except one.

I want you.

His hand slid from her cheek into the silk of her hair, still damp near her scalp.

The moment seemed to stretch out endlessly until finally their mouths met.

If their first kiss had been strange and sweet and the second reckless and passionate, their third was incendiary.

Hard and hungry and demanding.

Charged by the long wait, the many interruptions and obstacles, the strength of every second he'd spent longing for her. For this. Her heat and scent enveloping him. The taste of her filling his every sense until he felt like he would never be able to come up for air.

Lark's hands moved over his chest and stomach, sliding lower until they'd slipped inside his basketball shorts. Nick's breath hitched as she molded her fingers against the outline of his erection through his boxers. His hips reflexively curled into her touch, intensifying the friction of the fabric over his sensitized skin.

They were both panting. Mouths wet, their breaths mingling.

Nick dipped his head to sample the delicate skin of her neck, finding it silkier than he'd dreamed as he nipped, licked and sucked his way down to her collarbone.

Lark's fingers curled around his cock when he reached the swell of her breasts.

As much as he hated to lose the feel of her hand on him, Nick shifted to roll Lark onto her back, pushing up onto his elbows. Peeling the blanket back, he could see twin beads beneath the thin fabric of her tank top. The sight of the slightly darker flesh through the sheer fabric had hunger coiling around the base of his spine.

He lowered his mouth to tease a hardened bud through the

fabric. Breathing heat against it, he tasted clean cotton as he flicked and rolled the taut flesh with his tongue.

Lark sucked in a breath and arched into him in a silent plea.

One Nick fully intended answer.

In time.

He moved lower, leaving the garment in place as he planted kisses on her sternum, her stomach, pausing when he reached the hem. Nick pushed it up just enough to get his tongue under the edge, tracing the skin of her belly above the waistband of her shorts. Gooseflesh rose on her arms as he whispered a breath across the places he'd made damp. Her hips undulated, her stomach shivering and tensing beneath his lips.

Slowly, he worked upward again, this time baring her skin to himself as he went. He pushed the fabric back just enough to reveal a sliver of her dusky nipple on one side. He traced the puckered flesh with the tip of his tongue, deliberately avoiding the most sensitive parts until she was squirming beneath his touch. Only then did he swipe his tongue over the warm, taut bud.

Lark's whimper reached straight to the base of his heavy cock, making it twitch against his stomach. Ravenous for the sight of her, he peeled the tank top up to her neck, exposing her breasts completely.

Lark's smoldering look scorched his soul, fueling his own hunger. His mouth and hands were everywhere then, cupping her breasts, capturing her nipples to suck and flick them with the flat of his tongue. Her back arched as her mouth opened in a gasp, her fingers tangling in his hair and drawing him closer.

Nick was all too happy to oblige.

His hands roamed over her body, tracing the graceful dip of her waist, the softness of her stomach, the curve of her hips.

All the while, he teased her nipples, alternating between gentle licks and deep pulls, wanting to fill each second with the pleasure she'd been denied these long, lonely months.

Lark's eyes were closed, her lips lightly parted on short, shuddery breaths.

Nick retreated, sweeping his tongue slowly up her neck to claim her mouth again. But it was he who was claimed instead. Lark's fist tightened in his hair as she stroked her tongue over his, stealing the moan from his mouth and giving it back to him with one of her own as she ground her hips against his. He drew back only far enough to get his hand between them, slipping it inside her shorts.

God help him, he'd forgotten.

Forgotten that she'd removed her damp panties at the pond.

Forgotten she was naked beneath.

Lark bit her swollen lower lip as he settled his fingers against her. He found her slick with need as he stroked lightly over her most sensitive spot. Her cry was half pleasure, half demand. Nick repeated the movement, increasing the pressure until she was arching up to meet each thrust fingers.

Her eyes flashed open, desire hazing their stormy depths, and he could no longer deny himself. He needed to taste her. To feel her writhe beneath his mouth. Trailing kisses across her ribs and abdomen, he paused when he reached the waistband of her shorts. Nick looked up, meeting her gaze and asking silent permission with his eyes.

Her answer came in the form of her foot hooked behind his knee.

He unbuttoned her shorts and drew them down her smooth legs with excruciating deliberation. Her skin glowed in the moonlight, and she shifted beneath him, stomach tensing in anticipation.

"I want to see you too." They were the first words she'd spoken, and the demand obliterated the last vestiges of his control.

Nick's hands worked feverishly, hastily tugging down his own shorts before kneeling between her legs. "You're so beautiful," he murmured, his voice husky.

Pushing herself up on her palms, Lark raked him with a heated look that ended at his cock. "So are you."

Reaching out, Nick trailed his fingertips outside her thighs, feeling the tension in her muscled flesh as if it were his own. He grazed her skin lightly, tracing circles around her knees until she gradually relaxed. Then Nick moved between them with a single-minded purpose. Curling a forearm over her thigh, he eased her legs apart, the sight of her wet for him landing like a blow in his gut.

Nick moved his mouth up her inner thigh, feeling the subtle drag of his stubble against her delicious smoothness. Lark gasped as he split her with his thumbs to grant himself unfettered access and stroked her with the flat of his tongue.

Her back arched, lifting from the floor as her forearm fell over her eyes.

The muffled moan that escaped her damn near unstitched his soul.

Nick lifted his mouth from her and reached out to gently peel her arm away. "Look at me, Lark. Stay with me."

She opened her eyes, and the intensity of their connection stormed his senses. He could feel the need radiating off her as they maintained eye contact while he continued his exploration, alternating light, feathering strokes with long, languid licks. Nick's tongue flicked out again, this time circling the sensitive bud at her core. His movements were unhurried and deliberate, taking the time to learn what made her body shudder, made her hips roll in invitation.

Lark's fingers threaded into his hair, and the pressure on his scalp further wound his body like a bowstring. Nick increased the intensity of his onslaught as her thighs began to shake, trembling on the brink of release. He both wanted to draw the moment out forever and needed it to come as soon as humanly possible.

So he could do it again.

And again.

Until he'd wrung every last strangled cry out of her.

"Nick." Her whisper held the urgent plea of her inevitable undoing.

As much as he wanted to feel her contract around his fingers, Nick maintained the exact cadence that had brought her to the threshold. A fine sweat had broken out on her skin. Her stomach shuddered and her hips jerked as her torso folded upward. Nick felt her release crashing over her like a wave.

He rode the swell with her, only moving up her body when it had gone still and slack.

"I want you," she whispered against his neck.

And what those words did to him.

"I want you too," he breathed into her hair. "Come here." Nick offered her a hand and staggered them both to his bed.

And they were kissing again.

Soft, slow explorations that left them both breathless. Nick's hands slid up her body and settled on the curve of her hip, his thumb tracing the dip of her waist.

Lark wriggled closer, and Nick groaned as she grazed the length of his cock. Every nerve ending in his body was alive, electric with pleasure. And when she wrapped her hand around him, Nick thought he might lose it then and there.

"Easy," he warned. "I've only been dreaming about this for seven years."

Her eyes widened. "You thought about me even then?"

Nick pushed a lock of hair away from her sweat-damp cheek. "Especially then."

As if galvanized by his revelation, her hand worked faster. Stroking him. Stoking him.

Rolling onto his side, Nick opened his nightstand drawer and found the silver packet by feel. He'd torn it with his teeth and was about to sheath himself when there was a tap at the door.

They froze.

The tapping came again and with it, a hot bolt of irritation. Of all the fucking times.

"Yeah?" Nick grunted, hoping his mother mistook the thickness in his voice for having been recently asleep.

"Nick?" His mother's voice was a low, worried whisper. "Someone's here."

Nine

Panic.

It invaded Lark's body like an unnatural haze of shadow shifting, smoky and nebulous. A thick wave of nausea rolled in on its heels.

Her father stood in Julia Hoffman's small, tiled entryway. Despite the hour, he was showered and dressed in his usual uniform of creased khakis and a polo shirt. His silvery blond hair was combed back from his face, his mouth a flat line of disapproval against skin already bronzed from this summer's many rounds of golf. Cold blue eyes raked over her, pausing only to take in the rumpled tank top and tattered denim cut-offs. Lark didn't even want to think about what her hair must've looked like.

She felt exposed, raw and completely vulnerable under his scrutiny. Her father's gaze felt like ice against her skin, and she couldn't help but shiver.

"What are you doing here?" Lark asked, trying to keep her voice steady.

As if she didn't know the answer.

She'd broken her promise.

Failed to show up by the hour when she'd assured them she'd be home.

And she had fully intended to follow through.

But that had been before their adrenaline-inducing trip to the pond. Before she'd eaten a large meal of carbs and fallen asleep in Nick's bed. Before she'd woken up in the unfamiliar dark to the sight of him crashed out on the floor so she could rest undisturbed. Before a rush of ardor had her sliding under his blanket even before her eyes had been fully opened.

For all of that, she had no defense whatsoever.

Her father didn't speak right away, instead turning his attention to Julia. "I'm sorry to barge in like this, but I need to speak with my daughter."

Julia's expression was unreadable, but she stepped aside. "Why don't you two use the sitting room," she invited, running a hand through her sleep-squashed curls. "Nick and I can go into the kitchen."

Only in hearing his name did Lark realize she'd completely forgotten to introduce them.

Nick, this is my dad, Dr. Anderson Hockney, noted obstetrician. Dad, this is Nick, a burgeoning tech entrepreneur who occasionally teaches art down at the community college when he's not making random women have brain-melting orgasms.

The thought made heat rise to her cheeks.

"After you," her father said, motioning toward the small sitting room with a pointed look.

Lark walked past Nick and Julia, reminding herself to breathe.

Her father gestured to the battered leather couch, indicating she should take a seat, but after she had, he remained standing.

"I'm trying very hard to understand what's going on with you." There was a new, unfamiliar edge to his words that made Lark's stomach knot.

Lark didn't respond, her mind flashing back to Nick's bedroom. The way she'd touched him, the heat of his skin underneath her fingertips. A vivid reminder of how far she'd let herself drift from the person she'd once been.

"I've tried very hard to be patient," he continued. "I know

firsthand how difficult medical school is, how much pressure it can put on you."

Pressure, Lark was compelled to note, that had never caused *him* to have a psychological break and end up living in his parents' basement.

"Which is why I haven't pushed you about getting a job. But for you to tell us that you need more time to decide whether you're ready to go back to school, then take up with some stranger so you can stay out all hours of the night and worry your mother sick—"

"He's not a stranger," Lark protested, her voice rising in defiance. "His name is Nick Hoffman, and we went to high school together. We've known each other for years."

Her father shook his head. "And what about Reese? Haven't you known him for years as well?"

Lark felt the blood rush to her face at the mention of her ex-boyfriend/would-be fiancé. She hadn't said anything to her parents about their breaking up officially for exactly this reason. She knew they would attempt to talk her out of it. Encourage her not to make any "rash decisions." That "rash" described any decision undertaken from her current mental state was heavily implied.

"This isn't about Reese," she said, keeping her eyes on the wood floor.

"Then what is it about?"

For the first time, her father had asked her this question as if he might actually want to know the answer.

But when it came time to provide it, Lark's words froze on her tongue.

I'm not sure I really want to be a doctor.

You might have wasted an entire bachelor's worth of tuition on me.

I have no idea what I want to do or where I want to do it.

"I—" she stammered. "I don't know."

"You don't know," he repeated.

Her eyes welled with tears, blurring her view of the small army of plants lining the built-in cabinets.

The floor squeaked as her father approached her. She caught the familiar scent of his crisp aftershave, the ache in her chest deepening at the tide of memories it dragged in its wake.

Him hugging her when she'd made the track team. When she'd received the letter declaring her acceptance to his alma mater. When she'd stepped down from the podium after her valedictory address. When her parents had been bidding their final goodbyes after helping her set up her dorm room. When she'd been accepted into the medical school of her choice.

Or *his* choice.

"Let's head home," he said. "We can talk about this more when you've had some rest."

Enduring an awkward car ride home with her father followed by an emotional reunion with her mother was about the last thing she wanted to do. But what other option did she have?

Stay here with Nick? And do what?

Finish their torrid encounter and *then* go home?

Lark rose from the couch on numb legs and robotically followed her father to the entry, only remembering when they were almost out the door that her purse was still sitting on Nick's desk.

"Be right back," she said. "I just need to grab my things."

She quickly slipped down the hallway and into Nick's room, where she retrieved her phone and grabbed her bag. Turning, she found him in the doorway, his arms folded across his chest and his face tense with concern.

"Are you okay?"

Lark nodded. "I'm fine. I just need to go."

"Are you sure?" he asked.

"I'm sure. I'm really sorry about this."

"Hey," he said, crossing to her and taking her by the hand. "Look at me."

Reluctantly, Lark lifted her eyes to meet his.

"We didn't do anything wrong," he said. "*You* didn't do anything wrong."

How she dearly wished she could believe him. Wished that her father's presence didn't transform last night's sense of adventure into reckless impulsivity. Didn't make seeking physical satisfaction feel like selfishness. Didn't make her newly asserted independence feel like irresponsibility.

"I'll call you," she said, slipping out of his grip.

Nick stepped back, allowing her to pass.

Lark felt her throat tighten. Fear, guilt, remorse and resignation all fought for space in her chest, crowding out breath. As much as she wanted to sprint out of the house, she made herself stop in the kitchen doorway. Julia was there, standing at the sink washing last night's dishes.

"Thank you again for the late dinner," Lark said, forcing a smile. "It was lovely to meet you."

Nick's mother turned, and the concern in her large brown eyes threatened to make the tears spill down Lark's cheeks.

"You're very welcome, sweetheart," she said. "You come on by any time."

"Thank you," Lark said.

"*Any* time," Julia repeated.

Lark nodded and pushed out the front door before the kindness could shred her tenuous composure. Her father's glossy black Mercedes-Benz was already idling at the curb across the street.

Their ride home was gratefully silent save for the public

news radio her father always had on in the background. One of the many ways he managed to make even his transit time productive. He'd barely finished parking the car in the garage when Lark levered herself out and made a break for the stairs to the basement. She couldn't talk to her mother.

Not now.

Toeing off her sneakers and stripping off her shorts, she retreated to the safety of her bed and pulled the covers over her head. The semidarkness only reminded her of the pond. Of the silence and peace she'd found below the water's surface and then again in Nick's arms. If only she could have stayed in that moment. Liberated from the confining grip of her perfection-obsessed past self. Untouched by the looming threat of an uncertain future. In the circle of Nick's arms, she'd simply been a woman. Led by her body and its primal, uncomplicated needs.

And for that brief moment, she'd felt…free.

Lark deliberately shut out the memory until exhaustion overtook her, and she let herself be drawn down into a dreamless sleep.

She awoke sometime later with a profound sense of disorientation. In her subterranean cave, it was almost impossible to tell dawn from dusk. Judging by how groggy she was, it could have been either. Muppet lay on the bed next to her, his purr rumbling to life when he noticed she was awake. Lark rolled over onto her back and felt around her nightstand for her phone. The display revealed a number that seemed incomprehensible.

4:55 p.m.?

But they'd gotten home at 6:30 a.m.

She couldn't have slept for ten hours.

Blinking at her phone, she swiped the screen open and found she had five text messages.

Three were from Nick.

8:25 a.m. Just checking to see if you're okay.

12:04 p.m. Text a thumbs-up if you're alive

3:33 p.m. I get it if you don't want to talk, but please just let me know if you're all right

Was she all right?

She'd basically thrown herself at Nick. Her father had showed up pretty much at the exact moment Nick had been about to slide inside her. And Lark been too much of a coward to stand up to her father or to face Nick on her way out.

Now she'd gone an entire day without texting him back. No.

She was most definitely *not* all right.

The anxiety from earlier that morning came flooding back, compressing her lungs within her chest. Her mouth went dry and sour, her pulse thundered in the ear pressed to her pillow. Shoving herself up in bed, she quickly tapped out a quick text reply.

I'm so sorry. I crashed hard. Just now waking up

She hit Send and held her breath, willing the tiny dots to appear on the screen and show he was typing a response.

Nothing came.

With every second that passed, her apprehension increased. What if he was annoyed at her now? What if while she'd slept, he'd decided it would be better not to have contact with her at all?

It wasn't like Lark could blame him.

He'd arranged the most thoughtful date she'd ever been on, had shared a beautiful part of his childhood with her, had provided the most intense orgasm she'd ever experienced, only to be cockblocked by her father.

Lark pressed her face into her knees and hugged her shins, absently stroking Muppet. She so badly wanted to call Nick, to reach for an instant answer to quell the mounting dread.

Her phone pinged, and Lark jumped, startling Muppet in her haste to check it.

The rush of relief she felt at seeing Nick's name in the text notifications evaporated when she read its contents.

Glad you got some rest.

The words seemed casual to her, his tone cool.

I'm really sorry for not answering earlier. And for this morning. I shouldn't have rushed out like I did.

Another eternal minute passed before the three bubbles appeared.

Then disappeared.

Then reappeared.

No worries at all

Lark's heart sank.

Four words, but it felt like a dismissal and a confirmation in one. Something had changed. She waited, hoping he'd follow it with something lighthearted that would remove the lead from her chest.

Nothing came.

Lark had nearly sunk into her mire when her phone pinged again.

Coming to class tomorrow?

The question felt like a life raft, and she dove onto it with embarrassing gusto.

Wouldn't miss it, she typed back.

After an interval of hours that felt like the interminable stretch between Christmas Eve and Christmas morning, Lark began her ritual with a long, hot shower, scrubbing until her skin was pink and tender from the heat. Feeling more awake and alive than she had all day, she twisted her damp hair up into a towel and moved to her makeup table. Surveying the options, it was clear which colors of eyeshadow and lipstick she favored. Only one or two had been used, and then, almost down to the pan.

Taking a deep breath, she made up her mind to use at least one shade she'd never touched before. Peach and green instead of taupe for her eyes. Shimmery nude instead of matte pink for her lips.

Color.

She'd been thinking about it ever since Nick's lecture.

Lark wasn't sure when she'd begun to shy away from it, but almost every item of clothing she owned was either white, black or beige. A palette that could also be found throughout her parents' modern, minimalist home. Lark's attempts to buck this standard in junior high and high school by asking to paint her walls or acquire comforters or curtains in a bold pattern had been met with her mother's insistence that they wouldn't "go" with the rest of the house. Her dorm rooms had become an unwitting extension, frequently garnering admiring comments from visitors that the space looked like something out of an aesthetic reel.

Whose aesthetic? was the question she found herself asking as she confronted her own reflection in the mirror.

Her hair was another problem.

She didn't trust herself to cut it, but damned if she'd wear it long and softly curled the way Reese had liked it—that required first blow drying it to straighten it, then half an hour's work with a curling iron. Instead, she found an old bottle of wave-enhancing product under the sink and worked it through hair before diffusing it into big, beachy waves.

Onto wardrobe.

After rejecting anything khaki or cardigan adjacent, she wound up in the section she hadn't looked at since her summer internship at a family-owned insta-care clinic. Selecting a pair of wide-legged navy trousers, she paired them with a cleavage-hugging, pale blue scoop-necked graphic T-shirt for the Westchester Ballet that she'd kept around for painting when she'd been in high school.

When she was finished, she examined the outcome in the full-length mirror attached to the bathroom door.

It had been months since she'd bothered with more than a hasty ponytail and a quick flip of mascara. In fact, she'd made a point of avoiding reflective surfaces all together. But now, examining her reflection, she felt an odd sense of recognition. The sort of quick pop she might get when spotting a friend in an unexpected venue.

I know her.

Her mother, on the other hand, did not.

Sitting at the kitchen table with her laptop and a stack of mail, she did a double take as Lark crested the stairs.

"Oh, honey," she said, eyes moving quickly over Lark's face, hair and outfit. "You're awake."

"It would appear so," she said, heading for the fridge in search of iced-coffee components.

"It's nice to see you in something other than pajama pants," her mother said, clicking away on the keyboard.

"You should have been at Nick Hoffman's this morning." Ice clattered into Lark's travel mug as she held it under the dispenser. "You'd have seen me in cutoffs and dire embarrassment."

The clicking of keys ceased abruptly.

"Oh, Lark," her mother said softly. "I'm so sorry." She closed the laptop and looked up at her daughter. "I tried to tell him that wasn't the way to handle things, but you know how he is when he gets like that."

Lark stopped stirring her coffee and met her mother's gaze. "I know," she said quietly, taking a long sip from the mug and moving across the room to sit down.

Her mother nodded sadly. "He loves you, honey. He just isn't sure how to help."

"One small hint—confronting me about my life plans in my art teacher's living room isn't it."

Lark's mother traced a knothole in the oversized table with the tip of her finger. "Am I allowed to ask what you were doing at his house, or would that be a breach of boundaries?"

Even steeped in irritation, Lark felt a flicker of gratitude for her mother, recognizing terminology from one of their few family therapy sessions. Well, mother-daughter therapy sessions. Her father had sited a full caseload and the undesirability of both him and her mother being absent from their shared practice at the same time. The therapist's suggestion that he could attend the next session had been greeted with initial agreement, then postponed, then dropped altogether.

"Enjoying each other's company," Lark said, choosing a sufficiently vague answer.

Her mother reached out and put a hand on Lark's arm. "Just be careful, okay?"

"I will."

"Before I forget." Shuffling through the pile of mail, her mother plucked out an envelope and slid it across the table. "This came for you."

Lark didn't even need to read the address at the top to know who it was from. Her eyes had grown accustomed to the height and thickness of the letters. The curves and serifs of the font.

Geisel School of Medicine at Dartmouth.

She also didn't need to open it to know the contents.

Her palms began to sweat.

Another reminder.

Politely but insistently informing her that if she didn't respond to the college within the allotted time period, she'd be automatically disenrolled from the program.

"Thanks," Lark said, turning it face down.

Her mother arched a brow at her. "You're not going to open it?"

"I will," Lark said, pushing back from the table. "I just need to get to class early tonight."

Lark's mother glanced down at the Cartier watch that had been a twenty-fifth anniversary present from Lark's father. "I can be ready to go in about ten minutes if that works."

"That's okay." Ducking into the pantry, Lark grabbed a protein bar and tore it open. "I have a ride."

When she emerged, her mother's helpful smile had wilted. "Oh?" she asked.

Lark bit into the bar and nodded. "One of the ladies from my class lives about a mile from here. She said she'd be happy to pick me up on the way."

"Oh." Her mother had opened her laptop and resumed her typing. "Well, that's nice of her."

Lark's heart squeezed at the sight of her mother bravely trying to pretend it didn't bother her.

Early in the wake of her breakdown, Lark had resented her mother's constant fussing. But watching her mother struggle to support Lark's desire to get out of the house even when it had been the very thing Diana Hockney had hoped to achieve all along, Lark had an important realization.

Her mother's over-attentive hovering hadn't been a manic need to restore Lark's mental well-being. It had been about preserving her own. A way of assuring herself that her daughter would be okay. That she would arrive safe. That she would have the supplies she needed. That she knew someone cared enough to check on her safety.

Lark bent to kiss her mother's hair before heading down to the basement to grab her portfolio and purse. "Thanks, Mom."

Her mother's blue eyes blinked up at her, wide and startled. "For what?"

Lark reached down and squeezed her mother's hand. "For signing me up for an art class."

Linda arrived promptly at 6:30 p.m. with the convertible top rolled back, the air-conditioning blasting and Etta James's mournful voice warbling from the speakers.

"Don't you look cute," she said, her dark eyes taking in Lark's outfit.

"Thanks," Lark said, twisting to put her portfolio in the back seat before buckling herself in.

They backed out of the driveway and motored down the street. "So how come we're headed in so early?" Linda asked.

Lark debated for all of five seconds before spilling everything. When Linda remained silent, Lark was afraid she might have said too much. Inundating her new friend with drama too soon.

"How old is your father?" Linda asked at last.

"Fifty-four," Lark reported. "He's eleven years older than my mother."

Linda sucked her teeth. "That sounds about right."

They turned into the parking lot of the community college, and Linda pressed a button on the dash that had the canvas convertible top extending over their heads.

"I have thoughts," she said once the car was sealed. "But we'll need to unpack them after class. We don't have quite enough time." Cutting the engine, she swiveled in her leather bucket seat to face Lark. "For now, I'm going to wait out here, and you're going in solo. Your talking points are as follows."

Lark listened as Linda listed them out, feeling like she should be taking notes.

"You good?" Linda asked when she had finished.

"I think so," Lark said, gathering her things.

"Good. See you inside in about fifteen minutes. Text if you need me sooner."

Exiting the car armed with a solid strategy, Lark felt an immense wave of warmth wash over her. Twice in one week, she'd been the beneficiary of Linda's sage advice. She only hoped it would prove as effective this time as it had before.

As she made her way to the entrance, Lark looked down the hallway and saw light spilling from one of the classrooms.

Nick was there.

But the burgeoning confidence she'd mustered on the drive over was not.

Swallowing hard, Lark spun on her heel and made a beeline for the bathroom, sending an SOS message as soon as she was inside.

On my way pinged right back.

Only when she heard the percussion of Linda's stylish wedge sandals did Lark exit the stall.

"Pep talk, or pretend it never happened?" she asked.

"Pretend it never happened," Lark said, selecting the less intimidating option for coping with seeing Nick again.

"Got it," Linda said. "We'll go in together."

Lark gulped a breath and followed her friend into the classroom.

Nick was half-seated at his usual table at the front, his head cocked as he studied something on his laptop. He glanced up from the screen and did a very obvious double take that lit a fuse in Lark's belly.

The hand resting on the table had been in her hair, on her belly, between her thighs. The shapely mouth framing a nervous grin had been on the most intimate parts of her.

It all careened back into her consciousness with a force that weakened her knees.

Before she could collapse in an all-out swoon, Lark averted her gaze and sat down.

"Hey there," Nick said.

"Hey," Lark said.

"Well, don't you look like you stepped right off the pages of a fashion magazine." Tammy's warm, twangy voice announced her presence seconds before she slid into the seat next to Lark's.

"Thanks," Lark replied, managing a weak smile.

At the front of the classroom, Nick cleared his throat. "Since we didn't quite finish our lesson on color theory from last time, I thought we could start by continuing work on our paintings."

Receiving mumbled agreement from both Tammy and Linda, he turned his back to set up the Bluetooth speaker. When the first notes drifted out, Lark lifted her head. David Bowie's "Space Oddity." Her eyes met Nick's, and his mouth lifted in the lopsided grin that stole her breath.

Tammy and Linda chatted as they settled into their paintings, squeezing dollops of pigment onto the plastic trays Nick had set out for them and dabbling their brushes in the paint-flecked mason jars.

"You know what we need?" Linda asked when they took a break to rinse out their muddy water. "We need a field trip."

"Lord, yes!" Tammy clapped her hands, her voice bright and excited. "I've been so bored lately I damn near started to wallpaper my silverware."

"To where?" Nick asked, glancing up from his phone.

"DC?" Linda suggested.

"Please." Tammy waved her hand dismissively. "Anywhere that's got that many politicians in one place is bound to be as much fun as a box full of mosquitos." She paused to apply a glob of aquamarine to her canvas. "How about Baltimore?"

"That's not a bad idea," Linda allowed. "We could see the Baltimore Museum of Art, the American Visionary, the Walters…"

"My baby boy's hotel!" Tammy said. "He just got promoted to general manager, and I'd just bet he can comp us some rooms."

Lark blinked at her.

She'd pegged Tammy at mid- to late thirties. Forty at the outside. The idea of her having a son old enough to have climbed the corporate ladder to the managerial level seemed impossible.

"I'll even rent a van so we can all go together," Tammy said, clearly attempting to sweeten the deal. "What do you say, Mr. Hoffman?"

Nick set his phone aside. "I say we vote on it. All those in favor?"

Tammy and Linda's hands shot up, but Nick's hovered just above his denim-clad thigh.

Lark realized he was waiting on her to weigh in. That he would vote at she voted.

Escaping the confines of her parents' home for a couple of days certainly held an allure. As did the idea of extended contact with Nick.

Before she knew it, Lark's hand was floating skyward.

"Looks like we're going on a field trip," Nick announced, raising his own.

"Hot damn!" Tammy clapped her hands together. "I'ma text Bryce right this second." Her nails were already clicking over her phone's screen when she paused. "When are we thinking of going? I guess I'd better give him some dates."

"How about this weekend?" Linda suggested. "With it being the Fourth of July, I have Monday off."

"Works for me," Tammy agreed. "How about y'all?"

Lark pretended to check her phone calendar, not wanting to admit that pretty much any day would have been fine. "Okay here."

"Fine here as well," Nick confirmed.

"Then it's settled," Tammy said. "Let me just step out to make a couple calls."

"Actually, that reminds me." Linda pushed back in her chair

and reached in her purse for her keys. "I left a watercolor in my car that I wanted you to take a peek at. Be right back."

Lark was tempted to slide beneath the table. She only hoped Nick wouldn't pick up on Linda's obvious effort seizing the opportunity to leave them alone.

Thick silence held them until, unable to sit still, Lark rose from her chair under the pretense of rinsing her brushes. Her heart beat hard enough to feel in her stomach as she stood at the sink.

"So, um…how 'bout them Patriots?" Nick asked.

"They still suck," Lark replied, staring resolutely at the wall behind the sink.

Several more beats of silence passed.

Nick cleared his throat again. "And, uh…how much further along are you with *A Garden of Chimeras?*"

"Not far," she admitted. Possibly because she'd never even heard of the book.

"It's a great book so far," he said, his voice lower than usual. "Really captivating."

Lark felt herself relaxing, drawn in by his attempts at breaking the awkwardness with invented conversations. Unable to stand it any longer, she turned to face him, looking directly into his eyes.

"Listen, Nick—"

These were the only words she got out before he was on her. His lips were warm and firm, his hands gripping her hips. She felt a rush of excitement laced with fear. Tammy and Linda could come back at any minute, but Lark didn't care.

She gave herself to the moment. To him. To the pure loveliness of his tongue tangling with hers.

Fueling the ardor was her relief.

He still wanted this.

He still wanted *her*.

And badly, judging by the hard column pressing into her hip. Lark moaned into Nick's mouth as he ground his crotch against her and his hands traveled up her body, cupping her breasts through her shirt before making their way up to her face. Threading through her hair.

He pulled back, his eyes dark with desire as he gazed into hers. "Is it wrong to tell you that I want you so fucking bad?" he whispered hoarsely.

"All *riiiight!*" Tammy sang.

In the split second it took her to make it from the hallway to the door, Nick took a giant step toward his table and Lark spun to face the sink. Both of their backs were turned to Tammy while they recovered their breath.

And, presumably, control over their respective bodies.

The counter bit into Lark's belly as she sagged against it, arousal slackening her limbs.

How delicious it was to be wanted. To have something to anticipate with such single-minded ferocity. Lark curled the knowledge around herself like a blanket, banishing the chill of a day's worth of worry and doubt.

"It's all settled. I got us a block of rooms *and* a rental van."

"When and where are we meeting up?" Linda had returned empty-handed but with a very noticeable smile on her face when she looked at Lark.

"Eleven a.m. on Saturday right here in this parking lot," Tammy said. Then, turning to Nick: "You think we'll be okay to leave cars here over the weekend, or should we grab a Lyft?"

Nick glanced over his shoulder. "You should be fine. I have an in with the facilities folks."

Only when they arrived Saturday morning, they were astonished to discover that Tammy had not rented a run-of-the-mill van.

She'd rented a party bus.

"Surprise!" she sang, gesturing to the sleek black van with a gameshow-girl flourish. "I figure if we've got to make a two-hour drive, we might as well make the most of it, right?"

And it was, in fact, the very most.

The exterior featured sleek windows and bright lights that glowed in the dark. The interior was almost like stepping into a nightclub. Limo-style plush leather seating, multiple plasma screens, surround-sound stereo speakers on each side of the cabin, LED lights, a fully stocked bar...

And a stripper pole.

Lark gulped and tried to keep her expression neutral. She was damn glad she'd followed her gut instinct to take an Uber to the college as opposed to letting her mother drop her off.

It had been a strategic move on Lark's part. After the bitter fight with her father, she knew her mother would want to smooth things over. But Lark was in no mood for smoothing. Nor had she been in the mood to sit there while her mother fretted about Lark's being away from home for two nights.

Tammy had already cracked open the ice compartment and was filling glasses. "What am I making for everyone?"

"Not a damn thing," Linda said, relieving her friend of the tequila bottle. "We let you pour the drinks, and we'll all be lit before we hit Dumfries."

"Well, that's the idea," Tammy said, ducking to look in a cabinet. "Where the hell's the sweet-and-sour mix?"

Linda looked to Lark. "What'll it be?"

Glancing at her phone, Lark noted it was 11:11 a.m. "A mimosa, if they've got the components."

"And for you?" Linda's eyes flicked to Nick, who was

studying the placard of rules for the party bus like he intended to commit them to memory.

"I'm okay for right now," Nick said.

Tammy pooched out a glossy lower lip. "Come on, now. This here is a holiday weekend and this great nation's birthday. It's practically your patriotic duty."

Lark and Nick snagged gazes. Tammy was going to be a handful.

"I'll just have a beer, I guess." Shifting, Nick peeked behind the curtain sectioning off the last part of the bus. The restroom, Lark suspected.

"One cerveza coming up." Tammy squatted in front of the mini fridge as Linda seated herself beside Lark.

"Here you go," she said, handing Lark a plastic cup of what looked like a liquid sunset. "I added a little grenadine at the bottom," Linda explained. "My grandma always used to make them like that."

"Well, that can't be right." Bottles clinked as Tammy pawed through the refrigerator.

"What's the matter?" Linda asked, sipping her drink.

Tammy's forehead creased as she looked at her friend. "I don't see a single beer in here."

"It's okay," Nick said, sinking into a seat across the aisle from Linda and Lark. "I'm fine, really."

"You're not either," Tammy insisted, a whiskey sour in her hand and a determined expression on her face. "How can they even call this a party bus when they've neglected one of the mandatory categories of adult beverages?" Tammy sipped her drink. "Well, I was going to start our journey with a toast, but—"

The bus doors opened with a hiss, and they all swiveled to look as Julia Hoffman's mane of wild red curls came into view.

"Is this the party bus?" she asked.

Had Lark not glanced at Nick, she might have assumed he'd invited his mother along as Tammy insurance. Judging from his open-mouthed gape, she surmised this was not the case.

"Mom," Nick said, rising from his seat. "What are you doing here?"

"I invited her."

Lark recognized the gravelly voice before the stony face came into view.

Mike Donnelly.

Followed by David Garza.

Ahh. So, he *had* invited Tammy insurance. He just hadn't counted on his insurance inviting additional insurance.

Tammy and Linda both stared at Nick, whose cheeks were stained the blotchy red Lark found intensely endearing.

"I hope you don't mind," Nick said. "I figured since you booked me that deluxe two-bedroom suite, there'd be enough room for a couple of my buddies to join us."

Tammy's mouth ticked only briefly before spreading into a broad smile. "Why, of course not." Rising, she set her drink aside. "Tammy Devereux," she said, offering her hand to Nick's mother. "And this is Linda Cassidy."

Julia's lips pursed together as her eyes flicked over Tammy and Linda and then back at her son. "Julia Hoffman," she said. "I've heard so much about you." Amazing how different this phrase sounded when stripped of all warmth.

Nick finished out the introductions with Mike and David, both of whom seemed considerably less displeased to meet Tammy and Linda than Nick's mother had.

"Let me take this for you, Mom." Nick folded down the handle of his mother's carry on, his bicep bulging against the sleeve of his T-shirt as he lifted the bag. "There's a luggage rack back here if you need it, guys."

The men both nodded to Lark as they followed him back and stowed their overnight bags. Nick's mother, on the other hand, strolled around the bus with the authority of a drill sergeant inspecting a barracks.

Ever the stateswoman, Linda popped up from her seat. "Could I interest you in a drink? Lark and I were just having a Pussy Foot."

"A Pussy Foot?" Julia asked just as Nick emerged from the back. "What's a Pussy Foot?"

Nick's face paled.

"Grenadine, grapefruit juice and prosecco," Linda said.

"Oh, well, that does sound nice," she said. "If it's not too much trouble."

"No trouble at all," Linda insisted. Moments later, they handed out the drinks—the Pussy Foot for Julia and whiskey sours for the bus's other two male occupants.

"I would propose a toast, but we'll have to wait until we stop and get Nick some beer first."

"Always got to be high maintenance, this one." Mike chucked Nick affectionately on the shoulder.

"For Christ's sake," Nick grumbled below his breath. Stalking over to the bar, he poured the last of the prosecco into a plastic cup and turned to the group.

"Here's to those who wish us well," Tammy said, lifting her glass. "All the rest can go to hell."

They all bumped rims and sipped.

"Oh, that *is* nice," Julia said, smacking her lips. "A Pussy Foot, did you say?"

Nick drained the rest of his prosecco in one gulp.

"Should we get these wheels on the road?" Tammy asked.

"Knock, knock, knocking on Kevin's door," she sang in a surprisingly good alto while she waited for the driver to respond.

The tinted glass slid to the side. "Miss Tammy?"

"Take us out," she said, slicing a hand toward the windshield.

"If everyone could take a seat and buckle up until we hit the freeway, I'd be happy to get started," he said.

"You heard the man," Tammy said.

With there being seven passengers instead of four, leaving seats between occupants was no longer an option. Lark glanced at Nick hopefully, feeling like a silly teenager with a crush.

He managed to time it perfectly, waiting until David and Mike took seats opposite each other closest to the front of the bus. Tammy slid in next to Mike, and Julia, chess master that she was, plopped down next to Tammy.

Checkmate.

Linda sat opposite Julia, leaving Lark to resume her former seat and Nick to take the one beside Lark's at the end of the aisle.

With a hiss of air brakes, they were off.

She smiled to herself as the bus pulled out and onto the freeway to the soundtrack of occasional commentary from Tammy or happy chatter between Linda and Julia.

Lulled by the rumble of the engine and the gentle sway of the bus, Nick nodded off about twenty minutes into the journey. Which afforded Lark the opportunity to steal glances of his profile. His eyes were closed, his lips lightly parted as he breathed evenly in and out. Long, dark lashes feathered his smooth cheeks. She resisted the urge to remove his glasses and brush back a dark lock of hair that had fallen across his forehead.

Instead, she contented herself with the pleasant distraction of his arm rubbing against hers. Hard muscle and crisp hair.

A grouping of dark, flat freckles in a shape that reminded her of a constellation whose name she couldn't remember.

As they traveled farther away from town and into Virginia countryside, Lark couldn't help but admire the rolling hills and lush greenery. They passed farms dotted with grazing cows and horses. Hollows and hills. Beautiful as it was, Virginia had never felt like *her* place. But then, neither had Hanover. She'd half given up hope of ever finding one.

Rotating in her seat, she realized with a start that Nick was awake.

And watching her watch the landscape.

Tammy and Linda were busy fixing another round of drinks. Julia, Mike and David had fallen into a heated debate about Spring Valley's recent decision to rezone the greenbelt. No one was paying the least bit of attention to them.

The corner of Nick's mouth curled upward, as if he knew exactly what she was thinking. Nick's movements were so unassuming that even she almost didn't notice what he was doing until the tip of his middle finger slid beneath the fluttery hem of her skirt. He traced a small circle around a freckle on her thigh, and Lark felt a sympathetic clench at her core. Taking care not to draw attention to herself, she crossed her legs toward him to provide more cover in case anyone should turn around.

A strange electricity seemed to pass between them. His eyes roamed over her face, studying her features like he was trying to commit them to memory as he pulled his phone from his shirt pocket.

Seconds later, a notification appeared on her phone's screen.

Silence your phone.

Lark lifted the device from the seat next to her and thumbed the button to quiet it.

Another text quickly followed.

You're killing me in that dress.

Warmth gathered in her middle, the excitement of their road trip and the sweet, heady drink making her uncharacteristically bold. You should see what I have under it.

Show me.

Lark gave him a questioning look.

Nick's eyes burned from behind his glasses before he turned nonchalantly back to his phone. The fingertip that had been playing with the hem of her skirt now hooked it, drawing it upward in demonstration.

A quick glance at the others confirmed her suspicion. From their respective angles, they couldn't see.

Lark leaned over her lap, angling her shoulders to further obstruct the view. With her left hand, she held the phone out in front of her. With her right, she began bunching the silky fabric of her skirt, leaving her thigh covered but revealing a sliver of her left hip and the curve of her ass.

Nick's breathing had deepened. Quickened. He, too, sat forward, but for different reasons, she imagined. Holding his phone in his right hand, he reached across his lap with his left.

Lark's stomach muscles jerked as he hooked the thin elastic band of the barely there thong that rode over her hip. His warm fingers stroked the crease where her hip met her thigh. Only she could hear his low rumble of satisfaction as he ventured further.

Nick's eyes held hers, silently asking what she would do next.

She smiled, her heart racing, the idea already forming in her mind. Reaching up to tug the elastic out of her hair, she let it fall in a curtain around her shoulders. She rubbed a finger across her chin as if deep in thought, then trailed it down her neck to the dip between her clavicles, then to her sternum.

Nick's fingertips dug into her thigh as he anticipated her next movement.

One quick flick, and the triangle of her halter dress was pulled to the side, baring her breast to him alone.

The muscles in Nick's jaw flexed.

When his eyes traced over the rounded curve and lingered on her hardened nipple, Lark would have sworn she could feel it. Could actually *feel* the weight of his desire across the sensitive peak.

The bus bumped, and she quickly replaced the fabric as Nick snatched his hand back.

Her phone lit up seconds later.

How much longer until we get to Baltimore?

Lark consulted her phone's map. Forty-five minutes.

Meet me in the back.

The words seemed to jump off the screen and into her throat.

Nick pocketed his phone and adjusted his glasses before standing up and disappearing through the curtains at the back of the bus.

Lark hesitated before glancing at the rest of the crew. David had fallen asleep, but Julia, Tammy, Mike and Linda were all bent over Tammy's iPad, engrossed in a video of a new home she'd been looking to buy.

Should they be interrupted, she could stuff Nick in the bathroom and pretend to be looking for something in her luggage.

Or vice versa.

Lark took a deep breath and made her way to the back of the bus.

Nick wasted no time.

No sooner was she through the curtain than Nick pulled her in and crushed her lips with his. His hands roamed over her skin, down the curve of her back to her ass. Then back up to push her halter top aside. Lark could only whimper into his mouth as he palmed her breasts, gently pressing her sensitive nipples with the pads of both thumbs.

His mouth found her ear, sending shivers down her spine. "I want to make you come."

She was breathless, electric, her entire body humming like a downed power line. "That's not fair," she panted against his neck. "I've already— You haven't—"

"You will."

Grabbing handfuls of her skirt, Nick hauled it up her thighs, shifting back to drink in a thirsty glance at her emerald-green lace panties. The small, dark thatch of her sex was visible through the sheer fabric.

"Fuck," he growled against her neck. "Are you trying to stop my heart?"

One hand in her panties, Nick dipped to capture her nipple with his eager mouth. Lark's back arched, and she muffled her moan against his shoulder, gripping handfuls of his T-shirt.

Lark's eyelids lowered as she watched the sun-kissed pastures blur by out the window behind him. Her pulse pounded as her back pressed against the bathroom door, her sandals planted wide. The illicit, decadent thrill stirred something deep within her, something she'd never even dared to imagine.

She swallowed a cry as his thumb brushed across her clit, her knees threatening to buckle with the intensity. Already, Lark felt the charge building within her. Crackling like electricity seconds before a lightning strike. Her thighs began to tense, the deepest parts of her rippling with warning.

"Oh! There's even a john!" Julia's voice floated out from the other side of the curtains.

"*Fuck.*" Jerking his hands away, Nick quickly helped Lark rearrange her clothes.

"You get in the bathroom," she whispered, glancing down at the bulge in his jeans. "I'll take care of your mom."

Nick planted a quick kiss on her lips and shut himself in, throwing the latch that made a red Occupied sign appear next to the handle.

Lark busied herself in her carry-on case, frantically scrambling for her makeup bag and getting to it just as Julia came through the curtains.

"Oh, Lark. Is that son of mine keeping you waiting too?"

"Not at all," Lark said. "I was just…powdering my nose," she said lamely.

"Tell me about." Julia fanned herself. "These hot flashes, I'm telling you. The doctor wants to put me on hormones, but my friend, Judy, she went on them and then started to lose her hair and got the worst case of acne you've ever seen. Me, I've been trying herbs and whatnot, but I just don't know how much longer I can hold out. Of course, I need to get my blood pressure down before I can make any changes. But I'm not sure how I'm supposed to do that when cheesecake exists."

Lark bit her tongue to keep from giggling at the impromptu monologue.

"As good of a cook as you are," Lark said, "I don't know how you could ever manage that."

Julia flushed with a mix of pleasure and the effect from at least two Pussy Foots. "That's very nice of you to say, dear. You'll have to come back over for dinner one of these evenings." The hand she laid on Lark's forearm was warm and surprisingly rough. "I'll make you one of my specialties."

"I'd love that," Lark said, and meant it.

The bathroom door unlocked, and they both moved out of the way.

"Finally." Julia propped a hand on her hip. "If I didn't know better, I'd wonder if you weren't in there 'reading an article' just like you did when you were fifteen," she said, making exaggerated air quotes with her fingers.

Lark stifled a laugh at Nick's horrified expression.

"It's nothing to be ashamed of, Fenwick. In fact, I wish they would encourage teenage boys to do it more. Teenage girls too," she added. "It's surprising how many women my age didn't know what an orgasm was when they got married. I know I didn't," Julia said. "Luckily your father was a very patient man—"

"That's it," Nick said. "I'm out of here." He pushed through the curtains leaving the two of them alone.

"I know I shouldn't tease him." Julia elbowed her conspiratorially. "He just makes it so easy." She disappeared into the bathroom, and Lark rejoined everyone in the cabin.

There had been some spreading out of the seating arrangements now that everyone wasn't staying buckled, and Lark couldn't sit next to Nick without looking suspicious, so she eased down across from him instead.

Tammy, who'd somehow wound up where Lark had been previously, crossed her legs toward him. "I've got a question for you, mister. Is it true your mother and father met at one of those free-love communes in upstate New York?"

Without a word, Nick rose from his seat, walked to the bar, poured himself a shot of tequila and downed it.

"Now you're talkin'!" Rising, Tammy followed suit. "Anyone else?"

"I haven't yet met my bad-decisions quota for the day," Linda sighed. "Set me up."

"Set me up, too!" Julia had emerged from the bathroom and was headed down the aisle toward them.

Nick's eyebrows lifted in a look of alarm. "Since when do you do tequila shots?"

"Since I'm on vacation." Mike moved to accommodate Julia as she sat down, and there was a fondness in the gesture that Lark found touching.

"This isn't a vacation," Nick pointed out. "It's a field trip."

"For you maybe," his mother said, earning an uproarious laugh from Tammy and Linda. "Anyway, some teacher you are, taking shots with your students. I have a mind to tell the humanities department chair."

"You *are* the humanities department chair," Nick said through a tight jaw.

"Huh," Julia said. "Then I guess we're both okay to have a shot."

"I like your mama, Nick," Tammy said, handing out the miniature glasses. "She's got spunk."

Lark found that she liked Julia too. Though she couldn't have been any more different from Lark's own mother if she'd made a purposeful effort.

"She's got something, all right," he muttered under his breath.

"To Baltimore," Tammy said, and they all drank.

Declining the offer of a second, Lark and Nick snagged gazes when the rest of their crew enthusiastically accepted.

Upon leaving Spring Valley, the original plan had been to get to Baltimore, find somewhere to have lunch and check into their hotel. By the time they were thirty minutes outside the city, it was clear that plan would need to be amended. Three shots in and counting, Julia was receiving an impromptu pole-dancing lesson from Tammy while Steppenwolf's "Magic Carpet Ride" thumped through the bus's sound system.

"This is my literal idea of hell," Nick whispered.

Lark had noticed his tone had soured along with his mood when he pulled out his laptop and connected to the party bus's Wi-Fi.

Work? she wondered.

More than once, Nick's offhand comments about Moonshot and his business partner, Marshall, led her to believe friction between them might have something to do with why he'd come home for the summer.

"Now you just need to build up some momentum," Tammy said. "Here, lemme show you right quick."

Julia extracted herself from the pole, nearly taking a header into Mike's lap. The short, burly man caught her and guided her back a couple steps so Tammy could demonstrate. Lark's jaw dropped when the lithe blonde gripped the pole with both hands before scissoring her legs into a graceful spin followed by a complicated dismount.

"Where did you learn to do this?" Julia asked, sipping the prosecco that had magically appeared in her hand.

"From stripping," Tammy said casually.

"You were a stripper?" Julia's eyes were round as salad plates.

"Sure enough." Tammy sank into the seat next to Linda. "There weren't too many career opportunities available to a high school dropout with a two-year-old baby boy in Blue Ridge, Georgia."

The song ended, and their formerly merry company dropped into stunned silence in the wake of Tammy's revelation.

Julia sat down next to Tammy, placing a hand over hers. "You had a two-year-old at eighteen?"

"Yes, ma'am," Tammy said. "There I was, a varsity cheerleader, a full-ride scholarship to University of Georgia and *boom*." She clapped her hands together for emphasis. "I found out I was pregnant on my sixteenth birthday, Cole got himself long gone and my parents kicked me out."

Lark watched the interaction from the back of the bus, feeling a twinge of guilt. Even in her darkest hours, she'd never worried about not having a roof over her head or food in her belly.

"I stayed with a friend until I had Bryce," she continued, "then made my way to Atlanta. Started dancing at a club, made enough money to get my own place, got my GED, finished my degree at an online college and now here I am. Fixin' to take my LSATs in the fall."

"I'd say that deserves a toast," Julia said. "To Tammy the lawyer." She lifted her glass, and they all drank.

"Speaking of bad decisions..." Linda scooted to the edge of her seat to look at her friend. "Did I mention that I got an email from One-Night Stan?"

"You did *not*," Tammy said.

Lark watched, wide-eyed, as the two women laughed and

made light of their missteps. They talked with a carefree attitude that bordered on indifference.

What would that be like? Lark wondered.

She had always been so careful. So deliberate. So afraid of doing the wrong thing that half the time she couldn't make herself do anything at all. But here were Tammy and Linda—fearless in their embrace of life's ills and misfortunes and all the more colorful for it.

It was a kind of freedom Lark had never known. One she desperately longed for but had no idea how to emulate.

Nick heaved a sigh and snapped his laptop shut. "I'm just going to step to the back and make a quick call."

"I'm sorry, darlin'," Tammy said. "Here we are carrying on while you're trying to work."

"You're fine," Nick said tersely. "This will only take a minute." He stalked to the back and shoved his way through the curtain.

"Marshall, I'd bet."

The group turned to look at Nick's mother, whose jovial expression had flattened into a scowl. "That man," Julia said, her voice thick with disapproval. "Can't let Nick have a moment's peace."

"Well, obviously we hate him," Linda said. "Who is he?"

"Nick's business partner," Julia said. "And by partner, I mean Nick does all the work but Marshall gets all the credit." She tutted and took a sip of her drink. "All hours of the night Nick is working. Answering emails, writing grant proposals. I keep telling him he's going to work himself into a stroke."

"Why on earth does Nick put up with that?" Tammy asked. "Smart as he is, I'd bet he has a line out the door of people wanting to work with him."

"Been like that since he was a kid," David said, speaking

up for the first time since the shots had started passing around. "Always had a soft spot for a sob story, our Nick."

"Isn't that the truth." Julia's eyes rolled heavenward as if the answers would come streaming through the bus's skylight. "He used to give away his lunch money if any of the other kids showed up without theirs."

"Let other kids copy his homework," Mike added.

"Would take the fall if one of his friends got in trouble," David said.

"Do you remember the time in little league when he refused to tag a runner crossing home base because the other team didn't have any points yet?" Mike's shoulders shook with silent laughter.

"His father was furious," Julia said, tears of mirth in her eyes.

"What about the time he brought that stray kitten home?" Dave countered.

Julia broke out into a contagious cackle that had them all laughing along with her. "Three months he has this cat living in his bedroom, and I have *no* idea," she said. "Until one day I go to collect his laundry basket and find a litter of kittens in it."

As everyone around her gave into hysterics, Lark's chest tightened.

"And don't even get me started on his girlfriends," Julia continued. "They see him coming from a mile away, these women. He fixes them and breaks himself in the process." Julia shook her head sadly. "Just once, I'd like to see him with someone stable and put together."

The first night Lark had been in his class. How he'd found her sitting alone on the wall. How he'd chased her down and insisted on giving her a ride. His special assignment and how he checked in on her.

Was she just another of his strays?

Had the passion between them merely been a chance to give her something he thought she needed?

Lark sat there, feeling queasy as the laughter died down. Glancing toward the back of the bus, she caught a glimpse of Nick's beleaguered profile. Julia had said it herself. He'd been pulling all-nighters to keep caught up at work, giving time to Lark that he needed for himself. For his business. And now the stress was catching up with him.

She'd been greedy. Needy. So eager to lap up his attention that she hadn't thought about what it might be costing him. What he might be neglecting out of his worry for her.

Suddenly, the bus felt too small, the air too thick. Lark struggled to pull it into her lungs, to remember how breathing even worked. Racing thoughts took over as the sound around her went muffled, superseded by the thunder of Lark's speeding heart.

Please. Not here. Not now.

The telltale ache clutched at the base of her throat as tears stung behind her lids. Needing to distract herself, she got up and went to the bar.

"If you're going to have another, you might want to hurry," Tammy urged, glancing out the window. "We're fixin' to be at the hotel in about fifteen minutes."

"Not a problem," Lark said. Pouring some bottled water into her glass, she placed the small yellow pill her mother had given her on her tongue and swallowed.

I know you don't like to take them anymore, but your doctor prescribed them for a reason. It's better to have it and not need it than need it and not have it.

Once again, her mother had been right.

Coming on this trip had been a terrible mistake.

Ten

There was a special place in hell for the bastard who had invented karaoke.

Nick sat crowded around a table with his mother, Tammy, Linda, Dave and Mike, watching person after person humiliate themselves beneath the atomic glow of neon lights.

The bar was sticky. People were sticky. The floor was sticky. The fucking air was sticky. His lungs wanted threatened to revolt from the mix of beer breath, cologne, cigarettes and trying too hard. The place was packed full of bodies, and the noise was beginning to give him a headache.

The wages of guilt.

His call with Marshall and the team had gone long, and he'd spent his afternoon and half of dinner holed up in his hotel room. By the time he'd joined them, Linda had reported that Lark wasn't feeling well and had gone up to her room. Which was exactly where Nick longed to be at present. But instead, he'd agreed to this excursion to make up for his absence at dinner. Nick checked his phone again, wondering exactly how long he needed to stay to pay off the filial debt.

"You're almost up." Tammy, fresh off getting a little grabassy with Linda on the dance floor, wrapped a hand around his bicep and squeezed.

Nick pulled away, trying to keep the mood light. "Hard pass."

Tammy's face fell before she mustered a cajoling smile.

"One little song isn't going to make your hairline recede or anything."

"He has a beautiful voice," his mother chimed in most unhelpfully. "His father and I always said he could have been a canter."

Meanwhile, Mike and David remained annoyingly silent, watching him squirm like a worm on a hook.

"Actually, I think I'm gonna step out for some air." Nick pushed back from the table. "I'll just be a minute."

As soon as he stepped outside, the night air hit his face, clearing away the fug. Nick pulled his phone from his pocket, determined to get on with the real reason he'd escaped. To check on Lark. He'd sent her a text earlier apologizing for having missed her at dinner, but it had gone unanswered. He now stared at the stubbornly blank screen, debating whether a call would be the worst idea ever.

Fuck it.

Pulling up his recent text messages, he opened Lark's and punched the Call button. The tightness in his chest eased when she answered on the second ring.

"Hello?" Her voice was thick, raspy, deeper than usual.

"Hey," Nick said. "Did I wake you?"

She sniffed to clear a nose that sounded congested. "No," she said.

That's when it hit him. She'd been crying.

"Are you okay?"

"I'm fine." Her voice sounded shaky. "Just a little tired. It was a long day."

She was right about that for damn sure. "Listen, the ladies dragged me out to karaoke, but I'm planning a daring escape in the next seventeen minutes. If you want to talk or anything—"

"I think I'm just going to take a bath and crawl into bed, actually."

Nick couldn't say he blamed her. Given the accommodations, that was exactly what he'd be doing if he hadn't been delicately bullied into this outing. Like the party bus, their hotel had been another of Tammy's surprises. When she'd mentioned her son was the general manager of a hotel in Baltimore, she'd conveniently left out that it was the Four Seasons.

"Okay," he said, hoping his disappointment didn't carry through the phone. "Get some rest."

"Good night," she said and disconnected.

Nick sagged back against the rough brick wallpapered with posters advertising musicians who'd long come and gone. He willed his racing thoughts to slow, closing his eyes to shut out the lights and noise. The clicking of heels on the sidewalk snapped Nick to attention.

Tammy.

Nick turned his head and saw her sauntering toward him, her purse over her arm and a smile on her face. "Well, hey there," she said. "What are you doing out here all alone?"

"Just taking a breather," Nick said, trying to keep his voice steady. "It's a bit people-y in there."

"I know what you mean," Tammy said, moving closer to him. "I haven't been checked out so hard since that wet T-shirt contest next to the naval yard."

Nick didn't have any problem seeing why. In her hip-hugging skirt and cleavage-bearing top, she was a bombshell.

"Is everything all right?" Tammy asked. "You've seemed kind of upset since you got that phone call on the bus."

Nick reached up to scratch a nonexistent itch. "Everything's fine," he said. "Just a little trouble at work."

"Sure sounds like that Marshall's giving you a rough time of it."

Nick suppressed an eye roll. That comment had his mother's fingerprints all over it. "He's all right. We're just both under a lot of stress."

Tammy cocked her head at a saucy angle. "I think I know something else that could help us both relax."

Shit.

"I, uh—" Nick began, choosing his words carefully so as not to hurt her feelings. "I think you're amazing, Tammy, I really do—"

An uproarious cackle cut him off mid-sentence. "Oh, honey," she finally gasped out. "Lord, no. You're cute and all but *totally* not my type."

Nick's cheeks burned with embarrassment. "But you said—"

"I was tryin' to get you to sing 'Hotel California' with me," she said, lightly slapping his forearm. "Not go to bed with me."

He blinked at her, feeling like the world's largest ass. "I'm sorry. I shouldn't have assumed—"

"Don't you apologize," she reassured him. "I'm an equal-opportunity flirt, and it gives people the wrong impression. And anyway, you're so obviously hung up on Lark that you might as well be wearing a neon sign."

"I'm not sure what you mean," he said, already feeling heat rising from his collar.

"I *mean* that if they could bottle the sexual tension between the two of y'all, Virginia could significantly reduce its dependence on fossil fuels." Tammy parked a hand on her hip. "You plannin' on doing anything about it?"

Nick looked at her, assessing her motives. A relatively new

transplant to Spring Valley, he doubted Tammy would feed the town's gossip mill. But knowing how eagerly news of Lark had made the rounds, he wasn't about to take the risk.

"Probably not," he said. "Seeing as I'll be headed back to Manhattan even earlier than I thought."

Tammy stepped out of the way as a pair of men young enough to be her sons gave her a thorough once-over before entering the bar. She made a disgusted noise and rolled her eyes.

"Bet that gets old," Nick said, hoping to smoothly change the subject.

"Boy, does it." She sighed. "I tell ya, I sure am glad Lark didn't come tonight."

"Why's that?" Nick asked.

"Me, I have no problem handling men like that. I just crush their lil egos, and they follow their peckers to greener pastures. But *Lark*. She'd probably be all polite when they tried to hit on her. Let them buy her drink, most likely. Wouldn't want to be a bitch or anything." Folding her arms across her breasts, Tammy turned to face him. "I always try to look out for girls like that when I can. Run the bastards off." She gave him a pointed look, and Nick realized he hadn't changed the subject at all.

"I understand," Nick said.

"Good." Tammy's pretty face slid into its natural sunny smile. "See you inside, sugar."

Nick allowed her thirty seconds' head start. Pushing through the door back into the bar, he braced himself against the crush of noise, heat and people.

Just not the only person he'd wanted to see.

After his encounter with Lark on the bus earlier that afternoon, he'd been counting down the minutes until they could be alone. Right up until Marshall had stolen one hundred thirty-seven of them. Nick bit back the tide of bitterness that threatened to dump him straight back into his foul mood.

It was no use.

After the bombshell Marshall had dropped that afternoon, there was no bringing this day around. One of their top five venture-capital picks wanted to meet to discuss a partnership. But Nick would have to be back in Manhattan in ten days.

Either you're all the way in or you're out, bro, Marshall's voice repeated inside Nick's head.

When he'd left Manhattan, it had been with the assurance that he'd have a few months to cool his head. Think things through. Now he had ten days to decide whether he wanted to dissolve his and Marshall's partnership. Whether he was really prepared to walk away on the cusp of finally getting the funding they'd been chasing together for so long.

The timing seemed more than a little suspicious.

Every time the memory returned, he felt sick.

"You look like you need a beer, Nicky." Mike materialized at his elbow and grabbed the scruff of his neck with thick fingers.

"Actually, I need sleep. I'm going to head back to the hotel. You think you can make sure the ladies get back okay?"

"Ha!" His mother scoffed. "And how do you know we won't have to make sure they get back okay? Have you ever thought of that?"

"Damn straight," Tammy agreed. They high-fived each other and managed to mostly make palm to palm contact.

"Point is, we'll all get back okay." Linda met his eyes and flicked a glance at her drink, and he understood that what looked to be a gin and tonic was likely a soda water with lime.

He sent her a grateful smile.

"Ten a.m. in the lobby?" he asked, as much to remind them that they had a moderately early day tomorrow as to confirm plans.

"Yeah, yeah. Go to bed you, old fuddy-duddy," his mother said.

As much as Nick was tempted to point out that her use of the word *fuddy-duddy* was, in fact, a fuddy-duddy-qualifying event, his exhaustion won out. The cab ride back to the hotel was blessedly short. Nick let himself into his uncomfortably luxurious room and took a long, hot shower.

Just picture all your troubles melting off your shoulders and swirling down the drain, Nicky.

He felt mild surprise that his father's voice could find him here, even in this hotel room his father wouldn't have set foot in with a bayonet at his back.

The old man had known Nick was embarrassed of his parents. Embarrassed of their accents. Embarrassed of the civically responsible jobs that left them perpetually short of cash. Embarrassed that they couldn't even afford to hang on to the land that had been his father's whole plan for retirement. Not that he'd ended up needing one. He'd known that Nick was embarrassed of them, and he'd resented him for it.

So why, after all this damn time, was Nick hearing a dead man whisper encouragements and advice instead of criticism?

Delusion? Wishful thinking?

When his skin had pruned, Nick cut the water and toweled off, swathing his hips with a towel before walking to stand before the floor to ceiling windows. The moon was full over the Chesapeake Bay, smearing the inky-black canvas with silver, the city lights reflected in it like constellations of twinkling stars.

Nick found himself wishing Lark were here to look at this

composition with him. To describe it to him in the ways only she saw.

He made a circuit of the room, turning off the dozen lamps before plugging his phone in and setting an alarm for the following morning. Peeling back the sheets, he dropped the towel and slid beneath, sinking into oblivion the second his head hit the pillow.

His dreams were strange and surreal. Full of stressful thoughts and odd sounds. Claustrophobic spaces. Jaundiced lights. Off-key singing.

Knocking.

Nick sat bolt upright, the last threads of his unsettling dreams clinging to him as he felt around for his glasses. Not on the nightstand. Had he fallen asleep with them on? His search of the sheets and pillows proved fruitless. Meanwhile, the rapping continued.

"Just a minute," he called in a sleep-thickened voice.

Pushing himself out of bed, Nick found his discarded towel and wrapped it around his hips before proceeding with one arm outstretched to avoid obstacles. He let fly a florid string of curses when he caught his toe on the luggage rack and abandoned his plans of pulling on a pair of shorts. Fuck finding clothes. Anyone who pounded on a door like this at…whatever time it was deserved exactly what they got.

He quickly snapped open the deadbolt and opened the door a crack, squinting at the bright light in the hallway. Even without his glasses, he recognized the shape of her face. The pattern of light and shadow that formed her face, hair and body.

"Lark?" he said, rubbing his eyes.

"I—I'm sorry to wake you up. I shouldn't have come."

"It's okay." Nick opened the door wider and stepped aside, gesturing for her to come in.

She stared at him as if she had suddenly forgotten why she was here. Which was when he remembered he was wearing only a towel.

"Please," he invited, finding his jeans slung over the back of the desk chair. "Have a seat. I'm just going to—" He pointed toward the restroom and lifted the jeans aloft.

"Sure," she said.

Nick emerged a couple minutes later to find her sitting on the edge of the bed, holding out his glasses. She'd turned on several lamps, bathing the room in a rosy glow.

"Thanks," he said. Slipping them onto his face, Nick was finally able to see her clearly.

And then instantly wished that weren't the case. Her eyes and the tip of her nose were red and puffy. Her cheeks pale and drawn.

"I'm sorry to bust in on you so late," she said. "Or so early, I guess."

Nick took a seat on the chair opposite her. "It's all right," he said. "What's up?"

Lark exhaled and hugged her knees to her chest. In her oversized Dartmouth hoodie and sleep shorts, she almost looked like she wasn't wearing bottoms at all.

"I just wanted to apologize."

"Apologize?" Nick furrowed his brow. "For what?"

"For the way I spoke to you when you called," Lark said, her voice barely above a whisper.

Nick swallowed hard, the memory of their phone interaction flooding his mind. He'd been perplexed by her coolness. Confused as to the sudden shift in her mood. But now, seeing her in person again, he was annoyed to note that it didn't matter.

"It was no big deal," he said, trying to sound nonchalant. "Don't worry about it."

Lark nodded, but she stared at her hands. She was picking her cuticles again. Something he hadn't seen her do since that first night in class.

Nick rose from the couch and sat next to her on the bed. "What is it *really*?"

"Nothing," she repeated.

Nick shook his head, unconvinced. "No wonder you never broke any rules in high school."

She dragged her gaze up to meet his. "What do you mean?"

"You never would have gotten away with anything," he said. "You really are a terrible liar."

"That's part of the problem," she said, hugging her knees tighter.

Nick blinked at her. "I'm afraid I'm not following."

"My whole life I've done exactly what everyone told me to do," she said, toying with the pull string on her hood. "My parents. My teachers. Pretty much any authority figure, really. I've followed all the rules, I've never stepped out of line. And now, with you, it's like I'm this whole other person that I have no idea how to be."

Nick was silent. He'd only ever wanted to help her. The idea that he might have been the cause of some deep inner conflict made him feel like someone was cinching a metal band around his chest.

"Never in a million years would I want you to do one single thing that you don't want to."

"That's the thing," she said, her eyes wide. "I *do* want to. I just don't know how. I don't know how to be like Tammy or Linda. I don't know how not to care what people think of me." She shook her head, the tears that had been gathering in her eyes spilling down her cheekbones. "I hate knowing that my parents are mad at me for coming on this trip. I hate knowing that my father thinks I'm ruining my life. I hate that I used to be able to make myself turn in assignments early and take more classes than anyone else and get the highest scores on every test, and now I can't even make myself fold and put away my laundry half of the time. I… I just feel so lost." The raw vulnerability in her voice threatened to tear Nick's heart in two. "I feel like I'm ruining everything, and I don't know how to stop."

Lark lifted her streaming eyes to him, full of pleading for an answer that he felt ill-equipped to give.

Nick scooted back on the bed, turning his hips so they were face-to-face. "The day my father died, we got into a huge fight before I left for school."

Lark's eyes widened, her mouth tugging downward at the corners.

"We had agreed I would stay in Spring Valley and get my first two years done at the community college, where I'd get free tuition because my mom was part of the staff," he explained. "I didn't tell them I had applied to NYU. I honestly didn't even think I'd get accepted with my track record."

"But you did?" she asked.

"I did," he said. "And the second I got my acceptance letter, I knew I wanted to go. But I knew there was no way my parents could afford it."

Lark nodded.

"So I called the financial aid department at NYU. They talked me through the process of applying for grants and student loans, and I came up with this whole plan. I even made a PowerPoint presentation." He chuckled, remembering how diligently he'd assembled every slide. "Such a goddamn nerd."

She gave him an encouraging half smile.

"The night before the response deadline, I sat my parents down and gave them my spiel. The cost analysis. The contribution I would need from them to make it work. My dad sat through the whole thing and didn't say a word. When I was finished, he told me he thought I was going to tell them that I'd gotten a girl pregnant."

Taking a deep breath, Nick allowed himself to sink back into that version of himself. To let the feelings come.

"I was so angry," Nick continued, his face growing hot at the memory. "I had put in all this work to convince him that going to NYU was a good idea, and it didn't make any difference. I remember thinking about how unfair it was and feeling so frustrated that even though I had done everything right, I still couldn't make him see.

"My father said that if I wanted to mortgage my future earnings, that was my business, but he had no intention of paying for what I could get for free."

He was there now, at the part that always scalded him to remember.

"I told him that maybe if my parents had been capable of anything other than a mediocre suburban existence, I wouldn't need to get it for free."

Even now, Nick felt shame and regret pool in his gut.

He'd been hurt. Angry. An immature, hormone-addled teenager with warring drives and not enough sense. It was exactly the kind of comment that tens of thousands of other mouthy little shits had spat at their parents in tens of thousands of arguments. The kind of comment parents would give their kids shit for once they'd grown into adults.

But because of what happened next, Nick and his father would never have that chance.

"He took me to school on the way to the station. The whole way there, I hashed it over and over in my head. Saying even more clever and hurtful things." Nick shook his head. "I was so involved in my vengeful inner monologue I didn't see the car coming."

Nick remembered the sickening crunch of metal that followed, his bike flying off the roof rack as the car rolled. The wet, coppery taste of blood in his mouth, and the bright white pain that radiated through every inch of his body as the ground and sky switched places several times.

"Right before the impact, my dad yanked the steering wheel to spin the car so it would impact on his side instead of mine. The car rolled and landed upside down," Nick said. "We were both still conscious at first."

As soon as he said the words, he was back there, in that place.

Suspended upside down in the car, breathing felt like an effort. His neck had been wedged between the headrest and window, and his legs had hung limply from the seat belt that had held him in place. Nick's gaze had shifted to his father, who'd hung beside him. They had looked at each other in this vastly altered context, and the combination of fear and sadness on his father's lacerated face had been so intense it made Nick's heart ache.

"I told the grief counselor about it afterward, and she said something that's always stuck with me. What I saw on my father's face in that moment was love. He loved me so much." His throat contracted on the last words. "But the only vocabulary he had to tell me was yanking a fucking steering wheel."

Lark scooted into him, buttressing his body with hers.

"I don't pretend to have all the answers, but I do know that until you understand how to be this person, you're not going to know what she needs. And if you don't know what she needs, your parents are going to keep trying to give her what *they* think she needs. They're going to keep loving you with steering wheels."

When she spoke, it was with a confidence that surprised him. "I need *you*, Nick."

Nick pulled away, thunderstruck by this revelation. Given a thousand years, he never would have guessed these to be her next words.

Lark nodded, her eyes never leaving his face. "I need you," she repeated plainly. "I need to feel the way I only feel when I'm with you."

Their gazes lingered, and they closed the distance between them.

Her lips were soft and warm against his but tentative as they sat cross-legged opposite each other. Nick waited her out, matching only as much heat as she supplied. Letting her set the pace.

Holding his body still proved a considerable effort while feeling her satiny mouth move over his, the tip of her tongue teasing the seam of his lips. Lark's hands moved to his knees as she leaned further into him. Gently sucking his lower lip. Grazing his chin, planting kisses on his cheek bone and jaw before hovering over his ear.

"Why won't you touch me?"

Her warm breath caused an involuntary shiver to work through him. "Because you haven't asked yet."

He felt her smile against his cheek. "Will you touch me, Nick?" Her fingers twined into his hair, grabbing handfuls that caused chills to rise on his scalp and spill down his arms.

"Gladly." Leaning forward, he anchored his hands on her

hips and pulled her into his lap so she straddled him face-to-face.

Lark moaned softly against his neck as she opened her mouth to nip and suck his sensitive flesh. Her palms slid over his shoulders, his naked chest, pausing when she'd reached a small, white scar. Their eyes met as she traced it with the tip of her finger. Though he knew it was impossible, Nick would have sworn he could feel her touch straight through to his back.

More than once in his life, death had hovered in the wings, waiting to steal the daylight. In that moment, Nick felt glad it had failed. Glad that however long or short his life turned out to be, he'd been gifted this minute and the next, with Lark in his arms.

Pulling back, Lark stripped off her hoodie, taking her sleep shirt with it.

Breasts bared to him, Nick filled his hands and took one nipple into his mouth, swirling his tongue around the hardened peak. Lark moaned, her body rocking against his erection, dragging a low rumble from his throat. His palms moved over her body in a gentle exploration, tracing her curves and hollows as he kissed and nipped at her jaw, her neck and collarbone.

His fingers found the downy small of her back, sliding around the front to cup her sex through her sleep shorts. Feeling her dampness through the fabric sparked an urgency that made him suddenly ravenous. He wanted to be closer to her, skin to skin, heat to heat, heart to heart.

Gripping Lark's hips tight enough to feel the bones beneath his palms, Nick rolled them both onto their sides while never breaking the kiss. His knee slid between hers as he reached down to tug off her sleep shorts and his jeans before coming back up for air.

He trailed kisses over each breast before moving to the valley between them, down her belly to the emerald-green panties that had driven him half feral on the bus earlier. He pushed against the lace with the flat of his tongue, the earthy scent of her making him dizzy with want.

"Not so fast," she said, wriggling away to scoot down his body.

Nick felt a clench of desire low in his belly when he realized what her intentions were.

She kept her gaze on his as she traced the ledge of his hipbone with the tip of her tongue. Her beautiful hands followed her mouth, and Nick sucked in a breath when her fingers wrapped around his cock. Slowly, she stroked up and down before brushing her lips across his swollen, sensitive head.

Once.

Twice.

She teased him. Tortured him. Parting her lips to trace the rim with her tongue before flicking featherlight strokes along the underside.

"*Fuck*," he swore as she drew him into the wet heat of her mouth and began to move.

Nick's fingers tangled in her hair, his breath coming in broken gasps. His eyes fell closed, and he gave himself over to sensation. The smooth slide of her silky tongue and the hot velvet of her lips, the gentle fire in her hands. Tension coiled deep around the base of his spine, and he sat up before he lost himself entirely. Quickly molding his hand around hers at his base, he gripped hard.

"Wait, wait, wait, baby."

When he again had control of himself, he lay back on the pillow.

"Come here," he said quietly. Guiding her to straddle his torso, he slid her panties to the side and explored her every ridge and crease. He heard Lark's breathing quicken as he pressed his tongue against her swollen clit, circling and flicking until she bit her lower lip. Her fingers sank into his hair to hold him steady as she undulated against him.

Nick felt a surge of satisfaction to see her take control this way. To take from him what she wanted. One hand planted against the dip of her lower back, Nick slid the other up her taut inner thigh to her heated flesh.

Fuck. She was drenched.

A moan escaped her as he slipped first one, then two fingers inside. Curling his fingertips forward, he found the raised ridge along her inner wall and lightly pressed. Her nails dug into his scalp as she rocked faster against his mouth. She let out a ragged cry as she contracted around his fingers, her whole body quaking. Nick held her there while he drank in every last spasm.

At last, he let her sink until she was sitting on his thighs, his face nearly level with hers. A sheen of sweat kissed her forehead and flushed cheeks. Her eyes were glazed and as sultry as a summer's day. Her pleasure-slack limbs bent at unselfconscious angles. Nick wanted to draw her like this. Paint her. Sculpt her. To immortalize the vision before him so he would always remember the summer he'd helped bring Lark Hockney back to life.

"I want you, Nick," she whispered, her breath hot against his face.

Nick shaped his hand to her jaw, his thumb running over her lower lip. "I want you too."

He reached into the nightstand and extracted the strip of condoms he'd stashed there earlier.

Lark tore off one of the foil packets and opened it with her teeth, a smile playing about her lips and eyebrow arched at him in silent question.

"Did you plan this?"

"Of course I did," he managed to croak out as she sheathed him. "I've wanted you like this since you told me to fuck off, then ruined my gym towel."

"I didn't tell you to fuck off." Lark rested her forearms on his shoulders, tracing the cartilage of his ear with a fingertip. "And I didn't ruin it. I returned it in much better condition than I found it."

"Yes, you did." Nick's hands slipped beneath her thighs to position her above him. "I'll never be able to look at it without thinking of you."

He met her eyes, their features so close that he felt the warmth of her breath against his lips. Their mouths melded in pure hunger.

Lark's hips rolled forward, guiding him inside her. Sinking that aching, urgent part of him into her velvet heat straight to the hilt. She paused at the bottom of her descent, both of them adjusting as she contracted around him.

"*God damn*," Nick gasped, combing back her hair with his fingers.

With her hands planted behind her on his thighs, Lark began to move.

Slowly at first, letting him feel every inch, then gradually picking up speed.

And urgency.

Though it required every remaining ounce of restraint, Nick let her guide the pace. Quietly thrilling when the force of her downward strokes pushed him so deep he wanted to thrust up in response.

"Don't stop," he moaned as he blazed a hot, wet trail across her collarbone. "Please don't stop."

They moved in rhythm, each stroke and retreat accompanied by primal grunts of pleasure. Nick pressed the heel of his palm just above the hard mound of her pubic bone, feeling himself moving inside her through the muscle and flesh that sheathed him.

"*Fuck*," she sobbed.

It wasn't the first time Nick had heard her say the word, but hearing her say it in this context mad something within him snap loose and run free. He found her clit with his thumb and rolled it as he drove up into her, filling her with reckless abandon. He felt her body begin to quake, heard her cry out as she trembled in his arms.

"You're gonna make me come," he growled.

"Do it." Lark pressed her forehead to his, and her raspy, ragged words proved his undoing. "Give me everything."

And then Nick was gone.

Moaning and begging in a language that barely sounded human. Plunging into her, his body tensing, surrendering. A stark roar ripped from him as he spilled into her in hot waves, wringing him inside out. The air between them was heavy with their combined scents and the sweat that coated them from head to toe. His heart beat wildly against the wall of his chest.

Nick massaged her back, her neck and shoulders as his arousal began to wane, still buried inside of her. He wanted to stay like this forever, two parts of the same whole with no beginning and no end.

Lark's lips curved into a mischievous smile. "We should do that again."

"Yes," Nick said, rolling them onto their sides on the disheveled mattress. "We definitely should."

How many times?

Nick batted away the unwelcome thought only to have it return, dragging even more questions in its wake.

How many times before the summer was over? How many times before he returned to Manhattan?

Because whatever he decided to do with regard to Marshall and Moonshot, Nick *would* be returning to Manhattan. To his apartment. His work. To the life he'd built for himself there.

And what then?

I need you, Nick.

I need to feel the way I only feel when I'm with you.

He'd fostered that need. Had nurtured it despite knowing his time in Spring Valley was limited. The very thing he'd promised himself he wouldn't do. Not to soothe his ego or as a distraction, but because he couldn't *not*. He couldn't *not* stop when he'd seen Lark sitting atop the brick wall outside the community college. He couldn't not talk to her. Message her. Call her.

Kiss her.

He hadn't even been able to stop himself from telling her the story he'd only ever told one other living soul. What had happened the day his father had died.

Lark pushed against him, her body seeking his heat. When the palm of her foot pressed itself to the top of his, realization slammed into him with perfect clarity. Nick wasn't falling for her. He'd already fallen.

And for him, there was no going back.

Eleven

Lark woke to the sound of Nick's steady breathing and the faint light of morning. For a moment, she lay still, savoring the warmth of his body, taking in the evidence that last night hadn't been a dream.

The bed sheets tangled around their legs. Foil packets and empty water bottles littered the nightstand. Discarded clothing covered the floor. Delicious aches made a map of her body.

Carefully rolling onto her side, she blinked bleary eyes to look at Nick. Still fast asleep, his arms beckoned her to stay.

As if she hadn't stayed too long already.

Fumbling on the nightstand, she located her phone and swiped the screen. Nearly dead, it sported an accusatory stack of missed calls. All from her mother. Once last night at 11:43 p.m. Twice this morning at 6:30 a.m. and 7:15 a.m. No texts.

Lark's heart skipped a beat.

Something was wrong.

Setting her phone back down without even listening to the voicemails, Lark slipped out of bed and got dressed. She needed to call her mother back but couldn't do it from Nick's room.

"Hey." Hearing Nick's sexy, sleepy voice, her heart sank. "Where you going? Room service will be here any minute."

"I need to get back to my room," she said, voice trembling in spite of the effort to stay calm.

Nick sat up, his sleep-creased features bearing a mix of concern and surprise.

"What's wrong?" he asked.

"I need to call my mother."

Nick's mouth quirked in a grin. "I hear they have cell reception in all the rooms now."

"She called me after eleven last night and twice this morning," Lark explained, shrugging into her hoodie. "She wouldn't do that unless something was wrong."

The levity disappeared from his expression. "All the more reason why you should call from here, then."

He had a point.

"All right," she said, avoiding his gaze. "But I get self-conscious when people listen."

Understanding this was an invitation to busy himself elsewhere, Nick peeled back the covers and shuffled off to the bathroom.

Lark's hands began to sweat as she pulled up her mother's last missed call and dialed her back. It was answered on the second ring.

"Thank goodness," her mother said, her voice saturated with relief.

"Is everything okay?" Lark asked.

"Well, I wasn't sure. When you didn't answer my goodnight text, I thought—"

"You called me three times because I didn't answer a goodnight text?" Lark repeated.

"Well, I hadn't heard from you all day." Her mother's voice was edged with gentle censure. "After the way you left yesterday morning—"

"The way I left yesterday morning was with you and dad guilt-tripping me about a field trip for the class *you* signed me up for," Lark pointed out. That her reasons for going had more to do with the class's instructor than any desire to broaden her artistic horizons didn't feel important to mention.

"I was just concerned, sweetie. This is the first time you've been away from home overnight since you came back, and even though you've been venturing out more lately, I'm sure it's still difficult for you to be around so many people."

Only it hadn't been.

Remembering the hours she'd spent boxed in a small space with a group whose personalities were big enough to fill a lecture hall, Lark had been fine. Entertained, even. Right up until Julia's comment about Nick's past relationships had poked a particularly sensitive bruise.

The people it had been the hardest for her to be around lately were her parents.

When she'd been avoiding pretty much everyone, that truth had been easier to hide. But now that at least part of her seemed capable of tolerating social interaction, her mother was beginning to notice.

And bring it up in her own passively indirect way.

"I appreciate your concern, Mom, but I'm fine," Lark said, pinching the bridge of her nose and releasing a long breath.

"Are you sure, sweetheart?"

"Yes," Lark replied, glancing up as Nick poked his head out of the bathroom. She gave him the all clear, smirking as she noted the terry cloth bathrobe wrapped around his lean frame. The mattress dipped as he seated himself behind her.

Strange, how comforting it was to have him near.

"I'm sure."

The tension between them seemed to thaw. "Well, what do you have planned today?" her mother asked. In the background, Lark heard the familiar sound of the coffee carafe sliding onto the warming plate.

"We're headed to the Baltimore Museum of Art first," Lark said.

Nick's hand slipped beneath her hoodie, warm on the small of her back.

"Then we're having lunch at an Edgar Allan Poe–themed café."

The hand slid around to her rib cage.

"Well, that sounds nice." A spoon clicking against a coffee mug. "And this afternoon?"

Nick nuzzled the sensitive skin just below her ear, the stubble on his jaw making her squirm as his lips grazed her ticklish lobe. "Umm, we might go to the Walters Museum. Or—*unh*—" she said as Nick's thumb brushed her nipple. "The American Visionary."

"That sounds like a very full day." The delicate sound of her mother sipping.

Anchoring a hand in the hair at her nape, Nick turned her face toward the mirror at the end of the bed. Kneeling behind her, he pulled up the hem of her hoodie until she could see her own bare breasts in its reflection, could see his fingertips stroking lazy circles over the already stiffened peaks.

"Oh, it is," Lark sighed, beginning to lose her words and her breath. "It really is."

"Are you *sure* you're okay?" her mother asked. "You sound a little...off."

"Sorry." Biting down on her lower lip, she watched Nick's hand snake down her belly and into her shorts. "I'm just a little...tired." Her head fell back against Nick's shoulder as he began to toy with her.

"Maybe you can grab a nap after lunch," her mother suggested.

"Good idea," Lark agreed. "Hey, Mom, I'd better let you go. I'm supposed to meet my group downstairs soon," she said.

"Okay, honey. You have fun today. And just take it slow, okay? If you get overwhelmed, it's okay to step away and take a breather."

"I will," Lark agreed a little too quickly.

Her mother's pause seemed to last for an eternity. "I love you, Lark."

"Love you too."

Lark ended the call and dropped the phone onto the bed.

"Everything all right?" Nick's casual question had the same strangely erotic effect as carrying on a conversation while he touched her.

She nodded. "Just your basic overprotective-mother stuff. This is my first overnight outing since *the incident*."

"Except for my house," Nick pointed out, guiding her to her knees on the bed. He lifted the hoodie over her head and tossed it aside.

"That's right," she said. Reaching behind her, Lark slipped a hand inside the bathrobe and found Nick already hard. "But I'm sure that room has seen plenty of action."

Nick's chuckle vibrated through her back. "You're the first."

She glanced over her shoulder at him, not content to meet his gaze in the mirror.

"I didn't lose my virginity until college," he reported.

"Who was your first?" Lark didn't even know why she asked the question. Only that it seemed important.

"A teaching assistant for one of my freshman seminars," Nick reported. "How about you?"

"Reese was my first." The name fell easily off her lips, though it seemed like it had been years since she'd thought of him. "Junior year. We'd been dating since we were sophomores. My parents trusted him so much they let him stay at the house when they left for an OB-GYN conference."

"Huh," Nick said.

"He had planned the whole thing. Rose petals, candles, soft music playing from his iPad so his phone would be free in case anyone called. He even ran me a bath beforehand."

She could still remember the steam rising from the water of the garden tub. The pink rose petals scattered around its border. The scent of lavender from the bath salts to help her relax. Because she had *needed* relaxing. In the days leading up to a date they both had marked in their iPhone calendars, he'd been extra patient with her. Extra affectionate. Reassuring her that everything would be okay. Because she had *needed* reassuring.

"That almost sounds too perfect."

Lark froze.

Too perfect.

Too. Perfect.

The words suddenly unleashed a barrage of memories.

Reese's proposal.

Lark in a dress that had perfectly matched Reese's suit. The perfect weather, warm and sunny with a gentle breeze. The perfect table at the country club restaurant. His perfectly curated list of surprise guests, including all their closest family and friends, whom he had invited without her knowledge so they could share in this perfect moment. Their phones all aimed at her as he'd made his perfect toast to her perfect parents, thanking them for raising such an amazing daughter.

I could search the entire world over and never find someone so per-fect for me.

Perfect for *me*.

The perfect engagement ring slipped onto her finger be-fore she'd even given her answer. And, of course, it had fit her perfectly, despite their not having shopped for it together. The triumphant look on Reese's handsome face when every-one had begun to applaud. His mistaking her speechlessness for awe as she'd stared at the gigantic diamond.

It's flawless, he'd whispered to her. *Just like you.*

Lark felt her throat constrict just as it had then. Her heart hurling itself against her ribs. A raw, dry sound escaped her throat. Lark didn't recognize it as a sob until the tears came.

A deluge. A torrent. As if every single feeling depression had held at bay for the last several months arrived all at once, pouring out of her eyes in a hot, salty stream. Tears of frus-tration. Tears of humiliation. Of shame. Of rage. Of pain. Of fear. Tears that had nothing to do with Reese at all. Small hurts. Deep wells of sadness, loneliness she'd filled with re-lentless achievement. Capped over with accolades and hon-ors. Because if she'd ever let anyone close enough to *see* her, they would have known the truth.

That she wasn't perfect at all.

"Hey." Nick's hands were on her shoulders now and re-mained there as she curled over her own knees, burying her face in her hands. A ball of grief. She felt the bed move be-neath her as he shifted positions, his hand landing between her shoulder blades, the mattress shaking both of them with her silent, wracking sobs.

He said nothing. When her gale of grief had quieted down to a minor squall, he lay down on his side next to her. "Come here," he said quietly.

And she did.

At first, she could only roll onto her side with her back against his chest, the circle of his strong arms banded around her with her knees still tucked against her heart. But slowly, as the heat from his body seeped into her bones, she began to unfold. Muscles loosened in her neck, back and shoulders until she melted against him. He held her there, one arm beneath her head as a pillow. His breath a steady rhythm of reassurance against her hair.

They must have drifted off because when Lark next opened her eyes, the sunlight had crawled even farther across the floor. The Chesapeake Bay was a deep sapphire blue beyond the windows, the sky dotted with clouds.

Nick stirred behind her. "Shit. What time is it?"

Lark glanced at the bedside clock. "Almost 8:30 a.m.," she said, extending her legs in a full-body stretch.

As she did, she felt a familiar hardness pressed against the small of her back. Her body's response was automatic. A warm flush crept up her neck and spread through her chest. Her breath deepened, and her hips curved backward to press against him.

His sleep-deepened rumble woke gooseflesh that tightened her nipples against his forearm. "We only have an hour," he whispered, tracing the waistband of her shorts.

In her life BC—Before Crash—Lark's getting-ready process would have begun no later than 7:00 a.m. But whatever she'd purged earlier had cleared space for a desire deeper and more ravenous than she'd ever known.

It was going to cost her.

She might have to skip entire steps of her process. Show up unfinished by her previous standards. Lark knew all of this.

She wanted Nick more.

Lark covered the hand resting on her hip and moved it between her thighs, where she could already feel moisture gathering in anticipation.

"Shit." His voice was husky with desire and sleep, the words brushing over her ear. "God, baby. You're so wet already."

She moaned as he parted her with his fingers, finding the sensitive nub that made her hips buck and her insides flood with heat.

"You *make* me wet."

Never in all her years with Reese had words of this kind ever entered her head, much less exited her lips.

Nick's fingertips dimpled her hip. "Let me get something."

Lark grabbed his wrist. As much as she craved the feeling of him inside her, she couldn't bear the thought of losing the feeling of his body against hers.

"I have an idea," she said. Reaching behind her, she found his thick length and angled him between her thighs—against but not inside her. "I want you to…" She hesitated, unable to make herself say the words she was thinking. "Finish on me."

Judging by the sound Nick made, even the less graphic version was incentive enough.

He began to move.

Lark's pulse raced as he slid against her, teasing her entrance and then drawing back, deeper now, nudging her clit.

She couldn't think straight, couldn't do anything but arch into his touch and let herself fly. Her arms lifted over her head, her hands buried into his hair as he drove against her with long, slow strokes. She was so close, her core already clenching in fluttering ripples when he withdrew.

"Please let me get something, baby," he mumbled against her ear as he trailed fingers across her middle. "I need to be inside you."

At that moment, he could have asked her to swim home and she would have agreed.

"Get it."

Nick sprang from the bed, grabbed a foil packet and tore it with his teeth. She watched as he rolled it on. Lark's gaze traveled over his broad shoulders, down the length of his pale, freckled chest, the angular pectoral muscles, down his abs to where his erection jutted out from his body. She wanted to touch it, wanted to taste him, but all she could do was lie there and stare.

He flipped her face down on the mattress, aligning her with the mirror at the end of the bed before pulling her shorts and panties down to the backs of her knees.

"Like this," he said, pushing her thighs together and lifting her hips upward.

Nick straddled her from behind, one foot on the floor beside the bed, the opposite knee planted beside her hip. Lifting her wrist, he tugged off the elastic hair tie and gathered her hair into a high ponytail, securing it with surprising dexterity. His fingers ran down its length before he wrapped it twice around his fist and angled her face so she was watching them in the mirror.

Lark had just gotten her bearings when the blunt head of his erection slipped inside her. He stilled there before pulling out completely just to do it again.

In the mirror, she watched his bottom lip disappear between his teeth. A crease of concentration appeared between his dark brows. The hectic flush returned to his cheeks as his abdominal muscles tensed with the effort of his slow, teasing strokes.

Lark wriggled impatiently. Wanting, *needing* to feel him as deep as he could go.

"Please," she begged.

"Please *what?*" Feral, primal energy seemed to flood his features as he met her eyes in the mirror, and yet she felt completely safe in its thrall.

"Please." She swallowed. "Please fuck me, Nick."

His fingers gently gripped her throat as his spine curled and he filled her completely with a powerful thrust.

Something between a sob and a scream escaped her.

"I want to hear you make that sound forever."

He shifted his weight forward, and the thrusts came faster, deeper, and she thought for sure that her body would break apart with the intensity of the pleasure.

Nick released her neck and scooted them further onto the mattress. His fingers threaded through hers, his palms pressed to her knuckles as he moved inside her with a desperate, driving need. His mouth was hot and wet between her shoulder blades, his rough stubble scraping the back of her neck before he followed it with his tongue and gentle nips with his teeth.

Lark could feel her release building, coiling. Driving her face into the covers, she arched her lower back to take him deeper still. To seat him against the place he'd lit up like a Christmas tree the night before.

"Oh, shit," he ground out on a ragged breath. "You feel so. Damn. Good."

He paired each word with a thrust that drove her further and further toward the cliff.

Nick galloped right alongside her, his words melting into urgent, unfiltered, unbridled whimpers as his grip on her hands tightened.

Her entire body was ablaze with a powerful sense of feminine pride upon hearing the sounds of his pleasure. She'd never before known hearing a man reduced to this state could be so erotic. The waves of rapture built, tying her in knots until finally cresting in an orgasm so intense she swore time stopped. Her body convulsed beneath his weight as she rode the waves. His thrusts grew erratic, punctuated by a deep groan that vibrated through her body as he pulled out, stripped off the condom and lost himself in warm pulses on her back.

He collapsed on top of her, panting like a man who'd just run a marathon.

They lay there together, their bodies still joined, chests heaving and skin slick with sweat.

Nick lifted himself off her, flopping onto his back as his breathing slowed. Lark opened her eyes to find him gazing down at her with pure adoration in his eyes.

There were no words.

Limp and boneless, Lark rolled onto her side. The clock's glowing numbers reported a completely impossible 8:43 a.m.

"Shit," she said, launching herself from the bed and hurriedly pulling on her discarded clothes. "We're supposed to be in the lobby in half an hour." At this rate, she'd be lucky to squeeze in a shower, much less apply makeup or deal with sex hair.

"See you soon." Nick pulled her into a kiss before slapping her ass as she rushed out the door.

Lark flew through her morning routine, zipping from the shower to the mirror and back again in record time. Noticing the patchwork of red on her chest and neck, she was glad she'd brought a light, sleeveless dress with a high-necked lace collar and tea-length skirt. Winding her hair into a sleek chignon, she had enough time to swipe on mascara and lip gloss.

Blush, she might never need again.

With a few last-minute adjustments, she slipped into her

sandals, grabbed her purse and was out the door and on the elevator in no time flat.

It could have been the power of suggestion, but when she stepped into the lobby, it seemed as though a blinking *I Just Got My Back Blown Out* signed followed her. With great effort, she managed to mostly walk like a normal human despite the ache laddering up her thighs.

She was the last to arrive and couldn't look Nick in the eye when she saw he was seated on a lobby bench between Tammy and his mother. Both clad in splashy blouses and capris, they looked like they had coordinated outfits. Linda sat on the bench opposite, bent in deep conversation with David, whose ears were redder than Lark had ever remembered seeing them.

Interesting.

Tammy spotted Lark first, her lips stretching in a smile. "Don't you look pretty," she called. A filament of alarm rose within Lark as Tammy's blue eyes narrowed. "Something looks different."

Heat bloomed in Lark's cheeks, deepening her flush. "I, uh, slept in this morning. Didn't have much time for makeup."

"No," Tammy said, tapping her chin. "That isn't it." After leaning to one side, then the other to scrutinize Lark's face, Tammy's eyebrows lifted as she wagged a manicured finger at Lark. "Shame on you, trying to hold out on us. I know exactly what's different."

Don't look at Nick.

Do NOT look at Nick.

She looked at Nick.

"While the rest of us were out on the town singing karaoke, *you* were getting a facial."

Nick aspirated a sip of the iced coffee he'd been nursing, his mother clapping him on the back.

"Guilty," Lark said, feeling the word branded on her soul.

Tammy looped an arm through hers and steered her toward the lobby doors that two valet attendants leapt to open for them. "Tell me everything. Who was your aesthetician? What service did you book? Is there a friends-and-family discount? Because whatever it was that made you that glowy, I need five of them."

Under the pretense of turning her shoulders so they'd both fit through the door, she glanced over to find Nick's mouth slanted in a wicked grin that did nothing to help her furious blush.

The party bus waited in the valet lane, and everyone piled in. The drive to the Baltimore Museum of Art was short—and punctuated by Tammy's stream-of-consciousness chatter. They piled out onto the marble steps leading up to the classical Greek structure of tall, fluted columns and archways. Their voices echoed in the soaring entryway, the skylights streaming down pale, milky light.

Julia paid for their tickets, proudly plopping down a college-issue credit card. "I'm pretty sure this falls within the humanities department's community-outreach budget," she said, winking at Tammy.

They were each handed their visitor stickers and a gallery map before clearing away from the front desk.

"So how we doing this?" Julia asked, having become the trip's self-appointed mother hen. "We all sticking together or meeting up at the same time or—"

"I think we all ought to go together," Tammy suggested. "I feel like I haven't gotten to spend hardly any time at all with Miss Lark here. And we're going to need both the resident

experts here to tell us all about the pieces," she said, motioning between Julia and Nick.

"I'll second that motion," Linda said, raising her hand.

"All in favor?" Nick asked.

"Aye," everyone echoed.

"All right, then," Julia said. "Where we starting?"

"Modern?" Lark suggested hopefully. "They have a really
large Matisse collection," she added, trying to sweeten the pot.

"Modern it is," Nick said decisively.

They consulted the map and set out on the appointed path.

Noticing Nick hanging toward the back of the pack, Lark
made an effort to walk slowly as well. When everyone in the
group had passed them, Nick quickly bent and kissed the back
of her bare neck.

"Been wanting to do that ever since you stepped off the
elevator," he whispered near her ear.

The fine hairs on her arms lifted with a shiver. "Sir," she
said with mock outrage. "We are in an edifice of higher learning." And then, quieter: "Also, I had to wear my strapless bra
with this, and it doesn't have enough padding to hide if you
make my nipples hard, so I'll thank you to keep your arms,
hands and other appendages to yourself."

Walking a step behind her, Nick captured her wrist and
pulled her hand backward to press against the front of his
jeans. Her eyes widened when she realized he was already
partially hard.

"Try hiding that," he rasped.

"You're just going to have to become very interested in the
statues," Lark said, fanning herself with her brochure. "You
can hide behind them until that situation resolves itself."

"The situation isn't going to resolve itself as long as you're within twenty miles of me," Nick said, releasing her hand as they turned into the gallery behind the group.

They made their way through several of the headliners. Van Gogh, who Julia pronounced "overrated." Chagall, who rated as "kinda gaudy." Gauguin, who Julia refused to look at all "on account of his being a syphilitic reprobate." And finally, Matisse.

Walking into the gallery, Lark immediately spotted her favorite and floated over to it.

Purple Robe and Anemones.

Lark stared at the woman in the center of the composition, casually leaning on a settee before a table bearing an explosion of red, white and purple blooms. The expression on her face seemed so serene despite a background of bright mustard yellow with blocky red stripes on one side and flat, dense gray marked by pale squiggly waves on the other. A riot of patterns and movements, and yet so incredibly…calm.

A state that was destined not to last.

"I guess his mama never told him polka dots and stripes don't go together," Tammy said, appearing at her elbow.

"I guess not," Lark said, forcing a chuckle.

"You sure missed out last night," Tammy said. "Karaoke turned out to be a most enlightening experience."

"How so?"

Tammy's eyelashes lowered as her eyes darted to either side to make sure they were alone. "Let's just say I received a very interesting piece of information about a certain art instructor."

Lark's heart beat faster. "What's that?"

"Well, it seems this field trip is our last hurrah. He's heading back to Manhattan sooner than later."

"Oh?" The single syllable escaped a throat quickly going dry.

"Yes indeed. That asshole partner of his is putting the screws to him about some big investor."

"Huh." Lark was only half listening at this point. Her face felt like a numb, dumb slab pasted to the front of her skull. She knew it was ridiculous to feel hurt that Tammy knew things about Nick's future plans that hadn't come up while they'd been together.

And could she really be surprised?

She'd blown him off yesterday evening, then showed up at his door to trauma-vomit all over him and finished with a bonus round of morning mommy issues. She hadn't even remembered to ask him what had been bothering him on the bus.

They'd made no plans.

No promises.

So why did the idea of his leaving cause her instant, devouring dread?

For once in her life, Lark wished the answer wasn't so easy to find.

Because without him, her summer would have continued on exactly as her spring had been. Gray, suffocating sameness. And once he left, what was to keep her from sliding right back into that pervasive fog? Didn't the panic she felt now prove her worst fears?

Lark hadn't managed to heal anything at all. She wasn't getting stronger or braver. She wasn't learning to accept her imperfections. She'd only been distracting herself from their existence. Throwing herself headlong into the speedball of infatuation.

She wasn't healing. She was hiding.

This time inside another person instead of her parents' basement.

Her father had been right all along.

"Are you all right, darlin'? You look whiter than skimmed

milk." Tammy's voice seemed to come from the other end of a very long tunnel.

Lark swallowed hard against the nausea flooding her mouth with saliva. Before her, the textures of the painting twitched and swirled.

"I think I need to sit down," she said.

Nick must have spotted them because he came rushing over and steadied her with a hand against her back. "Are you okay?" he said softly, his eyes searching hers.

"Uh-huh," she nodded, pushing away from him and trying to force a smile onto her lips. "I think it's just low blood sugar."

Nick eyed her skeptically but took a step back as the group began to move "Did you eat any breakfast this morning?"

After you left my room being the part of the question he didn't say.

She shook her head. "I ran out of time."

"Well, there's your problem." Julia was already shuffling over to them, rooting through her giant shoulder bag as she walked. Sitting down next to Lark, she began evicting her purse's contents a handful at a time. Tissues, pens, lipsticks, receipts, gum, cough drops, mints, stain-removing sticks, bandages, tissues.

"Ha!" she said triumphantly, holding up a Snickers bar. "Always keep one on me in case of emergencies." The sound of her unwrapping it seemed especially loud in the gallery's cool, hushed atmosphere, summoning a uniformed security guard to their midst.

"Ma'am," he said. "I'm afraid you can't eat that in here."

"I'm not going to eat it," Julia said, handing Lark the candy bar. "She is."

"She can't eat it either. No food or beverages in the galleries." He pointed a stiff finger at a wall plaque with a hamburger and soda cup imprisoned in the iconic circle with a slash.

Julia narrowed her eyes with a keenly shrewd look. "I happened to see in this nice little brochure here that this museum regularly hosts events. Is that correct?"

The guard's lips flattened into a tight line. "I don't see how that's—"

"If you look at this little picture right here," she said, unfolding the guide, "it looks like this lady in the very loud jumpsuit is not only drinking a glass of *red* wine, she appears to be receiving an appetizer from this young man holding a silver tray."

"I'm really okay," Lark lied. "I feel better already."

"That's a paid event, ma'am," the guard said, ignoring her.

"Oh, a *paid* event."

"They also sign a contract stating that they're liable for any damages they or their guests might cause to the artwork."

Julia folded her arms over her impressive bosom. "G'head and bring me one of those contracts, then. I'll wait." Her electric-orange Croc tapped on the gallery's wood floor.

"Ma'am—"

"I mean it. I'm perfectly willing to be on the hook if instead of eating this fun-sized Snickers, this young lady wants to go draw a chocolate mustache on the *Mona Lisa*."

"The *Mona Lisa* is at the Louvre," the guard said. "In Paris."

"Oh, well, then it's in no danger of being defaced with a fun-sized Snickers by my son's lady friend."

Nick's head whipped toward his mother, the blood draining from his face.

"Lady friend?" Tammy shrilled at a decibel that could be heard four counties over.

"*Julia*," Nick snapped.

"What?" she asked, shifting her attention from the security guard to her son. "She spends the night at our house, and I'm not allowed to call her your lady friend?"

Now Lark didn't feel like she was going to faint, she felt like she was going to die.

"The museum café is on the second-floor west wing," the guard said. "Your son's lady friend is welcome to eat her candy bar there."

"She could barely walk to the bench, and you expect her to go all the way to the café to eat one lousy Snickers? What are you going to do when she falls and hits her head and gets blood all over the floor? The chocolate's not looking so bad now, is it... Dennis?" Julia asked, leaning in to look at his badge.

"If you need me to radio for emergency services, I'm happy to do that," the guard said.

"Please," Lark said, straining to be heard over the wrangling. "Don't—"

"In the time it takes them to get here, she could have eaten the goddamn candy bar already!" Julia shouted.

Lark attempted to draw in a breath, but her rib cage compressed her lungs.

"Lark?" Nick asked, crouching down in front of her. "Are you okay?"

Lark shook her head, unable to find the words to explain how *not okay* she was. She felt like she was on an invisible amusement park ride, the world spinning faster and faster as her stomach churned and her vision blurred. She gripped the edge of the bench to steady herself.

"Stop!"

Lark hadn't even realized she'd shouted the word until everyone stopped talking. They all blinked at her with expressions of concern.

"I'm having…" She wheezed, fighting with her breath. "A panic attack. Just please, leave me…alone. And I'll be…fine."

"Why don't we continue our tour?" Linda suggested, herding the others away. Hearing the kindness and consideration her voice, Lark was overcome with a wave of gratitude so fierce, it almost eased the sickening ache in her chest.

Julia began repacking the contents of her purse, muttering under her breath. She'd made it almost to the bottom of the pile when a square foil packet fell out of one the tissues and bounced off the toe of Nick's sneaker.

He and his mother stared at it.

"Don't get your boxers in a bunch," she said, snatching it up. "Tammy gave it to me last night. One of the bouncers was making eyes at me, and she said I should have it in case I got lucky. Which I didn't, thanks to Mike."

"What did… Mike do?" Lark asked, trying to focus her attention anywhere but her rioting body.

"Told the bouncer he'd better keep his greedy eyes off me unless he wanted them relocated to the back of his skull." Julia's cheeks glowed beneath their freckles. "Between you and me, I think he might have a little crush." Rising from the bench, she shot her son a look. "You call me if she gets any worse."

"I will," Nick said.

Julia turned and headed after the others, taking a giant bite of the candy bar *at* Dennis on her way.

Lark and Nick sat alone on the bench.

Already her heart had begun to slow, and he'd done nothing more than sit next to her.

"So…how soon?"

"We don't have to talk about this now, Lark. Not until you—"

"When were you going to…tell me?"

Nick's shoulders rounded on a defeated exhale. "Heading back to Manhattan early has only been in the mix since yesterday. One of the investors we've been courting is ready to bite, but Marshall won't move forward unless I'm there. I only mentioned it to Tammy because she was needling me about you. Asking me about my intentions, basically."

Even in the center of her current storm, Lark felt the flicker of gratitude. "She was?"

Nick nodded. "Apparently she suspects that there's something between us."

Suddenly, Tammy's casual mention of Nick's imminent departure made more sense. Lark had never been an especially good liar. She could only imagine what she'd been telegraphing when she'd rolled into the lobby on a tide of pheromones and post-sex satisfaction.

"I'm going to tell Marshall to fuck off, Lark." Nick scooted toward her, prying open her clammy fist with his warm fingers. "I'm not going anywhere. I wanted to tell you when you showed up last night, but—"

"But you could see I was already upset," Lark said and breathed into the sliver of space that had appeared in her rib cage. "And you didn't want to make it worse?"

Nick nodded. "Something like that."

Lark stared down at their clasped hands. She could feel his eyes on her, but she couldn't bring herself to meet them. "We both knew this summer would end."

"It doesn't have to." He leaned forward, his eyes burning with intensity.

Lark steeled herself against a swell of silly, childish hope for an easy solution. "No," she said. "This is easier, actually."

His eyebrows gathered at the center of his forehead. "Easier? How?"

Drawing in a deep breath, she searched the chaos at her center and found a kernel of resolve. "I'd rather that you leave me for Manhattan than leave Manhattan for me."

"Why?" he demanded.

"What just happened here," she began. "The way I reacted to hearing that you might be leaving… I didn't have any control over that. I can't stop it from happening to me."

"I know that," Nick said.

"But I can stop it from happening to you," she finished.

Nick flinched, his whole body bracing as if for a blow. And like it or not, Lark had to be the one to deliver it.

"I can't do this, Nick. I can't be with you when I'm still like this. I never should have been with you in the first place," she said. "But the truth is I just…wanted you. And it had been so long since I'd wanted anything at all that I didn't want to lose that feeling."

"Wanted," Nick repeated. "Past tense?" He looked at her with a thousand questions and a bottomless well of hurt in his eyes.

"No," she admitted. "Of course I still want you. But it's like you said last night—I don't even know what I need. And if I let myself, I could fall all the way into you."

"Why is that a bad thing?" he asked.

Lark waited, begging the right words to appear in her mind. "Because what I want is to fall *for* you, Nick." She made herself hold his gaze, willing him to understand. "I want…" Her throat tightened painfully with the realization that it was the strongest declarative sentence she'd spoken in as long as she could remember. "I want to be strong enough to swim by someone's side, not pull them under because I'm drowning."

"You're not pulling me under." Nick scooted closer, pinning her with the intensity of his look.

Lark squeezed his hand. "Not yet. But I could."

Unbidden, the image of her parents' tired, worn faces flashed through her mind. She'd been so mired in her own pain, she hadn't been able to imagine what witnessing her unraveling must have been like for them until she saw it reflected in Nick's eyes.

Nick lifted her hand and kissed it before holding it against his heart. "I held you while you cried this morning. I was inside you less than two hours ago." He searched her face as if trying to find anything that would make sense of her. "The fact that you're still healing doesn't make any of what we have less real."

"Which makes it even more dangerous," Lark said. "Because it looks like something you can build a life around. But I can't let you become my life preserver. I can't let you break yourself while trying to fix me. I can't be one of your strays, Nick."

"You're not a goddamn *stray*." His words vibrated with an intensity that surprised her.

"Then how would you describe how we became involved?" she asked.

Nick's shoulders were rigid, his hands balled into fists at his sides as his jaw clenched to hold back the truth. "Looking at you broke my fucking heart, Lark."

Words abandoned her utterly, her mouth and mind empty and stunned.

"Seeing you like that at the back of the classroom…" He shook his head. "It was like someone had—fucking—*stolen* the life from you," he said, his voice vibrating with emotion as his face contorted. Behind his glasses, his eyes filmed with a sheen that stung moisture to her own.

"Watching you try to draw, and you were so angry at yourself. And there was this...this pain radiating off you. I just wanted to make it better for you." His face was a portrait of anguish, illuminated by the sunlight streaming through the window.

She averted her gaze and then forced herself to lift her chin and hold his desolate stare. "You can't," she said, her voice resolute. "That's my whole point. No one can. I have to make this better for myself, and it's not fair to bring someone else into that process."

Nick's gray eyes burned with a sadness that nearly stole her breath. "What happens now?"

Placing her hand on Nick's cheek, she pressed a kissed to his lips for all the days ahead when she would need to remind herself of this good thing and why she was making this choice.

"Now you remember when to let go."

Twelve

Lark was blue.

And not in the hyperbolic emotionally chromatic sense.

Cobalt blue.

Phthalo blue.

Ultramarine blue.

Prussian blue.

The colors streaked her fingers, forearms and face as she frenetically attacked the canvas, pausing only to load her brush for another assault.

Her arm ached, her shoulder burned and she was reasonably sure her hand would be cramped even after she finally put down the palette.

She'd been painting all night.

Canvas after canvas, dragged from the basement storage room where her mother had squirreled them away when she'd left for college. Along with the easel, which Lark had parked in the tiled entry of the basement's walk-out door. Pristine when she'd started, the varnished wood frame now bore streaks similar to the ones smearing her arms, her nightgown and probably her face.

Despite all the pain and exhaustion, Lark couldn't help but feel a swell of pride when she looked at what she had created.

A mess, mostly.

But one that looked exactly like her.

One that reflected the bone-deep ache she'd felt since returning early from the field trip to Baltimore. Alone. And yet feeling Nick's presence stronger than ever.

He was with her as she worked, haunting the space between breaths. Endlessly making love to her in her mind.

Even now, blending the paint, she could summon the feeling of his hands on her. Of his breath on her neck. His steely cock filling her—

Movement in her peripheral vision made Lark jump. The paint-loaded brush slipped from her fingers. Lark watched in horror as it clattered off the tile and—in slow motion—bounced onto the carpet.

Landing at her father's Italian-leather loafers.

Lark's gaze traveled up the sharp crease of her father's pants, past the tucked-in waist of his pressed dress shirt to the co-ordinated tie and Windsor knot and then the clean-shaven jaw, tight with concern. Lark's mother stood at his side, her face pale above a beautiful cream-colored suit, one hand near her mouth, the other holding the unopened letter from Dartmouth.

Both sets of eyes looked from the brush to Lark.

She knew she should retrieve, it but she couldn't get her frozen limbs to cooperate.

Her father stooped to pick it up, fingers around a lone spot where her grip had kept the handle clean. Handing it back to her, she didn't miss his second glance down at the smudge it had left on the creamy carpet.

"Oh, honey," her mother said, breaking the silence. "That's—"

"A mess," Lark quickly finished for her. "I know. I'll clean it up when I'm finished."

Though she had absolutely no idea how.

"I was going to say *beautiful*."

Lark's father shot a pointed look at his wife, his expression mirroring the shock Lark had felt at the compliment. "There's something we need to discuss with you," he said.

Lark didn't need to think hard to guess what.

"I'm not going back."

The words smeared the air as haphazardly as the bold swath of paint she'd applied to the center of her composition with a palette knife.

This was not at all how she'd planned to deliver the news.

During the small hours of the night, when she'd played and replayed the scenario in her head, Lark had imagined herself scrubbed and shiny. Her hair in a neat bun and a leather planner perched in her lap. Wearing a blouse and pearls. Probably a cardigan.

"Please elaborate." It was a habit of her father's to be even more polite the angrier he became.

Lark's grip tightened on the brush as if it were the hilt of a sword. "I'm not going back to medical school."

Her parents traded a look that made Lark's throat go dry.

"If you need more time—" her mother began.

"I don't," Lark interrupted. "I don't need more time."

"If this is about that man you've been seeing—"

"It isn't," Lark said, cutting her father off. "At least, not the way you're thinking," she amended.

Because in a way, it *was* about Nick. It was about the way he'd made her feel. The way he'd led her back to parts of herself long buried, parts yet untapped. The way he'd helped her find pieces of her life she hadn't realized she'd lost.

Like art.

Like the dizzy, all-consuming rush of seeing your feelings made visible.

"This is about me," she said, her voice firmer than she'd expected it to be. "This is about what I want."

Her father folded his arms across his chest. "And what do you want?"

Lark's pulse thumped in her ears. "I don't know."

He gave a dismissive *it figures* snort that lit an invisible pilot light at the base of Lark's skull.

"How could I possibly know when my entire life has been laid out before me like some kind of..." She paused, searching for the right comparison when her gaze landed on the canvas. "Paint-by-numbers picture."

"You make it sound as if we've never given you a choice." Her father's eyes flashed a blue almost as bright as the one smeared on her knuckles.

"Oh, you gave me choices. Would you rather run track or take Debate, Lark? Would you prefer Harvard or Dartmouth for medical school?" Lark said, doing what she thought was a decent imitation of her father's authoritative voice.

Her mother's mouth dropped open. "Sweetheart, we only—"

"I *know*," Lark said, unable to endure the same reassurances that had choked every corner of this space for the last several months. "I know you only wanted what was best for me. I know you love me and want me to be happy. But how am I supposed to do that when I don't even know what makes me happy?"

"How do you propose to find that out?" her father asked. "Taking off whenever it suits you? Throwing away everything you've worked for to go on some kind of journey of self-discovery?"

If it was possible to make the suggestion sound more insulting, Lark wasn't certain how.

Setting the brush aside, she turned to face her parents. "By being given the freedom to try things without feeling like I'm failing you if they don't work out. Even if they're stereotypical or pointless. Even if you think I'm ruining my life. And maybe I will," she allowed. "But it's *my* life. It's the only one I get. And so far I've only managed to drive myself to the brink of a total breakdown trying to live it the way everyone else thinks I should."

Only when the air conditioner kicked on did she become aware of the tears streaming down her face. Lark swiped at them furiously, rolling on when neither of her parents spoke. "I can't do it anymore. I *won't*. And I'm not asking you to approve of whatever it is I choose to do. I'm just asking you to give me the space to do it." She was dizzy with adrenaline. Her heart fluttered in her throat and her palms sweated against her sides.

Her father studied her as if seeing her for the first time. A look not altogether warm or friendly but direct. So unlike the hesitant glances he'd slid her way lately. This was a look of acknowledgment. Of recognition. As if she was really there.

Holding his hand out toward her mother, her father took the letter and passed it to Lark.

The creamy envelope felt heavy in her hands as he turned and walked out of the basement.

It was as close to approval of her request as she was going to get.

Her mother predictably lingered behind, waiting until he was out of the room to speak. "You know, the Gartens still have an apartment in Paris," she said, angling herself to get a better look at Lark's canvas. "They usually spend August in Italy, so it will probably be empty soon. If something stereotypical is what you're after, running off to France to study art would be a decent start."

Lark blinked at her mother, unsure if she was hearing her correctly. "I'd be happy to give you their number, if you'd like to reach out about staying at their place while they're gone."

With that single sentence, it was as if her mother was letting Lark know it was now up to her to choose the path. Hers, the responsibilities. Hers, the consequences.

Lark threw her arms around her mother in a fierce hug. Only when her mother drew back did like realize what she'd done. The beautiful suit smudged with streaks of blue.

"Oh, Mom!" Lark gasped. "I'm so sorry."

Her mother only smiled and squeezed her hand. "Nonsense," she said. "This could be worth a lot of money someday."

Lark laughed, overcome with a gust of gratitude tinged with bittersweet sadness. In that moment, the only thing she wanted was to share this victory with Nick.

Thirteen

"Do you want to take a couple of these?" Nick's mother stood in the doorway to his room, her hands full of the miniature soaps, shampoos and lotions she'd snatched from the Four Seasons. "They could come in handy once you get back to the city, if you don't have time to go shopping right away."

"Sure." Nick dumped them into his bag. Easier than arguing. It had become sort of a life philosophy as of late.

Copping out, you mean.

Whatever else his return to Manhattan meant, Nick sincerely hoped the cessation of his father's opinions popping into his head would be part of it. His father was proving to be no more help in death than he had been in life. All the more reason to finish packing up and get the fuck out of here. Get the fuck on with it.

"It" being the meeting Marshall had scheduled for the two of them with the venture capital firm prepared to "launch Moonshhot to the stratosphere." Nick had listened to his partner's enthusiastic reassurances with bland ambivalence, unmoved by Marshall's formerly contagious enthusiasm. The prick could afford to be warm and effusive now that he'd gotten what he wanted. Nick's cowed cooperation. Or at least a reasonable facsimile thereof.

He was set to hit the road first thing the following morning and be back in Manhattan in time to meet Marshall for a preparatory dinner. It was nearly a four-hour drive, but if timed right, he should miss the worst traffic. Not that he especially cared. Like his agreement to come back, his decision to drive had been made the way everything seemed to happen in the aftermath of his disastrous summer fling. By default.

Now that Lark had suggested—no, *informed him*—that it would be best for them to have no contact for a full year, he didn't especially give a shit what filled that time. Hell, he *needed* something to launch himself headlong into. Even if it happened to be expansion of the company he no longer believed in. At least this way he could finally pocket some cash in exchange for his effort.

Copping out and *selling out*.

He chased the bitter thought with a sip of the beer his mother had brought him after pronouncing him cranky. *Cranky* didn't begin to cover it, he thought, zipping the duffle bag. "Jesus," he grunted, hefting it onto his shoulder. It seemed to be actively gaining weight on his way out to the car. He was wondering how the hell it had gotten so heavy when he heard a suspicious clinking as he settled it into the trunk.

"What the…"

He unzipped the side and dug through his stacks of clothing only to find jars of homemade Bolognese sauce and jam tucked into the corners. Written on the silvery lid of each was the contents, the date and *Don't argue with me* in his mother's distinctive slanted script.

Shaking his head fondly, Nick closed the trunk and nearly leapt back a full foot.

Lark stood next to his car, a flat, rectangular brown paper bag in her hands and a hesitant smile on her face.

Nick felt his breath catch in his throat. Not having to suffer the ache of losing her all over again had been the one upside of her cutting off contact cold turkey. Nick had respected her wishes, beginning and deleting at least a dozen texts.

The prospect of humiliating himself hadn't been sufficient to stop him. But the thought of compromising her healing process was.

And now here she was, showing the fuck up without warning.

As if it shouldn't devastate him as it clearly hadn't devastated her.

He grasped the thought with both hands, needing the anger. Needing it to shield him against the ache already opening in his chest at the sight of her. She was more beautiful than ever, he noted miserably. Her simple strapless sundress glowed a ghostly white in the dying light, the gauzy fabric clinging to her slim frame and revealing glimpses of her shapely legs as it lifted in the summer breeze. Nick wondered if she'd pulled her hair into a high ponytail just to torment him.

"Lark," he said, his voice barely above a whisper.

"Hi," she replied, a small smile playing on her lips. "I'm sorry to just drop in on you like this."

He didn't offer any absolution, only waited for her to justify her visit.

"There's something I wanted to give you before you left."

So, she knew. No big surprises there. Julia Hoffman, information-distribution specialist.

Lark held out the brown-papered parcel.

Nick stared at it. "What is it?"

"You could always open it and see." She ducked her head, grinned at him, and—who the fuck had he thought he was kidding—any defenses he'd thought he had dissolved.

Taking the bag from her, Nick opened it and pulled out a

rectangle of stiff canvas stretched on a thin wooden frame. A painting. Of the pond.

It was all there.

The giant willow tree. The rope swing. A lanky shirtless boy in swim trunks, his long, curly hair flying out behind him like a comet's tail, feet still clinging to the rope while his hands were already reaching for the sky. But not just any sky. Entire galaxies of stars tumbling from a giant red-gold nebula.

Nick stared at it, speechless.

"This way it can always be summer."

Lark had captured the essence of one of his favorite places in all the world perfectly. A season Nick knew he'd not forget as long as he was alive. But what struck him most was the color. A far cry from the silvery graphite and inky charcoals she'd hesitated to even put to paper, the composition teemed with vibrant hues executed in confident strokes.

And maybe, just maybe, he'd had some small part of that.

Nick took a deep breath and looked at her, his eyes stinging. "This is…amazing," he whispered, his voice hoarse.

"I'm glad you like it," Lark said softly, her eyes meeting his. "I wanted to give you something to remember me by."

Nick felt a lump form in his throat as he looked at her. Remember her? How could he forget her? In just the five days they'd been separated, his entire world felt…gray. Gray as the city he was returning to.

"Thank you," Nick said. Every cell in his body howled with the need to pull her into his embrace, but he resisted.

Lark's eyes were shining when she stepped back, her movements jerky enough to suggest that she, too, felt the pull. She cleared her throat, signaling a shift in topics. "So you got things worked out with Marshall?" she asked.

Fuck.

"Kind of," Nick said.

Lark's eyes narrowed. "What's 'kind of' mean?"

Nick provided the briefest summary possible. "So it makes sense to go along with it for now," he shrugged, winding down. "Once Moonshot is launched and off my plate, I can think about what I want to do next."

Lark, who had listened silently up to this point, glanced up at him with an impish gleam in her eye. "Or you could tell Marshall to fuck off, take your IP back and do what you want."

Nick blinked at her. "Who even are you?"

"I'm the woman you've been teaching how to be a rebel," she answered. "Question is, do *you* remember how to be one?"

Nick opened his mouth to speak but promptly shut it again.

"I'm also the woman who told her dad she was dropping out of medical school," she said, hugging her torso.

Nick was so taken aback he nearly dropped the painting. "You did?"

"Mmm." She nodded, her throat visibly constricting. "I—uh, got home from the field trip, and I couldn't stop painting," she said. "And somewhere in there I realized how much I missed it. Which made me realize that I hadn't thanked you." Her face contorted, lower lip wobbling.

"Lark—"

"Please," she said urgently, holding up her hand. "Don't be nice to me. If you're nice to me, I'm going to cry, and I'm afraid I'll never stop. I need to get through this."

Nick clamped his jaw shut.

A breeze made Lark's dress dance around her calves. "I never thanked you."

"For what?" he asked.

"What you did. I can't even begin—"

"You don't need to," Nick interrupted.

"But I want to—"

"Don't." The words came out more forcefully than he'd meant them to. "Please don't," he said, softer. "I'm doing my best, but much more of this and I'm going to lose my mind."

Standing there watching her try to be brave without being able to touch her, it hit him all over again. His earnest desire for her to be free, to follow her dreams, to heal, to grow—it in no way lessened the pain of losing her.

"Well, I just…wanted to you to have something, so." Lark drew in a shuddery inhale. "I'm sorry. This is—is really hard."

Unable to bear the sight of her struggle any longer, Nick stepped forward and folded her into a hug. Resistant at first, Lark melted against him by degrees until her arms slipped around his waist. With his chin atop her head and her ear against his heart, they stood there for a length of time Nick couldn't begin to measure.

"Fenwick Avram Hoffman," Lark said against the fabric of his shirt.

Nick lifted his chin. "Do *you* have a middle name?"

"Lark *is* my middle name," she said.

"What's your first name?" Nick asked.

"Meadow," she said. "Meadow Lark Hockney." She sighed and rested her head against his chest. "My mother had to go through fertility treatments. They agreed it would be their last round, and my mother told herself if she saw a bird on the way to the fertility clinic, her pregnancy test would be positive."

"And she saw a meadowlark?"

"A tufted titmouse. But neither of them was especially enthused about the nicknames for that one."

"I see your songbird and raise you a fishing reel," Nick said.

"What?" Laughter through tears made her eyes shine like diamonds.

"True story." Julia chimed in from the front porch. "Nick's father didn't tell me until *after* it was on the birth certificate."

How long she'd been there or what she'd seen was impossible to tell.

"Hi, Julia," Lark called.

"Hello, dear. Do you want to come in for some apple streusel?"

"I wish I could," Lark said, pulling out of his embrace. "But I really have to be going. I have a flight tomorrow morning."

"A flight?" Nick asked, gazing down at her. "To where?"

"Paris," she said. "My parents' friends have a place that'll be empty until November. After that." She shrugged. "I may head to Italy. Or Prague."

I'm never going to see her again.

"Isn't that exciting," his mother cooed.

Nick shot her a pointed look over his shoulder.

Ducking her head and mouthing *Sorry*, she slipped back inside.

Nick took Lark's chin in his hand, lifting it until their eyes met. Her green gaze was steady and warm, filled with an emotion he couldn't quite place.

I love her.

"Would it be super weird to ask for a goodbye kiss?" he said.

"Only if your mother watched."

They both glanced toward the front of the house where the curtains in the window next to the front door stirred.

"Julia!" Nick barked.

"All right, all right," they heard as a shadow behind the curtains receded.

Nick wound his fingers into the short silky hair at Lark's

nape, rubbing it between the pads of his thumb and forefinger to memorize the texture.

Only then did he bring his hands forward to trace the shape of her rounded ears before cupping her jaw. His thumbs strayed over her eyebrows, eyelids, cheekbones, lips, chin. Imprinting the memory of her face on a part of him more reliable than his eyes.

When their lips finally met, they struggled to sink into a shared rhythm. Their mouths moved to the strains of two different songs. Hers, a hymn. His, a lullaby. Until gradually, the building heat lifted them both into a ballad. Lush and sweeping. Passionate and pure.

Lark was crying again, and Nick could taste the salt of her tears. Could feel her smile turn to a grimace, then to a smile again against his mouth. Only when his lungs screamed for air and the pavement shifted beneath his feet did Nick break the kiss and press his forehead to hers instead.

I love her, and I'm never going to see her again.

Only with Lark in his arms and this thought in his mind did understanding finally coalesce. This fucking *hurt*. And before seeing her again tonight, that hurt had begun to poison him. Just as it had poisoned his father. Losing her was the most painful thing he'd ever experienced. But losing the part of himself that had helped restore the color to her world?

That would be infinitely worse.

That would be a hell of his own making.

Lark hugged him so tight he could feel his heartbeat against her cheek. He willed it to stay there like a brand. Reminding him of the kind of man he wanted to be.

"Okay," she announced. "I've got to go." She released him and took a step back, blotting her cheeks with the tips of her fingers.

"See you next summer?" he asked, his voice raspy with emotion. The question was wishful thinking. Nothing more.

Lark gave him one last look before climbing into her car, closing the door and starting the engine. Only after the red taillights had disappeared into the distance did Nick notice an additional detail in the drawing. There beneath the willow tree, almost hidden by a skirt of branches, was a dark-haired girl. A high ponytail, a simple white sundress just visible in the shadows.

Nick heard the screen door creak open and saw his mother's clogs appear on the porch step where he sat. She plopped down and pressed a cold beer into his hand before squeezing his shoulder. They sat there together in uncharacteristic silence.

"Lark thinks I should tell Marshall to fuck off," Nick said by way of a conversation opener. "What do you think?"

"You're asking me?" A crease appeared between his mother's dark brows.

"Yeah." Nick took a pull on his beer. "I am."

For all the times she'd offered her opinions without being asked, Nick would have thought she'd be quicker to respond.

"Well?" He nudged her with an elbow, surprised how much he wanted to hear her answer.

Julia set her own beer down with a satisfying *thunk*, scooting so she could see his eyes. "I think I like this one."

"I do too," Nick said. "In fact, I love her."

His mother only nodded, ruffling his curls before pushing herself up to go inside. "Don't forget to turn off the porch light before you come in."

"I won't." But he wasn't ready just yet.

Sitting on the front porch of the house he had resented, in the town he'd been so desperate escape, he was surrounded by reminders of the man whose stubborn pride was the very reason he'd met Lark Hockney.

If it hadn't been for the old man's obsession with a retirement that would never come, they'd never have moved here from Boston. If it hadn't been for his hectoring Nick about practical skills, Nick wouldn't have defiantly made a point of signing up for the art class where he'd first met Lark. Had it not been for his father's untimely death here, Nick's mother wouldn't have stubbornly set down roots in a community that hadn't always welcomed her with open arms.

And Nick wouldn't have come home for the summer.

Home.

The place from which you launched.

Spring Valley had been that place for him and Lark both, and for a season, it had drawn both of them back into its orbit.

Nick pressed the palm of his hand against wood his father had once spent a summer sanding and staining. "Thanks, Pop."

A rain-scented gust of wind rustled the trees and set the wind chimes singing. His pop always did like having the last word.

Fourteen

One year, twelve days, two hours later...

Lark took a deep breath, letting the electric energy of the city wash over her as she stared out the gallery window. The show's opening was fifteen minutes away, and her heart had taken up permanent residence in her throat.

"We already have a crowd," Sandra Sòng steered Lark away from the window and over to the table of canapés. "You'd better eat something before people start getting here because once those doors open, your hands and mouth will be busy," she said, swiping a caviar crostini. With her free hand, Sandra waved over a bow-tied waiter carrying champagne.

"Take one," Sandra urged, handing a glass to Lark before snagging one for herself.

Like her show at the Grey Art Gallery in Manhattan, having a designated dealer for her paintings could be listed among the more positive developments of the past year.

There were others, in no particular order: Having celebrated her one-year anniversary of her breakdown in Paris with a very friendly, and very handsome, group of students from Athens. Taking a job at an art-supply store in New York after her return from Europe. Being promoted to assistant manager. Signing the lease on her first non-dorm apartment—a two-bedroom prewar apartment in the Bay Ridge neighborhood of Brooklyn with a view of Owl's Head Park.

Five piercings. Three tattoos. Two panic attacks. Zero contact with Nick Hoffman.

Many times, she'd written out a late-night message recanting her request, only to promise herself she could send it in the morning if she still wanted to when she woke up.

Morning always came with her electing to delete.

But.

She'd asked for a year. A year during which they were both completely free to follow wherever life's path would lead, even if it meant away from each other. It had now officially been more than a year.

Not that she'd expected him to call the second the clock struck 7:22 p.m. on July 8th. For all she knew, he could be engaged. Or married. Hell, he might even have a child. A new-ish one anyway, given the allotted time. Of course, she hadn't contacted him either since the anniversary of their parting had passed. She couldn't even say why, exactly. An unwillingness to open a line of communication he might want to remain closed, maybe?

"Ready?" Sandra asked, dusting off her palms.

Lark's stomach tightened. "I guess?"

Confidence, Sandra mouthed. *Confidence*.

That had been a consistent theme in their work together. Efforts for tonight had included makeup artists, a personal stylist who had miraculously sourced a black halter-top pantsuit that made Lark feel like a Bond Girl and showed off her forearm tattoo, and a pair of killer four-inch stiletto boots. Grabbing one last glance at herself in the floor-length mirror on the back of the supply closet door, Lark couldn't help but smile.

They were all there.

The eight-year-old who had practiced piano until her fingers had blistered. The twelve-year-old who'd studied the dictionary until her eyes had crossed. The fifteen-year-old who'd run three miles a day before 6:00 a.m. The eighteen-year-old who'd sweated every tenth of a GPA point. The twenty-two-year-old who'd inadvertently set them all free by sitting down in the middle of the road and refusing to move until conditions improved.

The almost-twenty-four-year-old who'd learned to listen to them all.

Taking a deep breath, Lark raised her glass and brought it to the mirror, clicking rims with the woman smiling back at her.

"Oh, honey your *hair*." Dr. Diana Hockney's mouth dropped open in shock.

Lark sometimes forgot who had and hadn't seen her since she'd come home from Paris.

A karma-changing chop had been her first order of business when she'd stepped off the Metro. Second, technically, if you counted the warm crepes with Nutella. It had grown out to a messy chin-length bob that she wore wavy or sleek, depending on the occasion.

Tonight was messy, in honor of her gallery show's theme. *The Art of Imperfection: An Exploration of Too Much and Not Enough.*

Once the initial shock wore off, Lark watched her mother notice the details. The tiny silver nose ring. The colorful whorls of ink from her elbow to her shoulder.

Under her therapist's guidance, she'd not seen her parents in person for the first three months since she'd returned from Europe. The next three had been their choice. Spring was baby season, and their getting up to the city hadn't been feasible. But now, slowly, they'd begun to reopen the channels of communication. Inviting her parents to her gallery show had been a huge step. One Lark desperately hoped wouldn't end up exploding in her face.

"Hi, Mom," Lark said, bending to wrap her in a hug. "How are you?"

"Really great," she said, squeezing Lark's hand. "Your father's just hired two more nurse practitioners, if you can believe it. He actually said out loud the other day that he thinks we should be spending less time at the office."

Direct hit to her younger selves.

Still, as much as she wished he'd come to the realization sooner, Lark felt encouraged that he'd come to it at all. Progress, she supposed.

"That's great," Lark said. "Where is Dad?" she asked, glancing around the gallery.

Her mother's smile slipped. "He's so sorry, sweetie, but we had three different mamas go into labor last night. He really wanted to be here—he just couldn't make it."

And also hadn't called to let her know himself. She tried not to feel disappointed.

"Well, you *have* to be Lark's mother." Sandra cruised over to them with her hand extended. "Sandra Sòng. I'm your daughter's gallery agent."

"Such a pleasure to meet you," her mother said. "I think this is a wonderful exhibition you've put together here."

"Thank you so much," Sandra said, her crimson lips parting in a warm smile. "Would you like me to show you some of my favorite pieces?"

"I'd love that," her mother said.

"Right this way." Sandra winked at Lark over the shoulder of her tailored Chanel suit as they walked away.

Lark pressed her palms together and quickly bowed in

thanks. Taking several gulps of her champagne, Lark blinked her watering eyes and made herself mingle.

The gallery held the usual mix. A sprinkling of friends and business contacts. Local art critics and other visual artists. Assorted street traffic looking to score free cheese and champagne. Lark kept a smile fixed on her face as she worked her way around the room, pausing to greet as many guests as she could. When her cheeks began to ache, Lark waved to Sandra and excused herself.

She headed to the staff kitchen to check the phone that her pocketless pantsuit had no room for. Leaning against the counter, Lark woke the screen and sucked in a little gasp. A missed call and voice message from her father.

Her pulse pounding in her ears, Lark hit Play.

"Hi...um, this is your father."

Lark couldn't help but smile at his self-conscious greeting.

"I just wanted to say congratulations. I'm sorry I couldn't make it, but I know it will be a great success." An extended pause. "I'm very proud of you, Lark."

Even as stiff as it sounded, hearing her father pronounce the words drew tears to her eyes. Dabbing at the corners so as not to ruin her makeup, Lark sent him a quick reply via text.

Thanks, Dad. That means more than I can say.

A text he instantly replied to with a heart.

That her father, the busy doctor, might have been anxiously waiting to hear back from *her* was a strange turn indeed. Lark allowed the thought to lighten her heart as she took a deep breath and prepared to rejoin her party.

She'd almost made it back to her original spot when a squeal echoed through the gallery. Every head in the place swiveled toward the entrance where, standing by the door with her arms thrown wide, was none other than Tammy.

Lark rushed over to her. The familiar cloud of lemony-floral perfume enveloped Lark as Tammy crushed her in a hug.

"Oh, darlin', it's so. Good. To. See. You," she said, matching each word with a side-to-side torso wiggle.

"It's good to see you too," Lark said, surprised by the wave of throat-clenching emotion that swept over her.

Tammy took Lark by the wrists and pushed her out to arm's length. "Lord Almighty, look at you!" Tammy fanned herself with a hand. "You're hotter than a billy goat with a blow torch."

"Um, look who's talking," Lark said, giving Tammy a twirl. The red-and-black polka-dot 1950s halter dress flared out around her.

"This old thing?" Tammy waved a self-deprecating hand.

"Did you come all by yourself?" Lark asked.

Tammy's red lips stretched in a brilliant smile. "Actually, Linda's parkin' the car. We have some—"

"You *drove* into Manhattan?" Lark asked incredulously.

"Well, you see—"

The door swung open, and Linda sashayed in, incredibly sleek in a body-hugging black silk sheath dress accessorized with a red neckerchief and red high-heeled Mary Jane pumps.

Spotting Lark, she broke into a broad grin and threw her arms around her. "Congratulations, honey."

"Thanks so much," Lark said. "How cute are you two?" she asked, seeing that Tammy and Linda had clearly coordinated. "Are you two coordinating full time, or was this just for my gallery opening?"

"We're so precious I can barely stand us." The women shared a look.

"Actually…" Linda began.

"We're a couple now!" Tammy half shouted.

"You want to say that a little louder, babe?" Linda teased, lacing her fingers with Tammy's. "I don't think they heard you in Hoboken."

"Oh my God," Lark said, feeling delight on their behalf. "I'm so happy for you."

"Where'd Julia and Mike get to?" Linda asked, scanning the gallery guests.

Lark's heart thumped in her chest. "Julia Hoffman came with you?"

"She sure did," Tammy reported. "And that Mike fella she's dating now."

"Julia and Mike?" Lark asked. "Boy, am I out of the loop."

"Yes indeedy," Tammy said. "They've been datin' since… since we all did the field trip to Baltimore, wasn't it?"

"Pretty sure that's about when it happened," Linda agreed.

Just then, the couple in question made their grand entrance.

Lark performed another round of hugs and greetings and made a point of *not* asking Julia about Nick, hoping that history would serve and she'd offer the information anyway. Sure enough…

"Nick was so sad he couldn't be here," Julia said. "He's been working like a dog."

"On the AI start-up still?" Lark asked.

Julia's brow furrowed. "Goodness no. He and Mr. Marvelous went their separate ways six months ago now." She accepted a glass of champagne from Mike. "He's part of a team creating AI-based immersive exhibits now. They're actually working on a new program with the Met and—oh, there he is!"

Julia's eyes fixed on a point over Lark's shoulder.

The hair stood up on the back of Lark's neck, gooseflesh rising on her arms and spilling down her belly. The air around her seemed to thicken, refusing to be drawn into her lungs.

Turn around. Just turn around.

When she spun on her heel, Nick stopped short, a flash of heat illuminating his eyes before it was swiftly extinguished.

Nick wasn't as handsome as she'd remembered him. He was ridiculously, unfairly, devastatingly beautiful. He'd let his hair grow out again. Long enough for the ends to be sun bleached. His natural curls pulled into waves that fell just below his clavicles. He'd clearly been getting outside more as witnessed by the tawny glow of his complexion. Whether he'd been hitting the gym harder or absence had made her ravenous, the effect was the same. The forearms that peeked out of his sleeves revealed prominent biceps, triceps, veins and ropy muscles. His stance was casual yet confident—legs braced slightly apart, hands loose at his sides.

He smiled then, the same lopsided grin that had decimated her sanity only a year ago.

"Hey there." Nick's soft, deep voice hung in the air between them, and for a moment Lark felt his presence as if he were pressed against her back, his lips grazing her ear.

"Hey," she said.

"Hot damn! Look who it is." Tammy and Linda came forward and gave Nick hugs and kisses on the cheek.

"Well, if this isn't just like a reunion," Tammy said, sipping her champagne.

"Only the art is considerably better," Linda said.

"I wouldn't necessarily say that," Nick said.

"I would," Tammy laughed. "We were awful."

"Except for Lark," Linda added, gesturing around the room. "Which—these are amazing."

"Thank you," Lark said. "I was super lucky to find Sandra."

"Or vice versa."

Was it her imagination, or had his eyes flicked from hers down to the front of her halter? Backless as it was, she couldn't wear a bra beneath it, but you couldn't tell that two of her five piercings lived in that region unless you knew in advance.

"Should we go take a look around before everything gets bought up?" Tammy suggested. "We got all those walls to fill."

"We just bought a new house," Linda explained.

"I've been in the market for some new pieces myself," Julia said.

"Don't know where you're gonna put them," Mike teased.

"Just you never mind," Julia said. "Come help me look."

Nick shook his head at their departure. "Well, that wasn't at all obvious."

"Not a bit," Lark agreed.

"How've you been?" As before, the intensity of his gaze left her feeling exposed. Vulnerable. As if it didn't matter how she answered because he'd know the truth anyway.

"I've been good. You?"

"Good," he said. "Really good."

"That's good," she said.

"Yeah," he agreed. "Really good."

"You already said that."

"Did I?

"Yep."

For several strained beats, they watched the other patrons mill about before turning back to each other and speaking conflicting sentences at the same time.

"You cut your hair."

"You grew out your hair."

Their *jinx* chuckle was so awkward…

"Is it weird that I'm here?" Nick asked. "Because if I'm making it weird—"

"No," she answered way too quickly. "I was going to invite you, but then I thought *I'd* be making it weird, so I didn't. Which was super rude."

"I didn't invite you to my exhibition," he pointed out. "So…"

"That's so fucking rude," she teased.

He lifted a dark brow. "You say *fuck* now?"

Lark folded her arms beneath her breasts. "I said it before."

The lopsided grin returned. "I remember."

And then, so did she.

Please fuck me, Nick.

Nick leaned close enough for her to feel the tickling of his breath in her ear. "Careful, or everyone will know you've got new jewelry."

Lark glanced down to find that the beads on either side of her piercing bars were pushing against the fabric of her halter as her nipples hardened. She quickly crossed her arms, her cheeks burning.

"Don't suppose you'd let me see them for old times' sake?"

"Don't suppose I would," she said.

"Not even if I agreed to sneak you in to see my exhibition after hours?" he asked.

"Depends," she said. "Is it at the Met?"

"No," he said. "Sadly, it's not. But it's about six blocks from here. Easy to walk to after your gallery show is over."

Lark looked at him, feeling the days peel away as if they'd never been separated at all. "All right," she said. "I'm game."

Fifteen

Manhattan at night.

One of Nick's very favorite places in all the world.

The sea of lights. Glimmering skyscrapers. Trains. Sidewalks. Neon. Street performers. People spilling out of bars. The pulse and hum of it all. To walk through it with Lark at his side left Nick feeling alive in a way he hadn't since she'd last been in his arms.

And how she'd changed since then.

The way she dressed, spoke—even the way she walked down the street. She was more confident. More assured. Even a little…dangerous. What hadn't changed was the way he felt about her.

The second they'd locked eyes, the longing of the past year had careened into him like a freight train. The illusion that his life had been okay without her shattering.

"So how are you liking living in New York?" he asked when he could no longer handle the silence between them.

"How did you know I live in New York?" she asked.

"It was on your About the Artist plaque."

"Pro tip," she said, glancing up at him. "No one ever reads those."

Nick found himself occasionally slowing his gait, trying to get behind her even a step so he could admire the creamy expanse of her bare back. But it was what he'd seen beneath the fabric in front that came roaring back to his brain. Lark

Hockney, tattooed *and* with pierced nipples? Was this the work of cruel trickster gods determined to fuck with him?

"We'll make a right up here," he said.

They turned the corner, and the blocky four-story building came into view. Nick unlocked the side door, and they climbed two sets of stairs before they entered the main event space.

He had chosen an affordable—for Manhattan—space just off a busy street corner, with only two large windows on either side that had to be covered. The walls were painted stark white. In the center was an empty space waiting for his immersive exhibit to be completed.

As they stepped through the door and into the exhibit hall, Lark hugged herself and wandered around the cavernous space, staring up at the blank walls.

"I love what you've done with the place," she said. "I'm a big, big fan of minimalism."

"All evidence to the contrary."

Nick pulled his laptop out of his messenger bag and plugged it into the docking array connected to the giant projectors on the ceiling. Digging through one of the large plastic storage containers he'd brought just for this purpose, Nick came back with a sleeping bag and two pillows. He rolled them out in the center of the floor and indicated for her to make herself comfortable.

Kicking off her high-heeled shoes, Lark lost several inches of height but not one iota of presence.

"Ready?" he asked.

"As I'll ever be."

Nick cut the lights and pressed Play, then quickly jogged over to stretch out beside her.

The projectors flickered to life, and the entire ceiling and four walls were covered in swirling gray voids. The color deepened in patterns around the room, moving and stretching, rolling like the clouds. Slowly, darker gray lines appeared and multiplied until it became clear they were pencil lines.

Lark's pencil lines. Slowly, they assembled into the drawing he'd fished out of the trash her first night of class. Her small gasp marked the moment she realized exactly what she was looking at.

"How did you—"

But the lines were changing already. Thickening, darkening, smearing themselves into a charcoal sketch of a ship gliding along turbulent waters. Above it, clouds roiled to life, crawling across the sky as the ship dipped and crested upon the waves. Slowly, the sea turned from gray to blue and merged with the presentation he'd prepared for their unit on color theory, followed by the impromptu presentation on the color gray. The image of the moon floated above them and all around them, the craters darkening, turning golden until they had morphed into the painting she'd done for their color unit. The colors bled into a sketch of a pond on a summers' day. A tall, curly-haired man stood on the shoreline as a long-haired boy swung out on the rope, his hair trailing him like a comet.

Out of the willow fronds burst a girl in a white sundress, her ponytail swishing behind her as she climbed the platform, grabbed the rope and jumped in after him. She and the boy bobbed together as the man on the shore grew transparent and disappeared.

The bright yellow sun shrank and changed until it became a bright-eyed meadowlark and took to the sky, where it joined a giant flock that swirled and dove before sailing off into the blue.

When it was over, they lay side by side on their backs as

the show looped and began again. Nick rolled his face toward Lark's.

Shining tracks descended from the corners of her eyes, picking up the colors of the projection. "That was…" She hesitated. "Completely unfair."

"Unfair?" Nick laughed, rolling onto his side. "How?"

"Here I gave you a lousy little painting, and you make me a custom immersive exhibit? How is that even remotely okay?"

"Mine was probably easier to make, honestly," he admitted. "It's kind of the point of the company I started after I bought Marshall out of Moonshot."

"Julia mentioned that," Lark said, aiming a knowing smile at him.

"Of course she did."

"That must have been intense." An invitation to tell her more.

"It was." Nick leaned back on his elbows. "Especially when I showed up to the meeting Marshall had scheduled with the venture capital crew and pitched a completely different idea than the one we'd discussed."

Her eyes widened. "You didn't."

"Sure did. And turns out, they liked it even better."

"Somehow I'm not surprised." Sunshine yellow deepened, gilding her features. "So what does it do, exactly?"

"It's technically AI I trained using only my own art as reference material, and it takes original content and creates 3D imagery that can be used for custom immersive exhibits."

"Kind of like you did for me in class?" Lark arched a dark brow at him.

"Kind of like that," he admitted. "But we've also been working closely with several psychologists who are leveraging virtual reality as a healing modality."

"Like you did on our date at the arcade?"

He'd forgotten just how razor sharp her mind was. How easily she made leaps of logic that dizzied him. Nick cleared his throat, feeling the back of his neck get hot. "Basically."

"And the program allows you to mix digital art and scans of two-dimensional media like my pencil sketches and charcoal drawings?" she asked.

"Exactly," he said.

Her thoughtful look paired with the deepening purple playing over her features. "That's what the charcoals were about, wasn't it? And the gouache. And pretty much all the assignments you gave us once I joined the class. They were media that couldn't be perfect."

Nick cleared his throat. "Maybe," he admitted.

Lark sat up and ran her hand through the wild feathers of her dark hair. When she shifted to look at him, her eyes were luminescent with tears. "How did I sit there in Mrs. Keil's art class all those years ago and never know that three feet away was a person who would one day be the color in my world?"

Nick sat up, brushing a tear from her cheek with his thumb. "See, the problem is I was raised by a very supportive mother who encouraged me to be in touch with my feelings, so I'm not one of those men who don't cry. And if you start that, I'll start too, and it just gets weirder from there."

Lark's hands moved down to his jaw, tracing it with her fingertips. "I like weird," she said.

"You've chosen wisely, then."

For a length of time impossible to measure, they just looked at each other.

"I thought I was never going to see you again," Nick said.

"You were always going to see me again," she said. "Just

like I was always going to walk into your classroom and mostly mess up your life."

"Are you kidding me?" Nick scoffed. "None of this would exist without you," he said, gesturing to the space overhead. "Not to mention I would probably still have been putting up with Marshall's bullshit."

"How do you figure?" she asked.

It had taken him the better part of a year to fully internalize the revelation that had come to him only when she'd suggested he tell Marshall to fuck off. "I spent my teenage years trying to be everything my dad wasn't. Then I spent my early twenties trying to be everything that Marshall is. Somewhere in all of it, I'd forgotten that *I* exist."

Lark's lips twitched. "You can take the boy out of the philosophy club…" She trailed off.

She had a point. "What I'm trying to say is you were the first thing *I* wanted. The first thing that wasn't about escaping my upbringing or trying to impress the kind of people that run in Marshall's social circles. And when I couldn't have you, I had to figure out what else I could build a life around. For me, it's this." He gestured to the images still unfolding around them.

"Well, what are you going to do now?" she asked.

"What do you mean?"

Lark threaded her fingers through his. "Now that you can have both?"

Mesmerized, Nick took his time finding an answer. "Thank my lucky stars?"

Time seemed to stand still as Lark leaned in, pressing her lips against Nick's. In that one simple gesture, an entire year of separation was obliterated. A long, sad season gone as if it had never existed.

Nick pulled back before his hunger could rob him of all reason. "I showed you my exhibition."

Her lips curved into a seductive smile. "A deal's a deal."

Taking his hand, she guided it to her breast, running his fingertips over the hardened bud and the small metal balls on either side.

"Oh, baby," Nick said. "I have a feeling I'm going to have a lot of fun with these."

Her eyebrow lifted. "Just wait until you find their friends."

Nick hesitated and then reached behind her neck to untie the halter top. Lark didn't just let it fall but slowly moved the black triangles down in a delicious tease. By the time he saw the first flash of metal, Nick was rock hard.

"Get over here."

Lark squealed as he dragged her into his lap. Body meeting body, completing their reintroductions with lips and hands. Tongues and teeth. The tears on her cheeks mingled with the warmth of his skin as they kissed, lost to sensation.

Like the art they both loved, she lit his mind with colors remembered and invented. He'd paint the feeling of her tongue in decadent scarlets and smoky umbers. Their shared desire burned ash white and gray. Her growing need a green more opulent than any spring.

The mundane issues of buttons and belt were quickly dealt with. For this moment, Nick measured himself not by the weight of his past—his losses, failures or mistakes, but by the span of his palms as they slid up her rib cage and gathered her breasts. By the length of his arms as they pinned hers overhead. By his thighs as they pried hers apart. By the exquisite peace he felt with her legs wrapped around his waist. Their eyes were locked when he made his home inside her, and neither looked away. He took her like a man starved.

Their bodies were a tangle of limbs, slick with sweat. Lark's fingers trailed over his chest, over the heart that belonged only to her. Together, they moved in messy, beautiful, imperfect harmony, their passion burning brighter, hotter than the long summer night.

Lark rested her forehead against Nick's, looking into his eyes as colors from the projectors painted their naked, fevered skin. "You realize what's going to happen now?" she asked.

"What's that?"

Lark smiled, a radiant expression that lit up her face as the lights turned it scarlet. "We're going to make up for lost time."

"I was hoping you'd say that."

★ ★ ★ ★ ★

Look for Cynthia St. Aubin's next romance,
coming Summer 2025!

LOOKING FOR MORE

afterglow BOOKS

Try the perfect subscription for **sizzling-romance lovers** and get more great books like this delivered right to your door or digital bookshelf every month.

Start with a Free Welcome Collection with 2 free books and a gift—valued over $30.

See why over 10+ million readers have tried Harlequin Reader Service.

See website for details and order today:

tryreaderservice.com/afterglow